ABOUT THE AUTHOR

TARAH DEWITT is an author, wife, and mama. When she felt like she had devoured every rom-com available in 2020, she indulged herself in writing bits and pieces of her own. Eventually, those ramblings from the Notes app turned into her debut novel. Tarah loves stories centered around perfectly imperfect characters. Especially the ones who may have just enough trauma to keep them funny, without being forcefully cavalier. She believes laughter is an essential part of romance, friendship, parenting, and life. She is the author of *Rootbound*, *The Co-op*, and *Funny Feelings*.

Also by Tarah DeWitt

Funny Feelings
Rootbound

THE
CO
-
OP

TARAH DEWITT

PIATKUS

PIATKUS

First published in this edition in Great Britain in 2024 by Piatkus

1 3 5 7 9 10 8 6 4 2

A CIP catalogue record for this book is available from the British Library.

ISBN 978-0-349-43897-9

Typeset in 10/14.5pt ITC Mendoza Roman Std
by Jouve (UK), Milton Keynes

Printed and bound in Great Britain by Clays Ltd, Elcograf S.p.A.

Papers used by Piatkus are from well-managed forests
and other responsible sources.

Piatkus
An imprint of
Little, Brown Book Group
Carmelite House
50 Victoria Embankment
London EC4Y 0DZ

An Hachette UK Company
www.hachette.co.uk

www.littlebrown.co.uk

For the ones still working on it, whatever it is.
Whether finding your way, or finding yourself . . .
Don't give up. You're worth the investment.

And for Ty. Thanks for loving this angry girl when she
was a teen, and during every phase of me since.

AUTHOR'S NOTE & CONTENT WARNINGS

I started to write this book shortly after I began writing my debut novel, and ended up setting it aside simply because I didn't know if I had the chops to pull off what I was imagining.

I tried to start it again after *Rootbound* came out, but then *Funny Feelings* demanded to be written, even though I had about 30k words written in this. Obviously, I was a whole mess of doubts when it came to this story after that, and started to think that maybe it was just cursed. I had two other ideas in the middle that I almost abandoned it for again . . .

I thought anything involving home renovation and people living together through it, struggling to communicate, might not be very fun to read.

But . . . then I realized that this was the *whole point*. And reworking this thing almost felt meta in a way, with how much I had to restructure it and change it.

I truly believe it was worth it, and that this is the story as it was meant to be.

CONTENT WARNINGS:

-Parental Abandonment
-Emotional Abuse via a Parent

-Explicit Sexual Content
-Explicit Language
-Death of a Family Member (mentioned; occurs off-page)
-Infidelity (committed by a side character; occurs off-page

PLAYLIST

- "Sweet Dispositon", The Temper Trap
- "Calypso", Spiderbait
- "Rollercoaster", The Bleachers
- "Matilda", Harry Styles
- "July", Noah Cyrus, Leon Bridges
- "Suspicious Minds", Elvis
- "I Wish I Was the Moon", Neko Case
- "Beg Steal or Borrow", Ray LaMontagne, The Pariah Dogs
- "Leaving It Up to You", George Ezra
- "Under the Boardwalk", The Drifters
- "Now or Never", Elvis
- "Sugar, Sugar", The Archies
- "Coming Home", Leon Bridges
- "Come and Get Your Love", Redbone
- "Friday I'm In Love", Phoebe Bridgers
- "August", Taylor Swift
- "A Little Less Conversation (JXL Radio Edit)", Elvis
- "Good Vibrations", The Beach Boys
- "Jump In the Line", Harry Belafonte
- "This Magic Moment", The Drifters
- "Fade Into You", Mazzy Star

- "Like Real People Do", Hozier
- "Can't Take My Eyes off You", Frankie Valli
- "Heavenly", Cigarettes After Sex
- "Cry to Me", Solomon Burke
- "Unchained Melody", The Righteous Brothers
- "Something Worth Working On", John K
- "Rose of Sharon", Mumford & Sons

PROLOGUE

THE FOURTH OF JULY

LARYNN

All of my life's most mortifying moments have a soundtrack.

In ninth grade, at my very first homecoming dance, I came barreling out of the girls' bathroom, skirting updos and side-stepping a multitude of grinding, hormone-riddled bodies so that I wouldn't miss *my song*. Rihanna was thumping through the gymnasium sound system, singing about finding love in a hopeless place—almost *too* on the nose, if you ask me. I quickly made my way to the imaginary spotlight in the crowd where I dropped and I swayed, a corsage-adorned wrist held aloft in the air. . . .

And an entire corner of my dress tucked into my thong.

I thought my date had been trying to touch and dance with me. Turns out he'd been trying to get my attention. The butt cheek wasn't the true travesty, though. Oh, no. The very visible tampon string—the one that seemed to glow in the dim gym lighting—was the thing that solidified that moment in horror for me.

Then there was the time, during my second semester of college, when I was listening to a pretty racy audiobook in the library. I eventually determined that it was too distracting to successfully study to, so I switched over to my playlist. 311 was strumming on about amber being the color of my energy when I noticed the stares.

Turns out, when I disconnected from my tablet and switched over to the music on my phone, the device continued playing that book—out loud. Let's just say, the narrator was very talented and had excellent, *enthusiastic* inflection.

And, alas, the memory I most often try to suppress manages to be the one that forces me to cringe the hardest. The one that occurred a few years before the echoing erotica incident.

My father's irate, reddened face surfaces in my mind, followed by my grandmother's stricken expression, and my other summer friends all stuck in various states of shock and confusion.

My hands clutching a boy's shirt to my naked front while my father berated us, as we stood trial in the glow of his headlights. And that same shirtless boy's face, hard and unapologetic.

That time, above the faint sound of a warning alarm in the distance, it was "Fade Into You" playing on a loop in the background of my shame—me wincing each time it began anew. Likely the fault of an errant limb hitting repeat on the dash when Deacon dragged me across the console and into his lap, as he attempted to undress me along the way. We'd rapidly become too distracted to notice or care.

"But you two don't even like each other!" June, the only girl friend I'd had that summer, said, gesturing wildly between us.

"We don't," Deacon replied to her, and my head whipped his way as something heavy plummeted through the hollow of my chest. The last words I'd ever muttered to him before the pounding on the window began had indicated otherwise.

Had stated the opposite, in fact.

"It was just sex, right?" he'd said and shrugged, his eyes never leaving mine, hardening.

"The fuck, Deac?" Jensen, another long-lost friend of summer and June's twin brother, had replied.

"LaRynn Cecelia Lavigne, mets ton cul dans la voiture!" Dad shouted before he slammed his car door. Get my ass in the car, indeed.

I'd only snorted, threw on Deacon's shirt, and marched over to my dad's Mercedes, hoping I'd never see or hear from Deacon Leeds again.

That was the last time I'd ever said the words "I love you"—to anyone—all while that fucking song droned on.

SO *NOW,* AS BROWN-GRAY WATER gurgles up from the shower drain like Old Faithful, as I'm sprawled out naked on the tile and sputtering, screaming . . . I'm also aware of Elvis crooning from the record player in the hallway.

This song cannot be ruined for me. I refuse. I *refute* this.

I scramble to my feet, suppressing a gag at the smell, my wet and bedraggled hair making a sickening *kersplat* against my face. I heave and tremble like a raging bull.

This is it.

This is when the Lavigne rage breaks free.

La goutte d'eau qui fait déborder le vase.

I almost laugh at the irony. The English equivalent to the saying is "the straw that broke the camel's back." In French, it's the drop of water that makes the vase overflow—much more accurate given this particular scenario.

I feel my throat start to clog before I physically shake my head to clear it away.

I will not give Deacon that. He will *not* have my tears.

It's just—I can't believe that he's still doing this. That he is *still* fucking with me. I can't believe that I thought we'd finally, *finally* turned a corner in this arrangement, or that we'd at least reached an understanding.

Neither of us wanted this to begin with, that much has been clear, but we each have something to gain by working together. And while we've admittedly done a less than stellar job at making the best of it so far, I truly thought our respective tantrums were thrown and we'd start making some progress. The better we cooperate, the faster we can get this renovation done, and be done with each other.

My temper continues to pool and gather, two whole languages of fucking-infuriated muddling together as Elvis sings on.

I quickly try to get the water sopped up and under control while a kaleidoscope of images flash through my mind—a cord being snipped, a red cape being waved, a hatchet swinging.

Swing

Swing

Swing

Swing . . . Elvis is baritoning triumphantly that his love won't wait just as Deacon bursts through the door.

"Larry?!" he shouts, abject terror paling his tanned, perpetually smug face.

"*You*," I snarl, my voice unrecognizable, possessed. The last piece of my sanity unhinges as I rise to my feet, still naked aside from the rubber gloves I pointlessly shoved on. Still dripping in the curdled, filthy water.

He clumsily grapples to shut the door, his head swiveling back around like he might rather die and let his ghost flee through it.

At least the man has the good sense to be afraid . . . *No*, I immediately shake off the thought. *Not* a man. An overgrown child. An adolescent meatball in the body of a smirking, swaggering adult.

My unfortunate ticket to jump-starting my life.

The bane of my existence.

My dear, sweet husband.

The dead man walking.

ONE

TWO MONTHS PRIOR

LARYNN

Bent and broken stalks of pampas lay in scattered piles across the hillside, like the Pacific's discarded toothpicks.

The occasional glimpse of the ocean on the horizon is welcome after the winding, swooping, relentless turns through the Redwoods prior.

I was forced to submit to my car sickness awhile back and had to make Elyse, my dearest (and only) friend, pull off to the side of the road.

I've spent nearly half of my life's summers here, so I suppose I should've expected the nostalgia. As soon as I'd finished my puking, I looked up and was swept under a fresh wave of it, remembering the very same spot and circumstances from the last time I was sick there, nearly a decade ago.

"Merde, LaRynn. You are almost an adult. You should have outgrown this—this car sickness," my father had yelled out the open door, the slight French accent only deepening the disgust in his tone. As if I was still wetting the bed or sucking my thumb. As if I could even help it. A Dramamine and all the pressure points in the world couldn't make up for the

stifling, stilted tension in the car that day. The way my mother stared longingly out the window and leaned into it with her entire body, like she'd rather have been anywhere else. The way my father would make small attempts at conversation before he'd shake his head in dismay when those attempts weren't met with any level of enthusiasm.

My parents, who categorically did not enjoy one another, who spent more time wrapped up in their resentment—to the point that it took center stage in our lives—traveled every summer from the time that I was eight until eighteen, leaving me with my grandma. And until that final one, those summers were always restorative for them, too. They'd drop me off at the beginning of summer—usually some weekend in May when school would conclude—and pick me up around Labor Day, just before it would begin again. And things would almost seem better for them, typically until Halloween. A few years we even made it through Christmas.

Until that final summer, when my naiveté about love was cured once and for all.

Until that year, *this* was the place that'd been more home to me than any, with the person who felt more like home to me than anyone had, too. My grandmother, with her deep French accent and her cutting sarcasm and her laissez-faire freedom.

I'd never understood how my father came from her, opposite in every way.

I also still don't understand how one summer nullified so many. I can only guess that it was my age the last time I was here that made it feel so vital. Eighteen had felt so much bigger than it was, so much more exposed. I'd burned bright for those months. The temporariness of it all had made me so unapologetically myself. Like I knew I was on the precipice of the rest of my life before college and the world's plans for me would take over.

Maybe it's because it was the last time I felt that way—like a version of me I enjoyed being. For a small while, at least.

AS I FEEL THE CAR make the final descent into Santa Cruz now, I try (and fail) to keep other memories submerged.

The smell of cotton candy and sun-soaked skin.

Vanilla custard and deep-fried artichoke hearts.

The ringing of arcade games and bare thighs shifting on leather, car windows open to the sound of waves crashing.

Hunger and frustration blurring together over three heated, sticky months. Deep brown eyes that cut right through me. Dark, silky hair sliding through my fingers. Broad shoulders under shaky hands.

The scent of a boy's body wash, the taste of his Chapstick, the tear of a wrapper—

"Are you okay? Is this okay?" whispered against my neck. . . .

"Rynn—Jesus, are you going to be sick again?! You need me to pull over?" Elyse shouts, and I'm catapulted back into the present.

"What? Oh—no. No, I'm okay. Sorry." I give a feeble wave of my hand before it falls to my thigh with a clammy slap.

"Your lips are back to being all pale." She frowns, her gaze bouncing around my face in concern before it darts back to the road. "Are you sure? Maybe we should stop for something to eat?"

I search her face right back, gratitude blooming in my chest at having her here with me. That she took time off from her well-managed life just to come help me settle this whole mess. It's a miracle she could even get the time away from law school. I certainly would not have been able to afford the time, had I still been attending.

In a roundabout way, even though it took me years to gain the strength to drop out, I'm grateful that I'd originally resigned myself to the life that was laid out for me. Because if I'd never gone to college and majored in poli-sci, I'd never have ended up in the same classes as Elyse, and made a true friend.

"Yeah, let's grab a bite if you don't mind."

MY HEART CONTINUES TO STUTTER and jump long after I've finished my fourth glass of water and pushed my food around my plate for the seven-hundredth time. I turn to stare out at the boats bobbing lazily in the harbor and try to settle its rhythm once more.

Elyse's fork clatters against the table and my body jolts in its seat, chair legs scraping against the worn deck.

She sighs. "Alright, are you okay? You're jumpy as hell and have barely eaten," she says.

I blow out a breath and nod, but let it semicircle into an honest shake when her eyebrow quirks above her sunglasses. She lets out a small laugh and tilts her head. "Worried? Sad? What is it?" she asks.

"A bit sad. Worried, yeah. Anxious—that's just a general state of being at this point, isn't it?" I laugh bitterly.

"LaRynn, I'm sure it'll be fine," she says, ignoring my sarcasm. "Let's just go and assess what needs to be done and take things one step at a time."

I turn to look back out over the water lapping against the dock. "I'm less anxious about that, I think. It's just . . . being back here," I sigh, ready to come clean. *All* the way clean. She knows that I need to get it ready to sell, knows that I need to work that out with a secondary owner. "Elyse, the other owner of the place . . . I know—well . . . *knew* him."

She frowns. "Okay? And that makes a difference because?"

"For one, logistics." I grab a napkin and a pen from the depths of my purse before I start sketching in order to explain. "A lot of the older buildings in Santa Cruz started out as single homes and then were restructured to be multi-unit buildings. So, some of them have weird layouts. My grandma's has one single staircase with a shared laundry-slash-hallway area and a garage on one side, with one unit downstairs on the other." I finish outlining that portion as she crosses her arms and waits for me to continue. "Then there's hers—*mine,* on top, the last unit. It originally began as two units on the second floor." I draw their shapes above what I've already laid out, little Jenga pieces on top of the others, along with their respective veranda areas sitting atop the garage side, plus a little cutout on the next side for my grandma's other balcony. That one always looked like it was cut into the slope of the roof, like the ocean took a bite out of it. "Helena, my grandma's partner, was her neighbor upstairs before they got together. That's how they met in the first place. And after a while they tore down the wall separating their two units and made it into one. Did a full conversion. So, it's a stacked duplex now, but shares one main entrance."

"Okay," Elyse says with a nod, always a step ahead. "So, wait, why couldn't you split it down the middle?"

"The downstairs tenant, Sally, has been there since before I was born. So, I'm already . . . *apprehensive* . . . about selling the entire building and giving her the boot. And, according to the lawyers, since they didn't specify leaving us each a unit, I'll need him to sign off on anything, too." *God,* so much time with lawyers in the last six months to go through all of this . . . If I'd had any lingering curiosity regarding a career in law, I'm officially cured.

Elyse blinks at me again. "Here's where you tell me why that part could prove difficult."

I twist toward the boats again, considering. Unsure how to explain that I feel betrayed on multiple levels over the fact that Deacon even gets to claim an ounce of ownership over my grandmother's home. Part of me feels like I don't deserve to, either. "Helena was *his* grandma. Deacon and his mom moved to be closer to her just before the last summer I spent here." She wheels a hand through the air, subtly prodding me to get to the point and I sigh. I can't say he was my boyfriend because he wasn't. No one even knew about our little arrangement back then, not until we got caught. "I had a fling with him—he was my—" I sigh. "I lost my virginity to him."

This has her sitting up with an amused sound. I simply can't share in the revelry, so I give her a flat look.

"We all have a first." She chuckles, shrugging. "It's bound to be a little awkward, I'm sure, but I'd think some familiarity would help in convincing him to work with you. And this was what, a lifetime ago?"

"Eight years."

"Well, you're all grown up now, and both of you stand to make a great deal of money. Get him to sign over one of the units while he holds onto the other and does what he wants with it." She laughs lightly again. "I thought you were about to tell me the place was haunted or something."

"*That* is—" I retrieve the finger I've jabbed in her direction and level out my tone, already on edge at the mere reference to Deacon Leeds. "—that is exactly what he's like, Elyse. My own personal poltergeist. You don't understand. We spent 50 percent of that summer hating each other, and the other half we were out of our minds in another way. He was . . ." I inhale deeply through my nose. "He was judgmental and condescending and goddamn full of himself. He was annoying, constantly badgering. An absolutely shameless flirt, in any setting, with anything. *Anything.* That fucking squid on your plate right there," I say and nod down to her calamari, widening my eyes meaningfully. "With a dash of a New England accent thrown in, he'd have found some way of making that sexual."

"I don't kink shame." She holds up her palms with a toss of her shoulders.

"Elyse, I'm serious." I close my eyes and groan, nerves prickling to life. A storm of emotion starts gathering in my mind: overcast, ominous, and entirely opposite to the glittering ocean to my right. "He had this way of aggravating me. He would—he'd bring out the worst in me, and then he'd make sure to call me out on it. He'd make me feel prudish, and then have some way of acting scandalized when I'd try to loosen up." In front of other people, at least. In private, he was sweet and attentive. It gave me whiplash. "I—I don't know how to explain it. From the moment we met, nothing was ever simple or easy between us."

"I'm waiting for the part where this transitioned to you having sex with him. . . ."

So I tell her.

I tell her the story of how a lonely, haughty, and very angry girl and a sharp-tongued, infuriatingly charming boy saw each other a bit too clearly for one summer. How that girl had already begun to harden her heart against love and vulnerability, and how that boy was already too accustomed and numb to loss for his age. I leave out the part about accidentally falling for him, not wanting to give him that much credit, not wanting her to have some "Aha" moment because of it. *So that explains why you're this way, why you so rarely date and why you're such a viperish shrew,* she might think. Though, there are more layers to it than that.

Instead, I stick to a limited version of the truth. I tell her how two foolish young adults became reluctant friends, eventually bonding over their pessimistic philosophies on life and love, and how those two thought that these commonalities made them ideal comrades in sex. . . .

Since, theoretically, it would have—*should* have—been easy for them to say goodbye.

TWO

DEACON

Sally gasps, the wheels on her oxygen tank squeaking to a halt as she gazes longingly at the TV.

"Good Lord. I would let that man eat crackers in my bed. Off of my naked body," she declares in awe, making the sign of the cross with her free hand. Never mind the fact that I know she couldn't be less Catholic.

Dansby Swanson smiles down from the television, unaware that he's likely roping my eighty-five-year-old neighbor closer to her grave in doing so.

I shake my head and laugh at the woman. "Why crackers?"

"Have you ever rolled on top of crackers in your sheets in the middle of the night?" she asks, leveling me with a glare. "You'd have to really like what you were rolling toward to make up for the sensation, trust me."

"I'll take your word for it."

"You"—she swallows a breath and lowers herself in her chair before continuing—"you sorta look like him, actually."

"Okay, lady, enough flattery for today. And check your O2 levels. You're having delusions now."

"What? You've gotta admit, Deacon, the hair is similar."

"I'll refrain from having you committed for now, I guess. But, listen, Sal. If you'd called that insurance broker like I'd told you, you might not need me here patching up this stuff all the time. We've got to get a more permanent fix done. I'm doing my best, but I'm not a plumber."

"Plumber, electrician—you both work on the guts."

"By that sound logic, I could moonlight as a gastroenter-ologist and have enough money at my disposal to take care of this properly, Sal." I'm also a general contractor but I have a feeling the plumbing issue is beyond my means—skill-wise, and financially.

She flips up the footrest on her recliner, closing her eyes through another attempt at catching her breath. My own chest squeezes at the sight.

It feels like yesterday that I showed up at the courtyard gate out front, its arch covered in tangled vines and overly-bright flowers, the sight of them offensive in their stark contrast to my bleak, riddled-with-teen-angst mood.

We'd relocated to California just that winter before, and I'd been fairly-fucking-pissed at the time to be spending my first golden state summer with my nana and her geriatric friends. All dreams of baseball and river floats with tiny biki-nis were dashed away and replaced with the image of three old biddies working in their garden beds out front, the decidedly un-sexy sounds of sea lions echoing through the air.

Mom needed that summer to herself, though. Needed to escape and just be human for a while after Dad, to take care of herself and no one else. I knew that even at eighteen. My older brother, perfect prince that he was, remained off at col-lege back east on his full ride. While I was headed exactly nowhere.

So I stayed here most of the time. Spent my time between Nan's and the campground we were living in, where I also worked.

Amazing how wrong I was about that summer, though. How full it had been. Of bikinis, sure. But so much more than that, too. There may not have been any baseball, but there was volleyball on the beach, near-daily loitering at Neptune's Palace, a few months' hold on adolescence—even a bit of growing up at the end.

That summer became so pivotal to me that it fundamentally changed every summer for me since. The elated screams coming off of the Giant Dipper all sound like uptight girls with mile-long legs and long black hair. Dipped cones taste like the first time with her, every time. Like trembling, fumbling limbs and foggy windows and being verbally whipped and then sweetly kissed. Every jam-packed beach with out-of-towners ranging from the jean-clad to the perpetually barefoot all take me back to *that* summer. To being sad, angry, lost. To being completely in over my head with a girl who was way above my pay grade and never missed a chance to remind me.

To wanting more from life, but not knowing what or how to get it.

I'd been wrong about the biddies, too. Those three women had more vitality in them than even us kids back then. With my grandma and Cece gone, that damned gate and Sal are all that remain the same in this dilapidated place.

It's the first weekend that feels like summer, that's why my mind keeps wandering, keeps getting stuck in the past, I tell myself. It's the same reminder I always repeat, and it typically rings true. It always gets better after Labor Day.

Give me the fall, winter, hell—even the spring. When everything is a bit more mild, and a lot more peaceful. When parking's easy, rides at the Boardwalk are either closed or only open on weekends, and I'm able to fill my days with work while getting caught up on whatever's inevitably fallen behind, sans the heat.

"I did call that insurance broker," Sal, finally having found her breath, tells me. "They won't touch any of it. Owner's responsibility, they said."

Ouch.

"RIP Cece and Hel, this hit's for you," she adds before she makes a show of snorting in her oxygen.

"Aren't we spiritual today," I mutter under my breath.

"Any update on all that?" she asks. I know what she's referring to. As well as *who.*

"Not yet, Sally," I grumble. "I'll reach out soon."

I'm struck with the memory of seeing her name next to mine on endless stacks of paperwork, and the weird jolt that that alone had given me.

It's only the ties shared between us that make me the slightest bit curious about LaRynn and what she thinks of this situation, what her plans are. Despite our grandmothers remaining together until they passed, *she's* never been back here—at least not that I know of. Since the last time I saw her eight years ago, she's given zero indication that she gives a shit about this place. She always met Cece and Nana elsewhere, always forced them to come to her, regardless of the state of their health.

The idea of approaching her and asking for her approval, when *I* was the one here for them . . . when *I* helped them through sickness and grief and even jetting over here whenever they couldn't figure out their fucking TV . . . The fact that I have to ask for her permission on anything sets my teeth on edge.

I'll have to soon, though. Sal's rent barely covers the property taxes for the place, and it's been a money pit otherwise.

And every time I imagine that conversation with LaRynn, I'm sent down an exhausting whirlpool of pondering and wondering and reflecting, which is aggravating enough as it is. This is all before actually speaking with her. And yet I still manage to tie myself up in wondering what she thinks. How she feels about all of this. Wonder if the passionate girl I got glimpses of grew up to be a woman who knows her own mind or not.

Ridiculous. Ridiculous and annoying that my brain ever gets stuck where she's concerned.

I RUN THE FAUCET AND the shower at the same time to make sure things are draining, willing the anxious feeling in my gut to clear away with it. When things seem to be flowing smoothly again, I call over to Sal to let her know she's up and running once more.

She moves like she plans to get up and walk me out before I put my hand on her shoulder and ease her back down.

"Thank you, Deacon," she says with a sad smile.

"Need anything else before I go?"

"Just turn up the volume on your way out. The summer shitshow is underway."

It's then that I notice the chorus of honking and yelling filtering in through the open windows, and I turn up her music to drown it out before I leave.

It's the time of year when even the reserved-for-residents-only spots are stolen, and people circle around for ages trying to find parking, tempers rising with each passing lap. Summer

feels like it starts in May on this part of the coast, and typically ends in August.

Someone sounds like they supremely pissed people off this
time, though. There's a litany of curses in between honking
that grows louder with each step I take into the courtyard.

"*LaRynn,* just get back in the car! Come ON!" rises above
the noise and my feet stutter.

I didn't . . .

I couldn't have heard that right. My brain must be fucking with me again.

I drop my tool bag and carefully unlatch the gate. The
honking and shouting carries on, but my steps move like
they're underwater. I round the corner to the other side of
the building and take in the scene before me.

A white, blonde woman standing in the middle of the
street outside a loaded-down SUV, passenger door ajar,
attempting to direct traffic around.

My eyes skate down the sidewalk, along the fence that separates it from the side yard until, sure enough, they snag on
the back of a head. A head of black, waist-length locks. It's
ridiculous, that hair—in its abundance and in its impractical-
ity. It was a constant complaint of hers and yet, here she is,
with more of it than ever before. Because yes, of course it's her.
She stands up, and if I wasn't already convinced, the legs would
have clued me in. Five foot eleven at eighteen made her intimi-
dating, so she's damn formidable now. But then she kicks a
planter box and I nearly shout and blow my cover too soon.
The planters are one of the only things in decent condition
and she's kicking it like she fucking owns the place. *Brat.*

Oh, I think. *That's right. I guess she does.*

"I still don't understand how you forgot the key, out of
everything you brought!" her friend shouts in irritation.

"There has to be something here. They always left a key to unlock the garage, *always*!" LaRynn shouts back.

"A decade ago, maybe," I say. I smother the smile that wants to tug on my lips when she whips around and sees me, eyes and mouth both wide.

She reels in her expression. "Deacon." She nods coolly. I guess we're not pretending with niceties.

"Larry," I reply, and she immediately scoffs and rolls her eyes. *Two syllables*—that's all it took to rile her up and now I can't stop the smile.

"I suppose you're still an ass, then?"

"And I suppose you're still a princess—who cares that it's opening weekend and it's especially crowded, everyone else with plans and places to be can fuck off because *you* don't want to look for a parking spot?"

"We've been looking for forty-five minutes!"

"And after forty-five minutes traffic rules and regulations no longer apply to you?"

"Is that him?!" the friend shouts from the road. LaRynn shakes her head sharply and stomps back to the car. "He's so tall!" she continues.

"I'm him!" I shout back cheerfully. "Deacon!"

"Nice to meet you!" she replies with a wave. LaRynn snarls something before she hurls herself into the car and slams the door.

"Okay, well, we're gonna go park and then we'll be back!" Friend yells before she eases into the driver's seat and takes off.

Can't wait, I think, still smiling.

THREE

LARYNN

Oh, *God*. I should have figured he'd be lurking around here. Probably visiting Sally, being the precious grandson she never had.

I also forgot how it felt to be in his proximity. I've grown so accustomed to being as tall as the men around me, or taller. The sheer size of him makes me jittery, uneasy in a way. That advice we all got as kids before a nature-related activity pops into my mind: *If you see a bear, act bigger than it. Be bigger than the bear.*

And it just fucking *figures* he'd look the same, somehow. The same, but better. I've successfully avoided most pictures, and the only times I've (drunkenly) looked him up over the years, his accounts have been private. But all the things that needled me so thoroughly before are still there in all their glory. The same warm, dark eyes that trap you, the kind that make you curious enough to get closer, hoping to explore their depths.

Nope, now's not the time to slip down that particular mental spiral.

After failing to find a spare key, it takes Elyse and I another thirty minutes to park—three blocks over. We narrow down and prioritize the things we need to bring right away and start making the trek back to the building in a frustrated daze.

By the time we amble up to the corner of First Street, I'm sufficiently irritable and my various packs keep slipping down my sweaty shoulders.

"Oh, you're *shitting* me," I growl when I see Deacon leaning against the open doorway of the perfectly *empty* garage.

"Thought you'd changed your mind and gone back home," he says.

He makes no move to help either of us, but he does proceed to talk some more. "I'll keep it open and let you guys park here for the night."

"*Let?* We don't need you to *let* us do anything, Deacon," I say. I feel my temper rising already. "Except get upstairs and get settled before you and I are forced to interact much more." I can see the way he's aggravating in his effortless way, and I know I shouldn't give him this sort of power over me. I need to get my bearings, somehow.

"Even so, before you go—"

"Nah-ah. Settled, first."

"That's fine, *but*—"

"Bye for now." I avoid meeting his gaze for too long and wheel past him with my luggage, Elyse following behind. It's clear I need a minute to pee and collect myself before I can attempt a grown-up conversation with him.

"*Rynn*," Elyse whispers when we make it inside the hallway. "I think I should remind you that you need him to be agreeable, so maybe a little kindness wouldn't kill you?"

"I know," I groan back. "I just—need a minute."

We slip past the laundry area toward the stairs, luggage wheels rolling noisily over the tile. Everything, down to the washer and dryer, looks exactly the same, but something is . . . *off*. I decide I'll put my finger on it later and start trudging up the stairs, my bag knocking painfully into my heels with each step.

It feels so much more open than before, somehow. The window across from the landing looks out to the now-setting sun over the ocean, the pier jutting from its center.

And, almost as if I can't help myself, I pause, suddenly hopeful. And *grateful* that my grandmother left me this piece of her, deserving of it or not. It's a foundation for me to build my own life on. I'm nearly penniless, completely directionless, and barely speaking to my parents. But I have Elyse, and I have this shelter by the sea.

Elyse has pushed past me during my musing, so I snap to and catch up, frowning when I see the look on her face. "Rynn . . ."

"Hey, Larry," Deacon says to my right.

I look that way now and—

"What the fuck?! How the hell did you get up here?" I shout. I do a double take when Elyse catches my eyes with her dramatically widened ones.

"*Poltergeist,*" she whispers in mock-terror.

"I installed a fire escape," Deacon replies, vaguely bored and tilted against the skeleton of a wall that once held a mishmash of art. I recall the ceramic key hooks Helena made during her pottery stint and almost let a laugh escape, remembering Grandma rolling her eyes at Hel because *"Could we be any more cliché than coastal grandmother lesbians that garden and throw clay?"*

And now they're gone. Left this world mere months apart from one another.

A sharp ache burns through my throat and I will it to

harden into frustration, aim it back at Deacon instead. The emotional whiplash has me flailing for those bearings I needed to find and coming up empty.

"Where are the *rest* of the walls, Deacon?"

I look beyond him and see the majority of my grandmother's original place. Or, at least what's left of it. It appears to be freshly primed in the intact areas, patched in others. But . . . there are almost no cabinets, no appliances—well, aside from a mini fridge and an oven. The bare minimum as far as furniture goes . . . and more of the walls are gone than standing. There's not even insulation in some.

His brows inch down, confused. "You don't know?"

Obviously not, dick. I manage to swallow that remark down. "What happened?" I ask.

He stands up from the wall and walks our way, bringing with him the full awareness of a grown man at ease in his body.

I'm forced to acknowledge it, now—just how very much he is a *man* in comparison to the boy I spent a summer with. From the five o'clock shadow dusting his sharpened features, to the shoulders and arms and legs that have filled out . . . immensely. He was an athlete before. At six foot four it was to be expected. Brown hair with a slight curl, a tiny bit over-grown and arranged artfully in a way that's just fucked-up enough to look like he's not trying. Or like it was mussed by someone's hands clenching it while he eagerly buried his face between her thighs, inky-dark eyes peering up between them in smug satisfaction. It's all too easy for me to picture.

And even back when we were teens he dressed like some-one's uncle on vacation—a look that's somehow managed to become a style these days. He's wearing an unbuttoned red shirt dotted in tiny redwoods slung loosely over a plain white tank top that clings to him. I spy the Santa Sea Campground logo and quietly snort. *Looks like he's just as stuck as he ever was, too.* The ensemble's completed by dirty blue jeans and work boots. A smattering of chest hair peeks up from the neck of his top; something I notice when he reaches up to scratch something there, along with an octopus tattooed on his hand—*both new.* But gone are the vestiges of lanky limbs, replaced by ropes of broad muscle and even more assuredness than what he had as a teen.

"A fire," he replies. "Faulty wiring. I tried telling them for years, when things kept going wrong. I think there were too many corners cut when they did their original reno, LaRynn." His gentler tone throws me off, along with the use of my name.

"She never said anything to me," I explain, trying to keep the plea out of my voice. "I didn't know *anything* was going wrong."

But, I see it turn over in his expression. I've managed to say the wrong thing—again. Shit.

"I guess you *wouldn't* know, would you?" he sneers. "Since you never bothered to visit her, couldn't even make it down for her wife's memorial."

"I haven't—I was in law school, Deacon, I couldn't get out of it. Grandma understood. Besides, no one would've let me." It's a poor excuse and I know it, but I can't stand his judgment on top of my own.

He just shakes his head at me and snorts in disgust. "You were an *adult,* Larry."

"Excuse me," Elyse cuts in before I can respond, "but where can we put our shit?" She swipes exasperatedly through the air with her free hand.

"The Dream Inn is a block away," he offers.

My head twists in his direction with the menace of a haunted doll. "*I* own fifty percent of this," I remind him, gesturing to the disaster zone around us. "I'm not going to a hotel."

His chin dips, dark gaze lazily sliding its way up from my feet to my face. I resist the urge to adjust my shirt or hair or perform any other nonsensical tick under his assessment.

He narrows his eyes. "I was understandably concerned about Sal living here after the fire incident, in addition to the plumbing issues—"

"*Plumbing* issues?"

"—so, I've been staying here." He points in a circle around him.

"So technically you're living in *my* place?" I ask.

"Technically, I'm living in the one *we* own. The one that *both* of our grandmothers moved into when they got together. If you want to argue it out then fine, I don't have a signed agreement for this and yes, I'm sure some court, somewhere would evict me for the time being. But this is California, Princess— even squatters have rights." The corners of his mouth shrug up. "So if you want to do the dance in court, I'm more than happy to do that with you. Hell, let's take care of everything you need to pay to fix up your end of the deal here and make this place livable again while we're there, two birds one hearing."

I bite back the retort that starts to boil out of me, imagine gripping the proverbial wooden spoon between my teeth to halt it. "Where'd her furniture go? Did everything get destroyed?" I ask, voice hitching.

His expression stutters and softens, reading the catch for emotion, I'd wager. He was always too good at seeing me too clearly. "A lot of it, yeah. What wasn't is in the garage under storage blankets."

Elyse shoulders past me. "Does your couch fold out?" she asks him.

His face buckles into a frown. "Uhhh . . ."

"Because even if it doesn't, I'd advise you to at least offer her a place to stay, otherwise provide a bed, a cot, a mattress—anything—because she's not going anywhere."

Deacon balks at her. "Who are you, again?"

"Elyse Kemper, LaRynn's best friend and future attorney." She smiles brightly and sticks out a hand. He straightens himself up to his full height and struts her way, loose-limbed and confident. He takes her outstretched palm in both of his and cocks his head with a smile. I suppress the urge to roll my eyes. *Here he goes.*

"Nice to meet you. Sorry we got off on the wrong foot." His dark stare crinkles at the corners before it dips just so, just enough to have Elyse tipping her shoulders back, a blush creeping up her cheeks. He maintains eye (and hand) contact with her as a lock of hair flops to rest against his brow. "Did you two meet in college? I would've remembered if she'd told me about you before," he says, smarmy grin intact.

"Oh because you were such an *avid* listener when you were *eighteen*?!" I scoff, and he throws an arm casually around her shoulders as he turns my way. Elyse, bless her soul, remains gaping doe-eyed back up at him.

Okay, if she's not going to answer—"And yes, we met in college."

"I figured. I have a *superb* memory." A satisfied sigh. "So many memories," he continues to sing, his gaze scaling the length of me again. And to my brain it sounds exactly like *I remember the footprints you left on the interior roof of my Nissan Pathfinder due to the frequency with which I had them in the air and spread that way.*

I smother the urge to stomp my feet and smile back, cruelly, instead. "Oh, yeah? Like the time you came in your pants in that stairwell right there without so much as a stroke?" Something explodes in my chest at the way his smile falls dead. A laugh sizzles out of me, and Elyse coughs to cover her own.

"Why are you *here*?" He takes his arm back and folds both across his chest.

I sigh and sort my thoughts, school my tone into something unassuming and friendly. *Here goes nothing.* "Mind if we go to your place to talk?" I gesture toward his pseudo living room.

And with a begrudging sigh, he leads the way.

FOUR

DEACON

"So, let me get this straight. You're asking me to just sign away half of the building, because—despite the fact that I've been staying here and trying to keep it from crumbling apart—you want to show up now and sell it for the money?" I ask.

She's shielded herself in all her long, folded limbs, swinging a crossed leg in annoyance. *Jesus, she's annoyed? What about me? I haven't been able to run the dishwasher in the six months that I've been staying here. I haven't taken a shower without a hefty side-helping of fear, either. I don't even want to let myself think about all the electrical issues. . . .*

"Yes, correct," Elyse responds on her behalf, *"but . . ."*

LaRynn rips her gaze over to her and widens her eyes as Elyse continues, "I'm saying this as your future attorney and just as a generally decent human." She gives her an uncomfortable smile. "Since you *are* just as responsible for the cost of the repairs, you need to take care of those before you sell."

LaRynn shakes her head. "No. I'll just give him some money out of the profits after we sell," she responds, not even looking my way. A flare of anger burns hot and bright at the confirmation that this place really doesn't mean a damn thing to her. How easily dismissed it is.

"No. I won't sign off on any sale until *all* the repairs are done."

She narrows her eyes at me. "Have you even reported this to insurance and figured out what's covered or have you just been squatting here?"

"*Squatting*? Seriously?!" God, she's infuriating. "Once again, I fucking *own* half of it, Larry. The insurance money barely covered getting it to a state that was deemed safely livable by the county. They were technically at fault! There is no more money."

"You said it was faulty wiring!"

"Wiring that they should have updated!"

"*LaRynn has a trust fund!*" Elyse shouts over our voices from her seat. Which is when I realize we've risen to standing, the coffee table the only barrier between us. She turns to look down at Elyse and attempts a silent conversation. The shift of her hair sends a gust of her scent my way, and I close my eyes against the invasion. Surprisingly sweet, like it always is, completely at odds with the woman it belongs to.

"Rynn, *plan B*," Elyse urges before turning back to me. "Cecelia left LaRynn a trust fund in addition to half the ownership on the property," she finishes, words in rapid succession.

"Plan B was a JOKE, Elyse!" Rynn cries.

"But, it *would* work! You'd have money for the repairs, and could do the updates and would make all of it back times ten, at least, when you sell!" Elyse placates.

"I'm not—" She turns to look back at me. "I can't even access it."

"She can access it when she gets married!" Elyse squeaks

even more rapidly, and I'm certain she can feel the burn of LaRynn's glare through the back of her head.

"Then, no. I'm not sitting around waiting for you to find some dumb schmuck to marry you," I supply. Some poor sop that'd be.

LaRynn throws her a look that clearly states *See?! He IS still an ass,* but Elyse presses onward.

"I am the dumb schmuck," Elyse says with a grin. "I will be marrying her."

I look between the two of them. "You introduced yourself as her best friend?"

"And isn't that what the best partnerships are made of?" LaRynn replies, baring her teeth.

"It's just to get around the clause," Elyse clarifies, and LaRynn's expression pinches.

"So, you're not . . . ?" *Dating? Together?*

LaRynn sits and falls back against the couch with a huff. "No, we are not romantically involved. We both suffer the incurable affliction of being attracted to men," she says.

"Yes," Elyse adds with a sigh, "despite being well-educated and certifiably brilliant, we are sadly heterosexual."

"Oh—kay?" is all I come up with.

"It's only a little over a hundred grand, give or take," LaRynn states with an annoyed sulk, and I have to bite back the fierce urge to call her a spoiled brat. "Definitely not enough for everything," she adds before she begins refolding her limbs, the scowl returning. It occurs to me that she might not be pouting over the state of the place or that she doesn't have enough money in her trust fund, but because she *needs* someone else in order to access it. She never could stand being vulnerable.

Still, she's too goddamn irritating for me to think clearly.

"There's an air mattress in the hall closet, otherwise there's the couch. The other bathroom toilets are out of commission, so you'll have to use mine. I need to head out for a bit," I tell them. I grab my keys and jet before either can argue.

I just need a minute and some space to sort through my thoughts on this, to come up with a plan. I *should* probably go to Sal and talk it out since she is the closest thing I have to my grandmother these days, or I could go to Jensen . . . Definitely not my mom. But, I feel like this needs to be something I work through on my own. That everyone else's opinion on it would have too great of an effect on what should ultimately be my—*our*—decision.

I know that I don't *want* to sell a damn thing, and the ease with which LaRynn can toss it aside disgusts me. But, it's also in line with what I know of her character. She's always been a spoiled and spiteful thing. Even at eighteen, half a step into adulthood, she was permanently on the verge of a fight, nothing and no one around her ever good enough.

Not even herself, I recall.

I REACH THE BEACH, THE cries from the last of the theme park goers piercing the air while dusk begins to crawl across the sky. It's movie night just outside the Boardwalk, so people begin to filter in and arrange their blankets in the sand as the screen is erected.

It's earlier in the season than it was back then, but it's not *un*like the night my and LaRynn's relationship took a turn eight years ago.

Back then, some horror film had been playing, and in our attempts to discreetly avoid watching, we caught one another doing the same.

"*Talk to me,*" she'd whispered.

"*Excuse me?*"

"*I mean, pretend to talk to me so we have an excuse not to watch this!*" She managed to yell it under her breath somehow.

"*Fine.*"

"*Fine.*" She held eye contact.

"*Your hair looks pretty,*" I'd said—a knee-jerk reaction to being put on the spot, and her response was to look away with a gag. Until something flew across the screen and she flinched, looking back at me with terror shining in her eyes.

"*Don't try to flirt with me,*" she growled, eyes narrowing.

"*I paid you a compliment, Larry.*"

"*Your opinion isn't so important that I consider it as such, asshat.*"

"*Jesus, I'll take the nightmares over this,*" I replied. And this time it was I who turned back to the screen.

I felt her eyes stay on me, tracking my every move.

"*HA!*" she shouted a minute later, and was immediately shushed by everyone around us. "*You're not really looking at the screen.*"

"*Yes I am.*"

"*No you're not. You're looking past the left-hand corner of it, I can totally tell!*"

The denial was there on the tip of my tongue, but a laugh rolled out of me instead. I was caught and called out. And then, the bigger surprise, she'd laughed back, the sound so foreign and pretty. So I'd turned, and our gazes locked. Understanding passed between us. We both were scared of the scary movie, and neither of us wanted to admit it.

"*Wanna get out of here?*" I asked. And to my astonishment, she agreed.

We spent the night walking along the beach and around

downtown Santa Cruz until the sun came up. Talking and laughing. Lightly jabbing, mildly bullying. It felt like our normal back-and-forth of the previous month, without the acidity. *With* the added occasional smile. It felt like we finally *got* one another.

But, that didn't change the fact that she was a spoiled rich girl who cared too much about her parents' approval. An only child, insular and pouty. Downright mean when she wanted to be. And she couldn't hack it when anyone called her out on her bullshit.

What we had in common could be counted on one hand: an intensely competitive streak, parent problems, and a hatred of scary movies.

It was enough to become . . . friendly. Though I don't think either of us would've categorized us as friends.

Even when sex came into the picture later on, I knew it wasn't born out of some heavy longing for one another. She was breathtaking—still is, but then she opens her mouth and proceeds to crush good feelings wherever they arise, like she's caught in a perpetual game of whack-a-mole.

No, even when things took a turn for the physical back then, it was that competitive streak that spurred it on, I think. The high of winning, and a small concession on both of our parts, and we were peeling off clothes in the back of my SUV. . . .

"You're sure this is okay?" I'd asked, searching her green eyes. Eyes like sea glass. *"You don't want to wait for someone—"* I swallowed and tried not to cringe. *"—special?"*

"No. I want to know what the fuss is about. I've never been able to—" She swept her hair over her front before continuing, *"Not even for myself. Sometimes something feels good but then it takes too long and maybe I just want to know if it's me."*

"It's not—I mean, I've only got a few years' experience, but what I know of girls is that it's not always easy for them to—you know." Jesus. I bury my face in my palms remembering how awkward I was, sitting in the backseat beside her, parked in an alcove off of the campground, looking out over a cliff at the sea.

"So it's not just because I don't love myself?" she said with a forced, trembling smile, something that sounded as if it wanted to be a laugh. God, I thought, she must be nervous if she's actually making a joke at her own expense. It was so unlike what I thought I knew of her, such a naked statement disguised as sarcasm.

I slid my fingers into her hair and shifted closer to her, pressed along her smooth collarbone with my free hand, and up to her ridiculous, full upper lip. I thought of what I could say to ease her, scared she'd retreat because I was suddenly achingly desperate for her, for the chance to make her come undone, to watch her discover something new. I'd never wanted to prove myself to anyone more than I had in that moment.

"I'll do whatever you like. You don't have to worry about sparing my feelings, not ever."

"Since this is just sex, and feelings play no role," she said, nodding like she was confirming it to herself. Trying to take back a piece of that vulnerability, I think.

I nodded back, still stuck on that desperate feeling. "Yeah. Just sex. Just . . . tell me everything you like, anything you don't. I'll follow your lead."

She leaned into my hand subtly. "One of us should know what they're doing."

I didn't dare laugh. "I know where to start." And then I kissed her.

* * *

A BICYCLE BELL STARTLES ME back into the present and I realize I've stopped on the pier. "Hey, Glen," I say to the glowing bike taxi. The driver's friendly eyes meet mine. I note her pink, puffy dress and pointed hat, both glittering in new LED lights she's decorated them with.

"You didn't compliment my new sign!" she chides. I take stock of it now, and the rest of the upgrades to her rig.

"Glenda the Good Hitch, huh?" I say. "Cute."

"I'm definitely getting the vote this time," she says, adjusting a ruby-red sneaker. She's been fighting for the top spot on the Boardwalk's best-of list for the last three years. Bike taxis are hardly a saturated category, but for some reason Glenda hasn't been able to crack the top three.

"I bet this is your year, Glen," I say.

She smiles and pedals toward the edge of the wharf until she's flagged down by a couple spilling out of a restaurant.

I love this weird, funky place. In spite of the tourists and the crowds. Love the proximity to the mountains and giant trees, to Silicon Valley in the north. I love that every kind of person gathers here. Sometimes, I even love the overly-packed beach—in small doses. Might just be because people watching is free entertainment, and getting internet and cable at the house has been sitting on the bottom of my priority list. Still . . .

LaRynn's face comes to mind—the way her lip stayed curled in permanent disgust today. And it's easy for me to picture her abandoning it all at the first sign of difficulty. That, combined with the lack of interest she's shown in recent years, makes me think it's *likely*. When something doesn't go her way she'll take her money and leave me in the lurch. And it's this thought that sends a surge of protectiveness bleeding through me.

It's not some small town by any means, but our grand-mothers' building, between them and Sal, felt like its own microcosm. The first real home I'd ever had in my life, after my dad died and took a piece of my mom with him. And even before that when he'd broken us all. This is the only true home I've had where not every memory is tainted, and I don't want to let it go for nothing. Want to make it count.

That money could go toward many things. I'd finally be able to hire a crew. Maybe even hire someone other than my mom for bookkeeping. Not just the odd handyman job here and there; I could start a real business. One that's my own.

I'd also want to make sure Sally has the rights to a lease, or at least has time to find somewhere else. Maybe I could set her up in one of the long-term rentals over at the campground.

I roll my shoulders and try to rein in my mind.

LaRynn can't be counted on to see this shit through, that's all I know for certain. I don't care if she wants to sell when all is said and done. I *welcome* it, in fact, even if it hurts to think of letting it go. There's so much I would be able to do with those funds . . . but there's only one way to ensure she can't take her money and run. And I've already dumped enough of my own into the place as it is. . . .

The street lights lining the planks turn on as the pieces of a plan fall into place.

Fuck, this is gonna hurt . . . again.

FIVE

LARYNN

"How difficult is *it to clean your disgusting hair trimmings out of the sink?!*" I howl when I step into the bathroom and see his mess.

"I imagine it's about as *difficult* as it is for you to not leave your *disgusting*, three-foot-long strands of witch-hair plastered all over the shower walls!" Deacon replies, a vein pulsing in his temple, his hair still damp from the shower.

Safe to say, living together is going well.

"Alright, lovebirds, we need to be on the road in forty-five minutes!" Elyse calls from the living area. She pokes her head in the doorway. "Deacon, since you appear to be ready, maybe you could go get coffee for everyone?"

"I'll take an extra shot in mine, *mon crétin*," I purr, low enough for Elyse to miss.

"I'll be sure to spit in it, *sugar*," he parrots my tone, and the old accent makes an appearance, that *R* falling off with lazy contempt.

"Looks like you missed a spot on your back, by the way."

"I don't shave my back," he snaps back with a glare. I don't miss the small turn he does before his eyes flick past me to check in the mirror, though.

I bark out an evil laugh when I catch him. "Guess that explains it, then." I shrug innocently before I slam the bathroom door on his stupid, freshly shorn face. I turn and lean against it as I try to catch my breath, not even his dumb expression bringing me adequate joy.

I've had a lump in my throat for days now, since the reality of this situation started to settle in. A fist that only seems to grow tighter, slowly cutting off my airway.

When Deacon came back after bolting the other night and briefed us on his plan, I'd started out angry. Angry because he *knows* that putting me in a position where I feel like I'm being controlled, like I'm without a fucking option . . . He *knows* it's the worst position he could put me in and he couldn't care less.

"*You can't sell it as is, anyway. It's not safe and you're going to make yourself liable—not to mention, I simply won't sign off on it,*" he'd said, smiling like a jackass. "*If we work together we streamline the whole process and make it a whole lot smoother for ourselves.*"

"*What do you mean by 'work together'? Don't you work at that campground still?*" I pointed to his shirt.

"*I'm a licensed contractor and electrician, Larry,*" he'd said, like he was explaining it to a two-year-old. "*I run the campground, but I'll only need to be there Friday through Sunday. I'll even stay there those days so you can have this place to yourself. Then I'll work here during the week. I'll do everything at cost.*"

I frowned, immediately suspicious of whatever was coming out of his mouth next. . . .

"*It's the only way you can afford to do it. Permits alone in this county will cost a quarter of your budget. Plus you'll make all of*

*it back times ten, like Elyse said. I'll do all of the work, all of it,
for free. You'll only pay for materials."*

I waited, bracing myself for the catch.

"Why? Why would you do this?"

"Because," he said as scratched the back of his neck uncomfortably. *"Because I have what you need and you have what I
need. With $100k, we'd be able to finish this place, but that's it.
Labor for everything—paying anyone else—and we won't.*

*"Therefore, I need your money to finish fixing things up, and
you need my skill set because I'm all you'll find within your budget,
and you also need my signature. And lastly, to put it bluntly, I
won't sign away a fucking thing unless you agree to all the terms."*

Venom coursed through my body as I put it all together. I
hated that I saw the merit in the arrangement, hated that
he'd trap me this way. *"You're a dick."* I looked away after I
said it, annoyed that he'd gotten the better of me again and
that I couldn't control myself when it came to him.

But then, the floor was swept out from under me. *"And
that's why you'll marry me instead."*

There was yelling and expletives and violent eye-rolling,
but in the end, he made it clear he wouldn't trust me to hold
up my end of the arrangement unless we were *legally* bound
to one another.

"It's just a piece of paper, LaRynn." He clasped his hands
together. *"Do this with me, and for $100k you'll get back half a
million when you sell. We'll put all of this in a prenup,"* he'd
urged, even though he knew he'd won by then and I didn't see
the point in him trying to make me feel any better about it.

I didn't respond, just got up and started toward the door
as he continued. *"You can pick everything. I'll do it all however
you want. Down to the lightbulbs."*

"Whatever gets this started and over with as quickly as

possible," I'd replied, defeated. And then I marched through the doorless doorway and went for a run in the sand, the night blanketing around me.

THE ANGER HELD ON FOR a few days until it molded itself into this . . . this desperate frustration. Until the license and prenup were completed and showed up three days ago.

Today's the last day before Elyse has to head back home to Sacramento tomorrow, so it's also the day we have an appointment to get married at the courthouse in San Francisco, since the one in our county had no availability for another month. And I continue to feel like a cornered animal, even as I stand here and delay turning on the shower to get ready.

This is when I see his toothbrush on the counter. It's the first time he's left it out in these last days, and it makes me fixate on the baser reality of this situation: my toothbrush next to his for likely the next six months, or at least until I get my own bathroom.

I've given up so much of my dignity to him already and I can't believe I'm in this position where I'll have to share a goddamn *toilet* with him now. The last time I showed up here, ready for one last summer at *my* place of solace, it and my friends and even my grandmothers had all been overtaken by him. Him and his charm and his ease. The way he was good at everything, casual and cocky and so naturally warm—to everyone but me—it burrowed and festered under my skin, a virus that replicated in my cells. Then we tackled a few things together—nothing worth building a relationship on. Some dumb tournament and a few chores assigned to us by our grandmothers. . . .

Oh god, I bury my face in my hands and groan when

memories start to rear up. When I recall how *adult* I thought I was when I'd believed I could handle sleeping with him.

"*It's just sex.*"

"*It's just a piece of paper.*"

I can't believe I've accomplished so little on my own in this life and have waffled and failed only to get to this desperate place where once again, my choices feel as if they're being made for me. Because that's the root of all this, really. The fact that while I knew I definitely didn't want to finish school, and eventually worked up the guts to drop out, I still don't know what I'm doing with my life.

I thought this place represented a fresh start for me, a new beginning. Money equals comfort and time to figure out what I want to do, where I want to end up.

But more than that, this place belonged to my grandma before it belonged to either of us. *My* grandma, who was my person, the one in my life whose love bolstered and tethered me. Who made me believe that people had the ability to change directions whenever they wanted to, reinvent themselves countless times in order to stay truest to who they were. This is my opportunity to have closure and to work through the grief I've been suppressing.

So, while I don't love being pigeonholed into this by *Deacon,* even though I hate that I need this . . . maybe part of me wants this, too.

WHEN I EMERGE FROM THE bathroom a while later in head-to-toe black, Elyse frowns.

"I don't feel like I'm doing my job as your friend unless I tell you to go get changed. You can't wear black to your wedding."

"Don't call it that," I groan.

"Call it what? Your wedding?"

"Yes, that. Stop it. This isn't my *wedding,* wedding. I refuse to think of this as my wedding."

"Well, you can't look like you're going to a funeral."

"Aren't I, though?" I say grimly.

She looses a sigh my way. "Alright, LaRynn. Enough. The last thing I want to do is gaslight you here, so I'm sorry if that's what I'm about to do. I get how you're feeling and it's valid. But you know what, if I'm being honest, I can't muster up sympathy for you. I don't feel *sorry* for the fact that you have to temporarily marry an obnoxiously hot man, all so you can eventually collect a large sum of money. Call me crazy, I just don't."

"Elyse—"

"Nope. Listen, I know how you're feeling. But one man's control is not the same as one man's *partnership.* And I think that's how you need to look at this, if you're going to get through it."

I cross my arms and close my eyes, searching my brain for the falseness in her words. I come up empty.

"I guess . . . I guess I can look at this as marrying myself. I'm choosing *myself* today—choosing a life-adventure, without worrying about disappointing anyone else." It's a stretch, but it's also a start.

"That's my girl. Now go get changed."

I draw the line at that and keep the black ensemble.

THE DRIVE TO SAN FRANCISCO is devoid of conversation and I'm grateful for it. Less chance for me to say something regrettable, and less chance for me to say something Deacon could take advantage of, too. He doesn't put the top up on his

Bronco, so between the roaring engine and the wind whipping through our ears, there's no point in trying.

Even this car feels like sandpaper against my nerves. I remember this being a hunk of rusted metal rotting under a carport at the campground that he'd sneak me into. I probably should have gotten a fresh tetanus shot after that summer, come to think of it.

Now it's completely restored. Buttery yellow paint, with creamy, pale leather seats. A radio that plays clear and loud. How lovely for him, that even junk turns to treasure in his hands. That he can take a thing, a place, and make it his own, where I only seem to leave disappointment or failure in my wake.

THE CHECK-IN PROCESS AT THE courthouse is strangely anticlimactic. You'd think that there would be a more official-feeling vibe for people entering into a life-altering contract.

Instead, before I know it, we're standing in front of a cheery officiant, the court-provided witness at Deacon's side, Elyse at mine.

"Do you have the rings?" the officiant asks, and I'm slung into the present, right into the feeling of his warm palm against my clammy one.

"Oh, no. Um, we aren't . . ." I stammer just as Deacon starts fumbling in his pocket with his free hand.

"Hang on," he says, taking back his other palm. He rapidly begins pulling keys off of a key ring. "I only have the one, but that's fine, right?" he asks the officiant as I notice the sweat gathering around his hairline.

"Oh—well, you don't need *any*, really," the officiant says with a light shrug.

"Just"—I try to say it gently, but it comes out impatient and rude—"just, *here*." I strip my grandmother's ruby ring from my right hand before I slap it into his palm. "Give me the key ring."

He hands it to me, a muscle rippling up his jaw. *Oh, sorry, mon amour, did me snapping embarrass you?* Good, hanging onto irritation is better than letting myself fall for the streak of nervousness I think I detect in him.

I inhale through my nose and look back to the officiant with a nod.

The rest happens in flashes. Pulse beats that I try desperately to detach from. More words are said, more words agreed upon. He slips on the ruby ring and I slip on the key ring, just barely too big given the size of his fingers. And then we're told we may kiss and I want to ask if we *must*, but his face is already approaching mine and my heart is catching in my throat. He steps in close, his eyes darting almost fearfully between my own before they dip down to my mouth. His throat bounces on a swallow and any gentleness disappears, replaced with something cold and hard.

Teenage Deacon was sly, but *this* Deacon . . . this Deacon is *dangerous*, with eyes that look like they see right through me, past the barriers, cutting right to my soft center where they find me *lacking*. But then his tattooed hand slips up my wrist and around to my back and he gathers me in closer, his chest rattling against my own. I hate that I love the feel of his body against mine, deliciously filled out and hardened over the years, pressed to everywhere I've softened. He dips and our lips meet, both of us inhaling sharply through our noses at the same time, a small swish of a sound that echoes through the little chamber.

It's a dry press, but it's soft enough that it still forces me to consider what he normally kisses like. Something ingrained into my memory only because he was my first, not because it's the standard I've pathetically measured every kiss against since.

It's when we pull apart that I notice the music lightly playing, some quartet version of "Wrecking Ball". Another score for the soundtrack of my life.

And then it's . . . done.

I'm a married woman, in a parking lot in San Francisco, climbing into the back of my new husband's SUV because sitting in the passenger's seat feels too official and real and couple-y.

We pick up lunch to go and pull over at a park that looks out over the Golden Gate Bridge. And while Elyse walks around on the path, I'm tearing off the pieces of my bread bowl that have chowder deliciously soaked in, tackling it with intense precision because it's the only thing I can control at this moment. I'm putting all my hope and energy into this meal, letting it be the thing I exist for rather than letting my mind wander, when Deacon bursts my happy bubble, walking over from where he'd just been eating alone. He sits down at my side and holds up his plastic spoon my way.

"Cheers?" he asks, and despite myself, maybe because I'm still numb, I want to laugh. Maybe cry. I manage to not do either.

"Cheers," I concede. "And, uh, thanks for lunch." We click our plastic spoons together. His cheeks are flushed with the breeze coming off of the water, his five o'clock shadow already apparent even though it's only a little past two. He catches me looking and takes it as an invitation to search me in return.

"So," I say, cutting through the silence. "When and how do we get this going?"

He sighs and looks back at the bridge. "Permits, first. I made an appointment to get everything submitted at the county office tomorrow."

"Do you not have to work?"

He tosses a piece of bread back down into his bowl. "I do *work*, Larry. I work so hard that I've afforded myself some flexibility, in fact. What about you? Any plans to get a job?"

"I didn't mean it like that, Deacon, *Jesus*." I throw the rest of my food into the nearest bin and start walking toward the car. It's better to just separate myself than to try.

"I'm sorry, alright?" he calls from behind me, the words bursting out of him. "I'm just . . . Maybe I'm struggling with the idea of answering to *you* all the time, too."

I whip around to face him and his eyes round before he puts his hands up.

"Really. I'm not trying to be a dick, I swear. I promise to try to be less defensive."

I nod, but can't bring myself to promise the same.

I start toward the car again, but turn back after a few steps.

"I already put in an application at that coffee shop on the corner, plus a few others I can walk to." *Since I don't have a car,* I don't say. *Since I have nothing but this place and the hopes that I can buy myself some time with it. Since I dropped out and was cut off and since I have no other real work experience and rent was impossible at minimum wage and—*

"Spill the Beans?" He throws away his trash and slides his hands in his pockets.

"What?"

"I mean, you applied at Spill the Beans?"

"Oh. Y-Yeah."

He nods. "I'll make sure they hire you."

My first reaction is to scoff and roll my eyes. *Gee, thanks, oh powerful one.* I swallow the sound and nod my thanks, instead.

"June owns that place," he explains.

Oh. "You're still friends with June?"

"Yeah. Jensen, too. They're both still around."

"Okay," I say, dully. "Um—thank you."

He steps closer to me, his hands still encased in his jeans. The same dirty workwear ones he dons every day. Today's shirt is a solid dark gray, and is buttoned up almost fully, I'm just realizing. Like he actually bothered to put forth a modicum of effort.

"*There.* Was that so hard?" he says with a smug grin.

I clamp my teeth together and refuse to let him bait me. He breezes past and strolls into the parking lot.

WE RIDE BACK IN SILENCE again, until Elyse decides to prompt conversation.

"So!" she yells, since the top remains down. "Tell me about the first time you met!"

Jesus Christ.

He chimes in before I can. "I gave her a gift and she chucked it into the ocean."

"It wasn't a *gift*, it was a sand dollar and it was still alive! I saved it. Just because you plucked it from the ground doesn't give you ownership of it!" I see him laughing at me in the rearview mirror, still thrilled every time he annoys me. Most people don't know that sand dollars are living things. "And," I add, "you very well know that wasn't the first time we met."

His laugh dies. "*That* was an accident!" he says.

"You broke my nose!"

"*Fractured!* And an ACCIDENT!*"

Elyse guffaws. "How'd he break your nose?!"

We pull up to a stoplight then, the quiet deafening in comparison.

"It was my first day back—first *hour,* in fact," I say. "And I was happily walking to the beach without a care in the world when Prince Charming here spiked a volleyball into my face. I spent half that summer deformed."

His knuckles go white on the steering wheel. "It was *maybe* three weeks of bruising. You were *not* deformed." I feel his eyes through his sunglasses. "I spent *months* saying I was sorry," he adds, and the light turns green. I shift away from his grooved reflection, and back to Elyse.

"Imagine my delight when he spent that night in the ER with my grandma and me," I tell her. I remember her going on endlessly about Deacon as I held an ice pack against my bloodied nose. "*Deacon was recruited to play first base before his injury. Deacon helped build our planter beds for the courtyard. He's going to build us two more matching ones. Deacon fixed the gate. Deacon showed me how to use the DVD player. Deacon works at the Santa Sea campground, sounds like a fun summer gig, I'm sure he would help you get on there if you wanted to, ma fille. . . .*"

"Oh, god. I'm sure *you* were the delight," Elyse laughs.

I laugh back, though the sound is forced. "What's that supposed to mean?"

"You don't want anyone *near* you when you're sick or hurt. You bit my head off when I brought you soup after you had *pneumonia,*" she says. Deacon snorts knowingly from the driver's seat. "She ended up hospitalized and only told me when she got discharged and needed a ride," she explains. I fidget uncomfortably when I notice his brow furrow in the mirror again.

"It was the day after that—the nose thing—when I followed her on her walk and tried to give her the sand dollar,"
Deacon supplies, and I'm struck with being grateful for the
way he steered the conversation back, as if he could sense my
discomfort somehow.

The reminiscing dies off from there, and the remainder of
the ride drifts into melancholy.

WHEN WE PULL INTO THE garage, he quietly says something about
going for a walk before he leaves Elyse and I to pack up her
belongings.

And as I help her, I smile and aim to seem light again.
Maybe if I can put a positive spin on things with her, it'll help
all of this feel real for me later. The last thing she needs is to
worry about me and my bullshit. I've burdened her with
enough as it is. She already housed me for half a year before
this, nearly for free.

"Hey," I say. "You know I'm grateful for you, right?"

She zips up her suitcase and wraps me in a hug. "I'm just
as grateful for you, don't you fucking forget it."

I don't know why, she's only going to be three hours away
after all, but I still can't hold back a few tears. She'll have to
buckle down and focus on school and will have little time for
anything else, and I decide in this moment that I certainly
won't give her anything to worry about when it comes to *me*,
either. I already don't know what I bring to this friendship,
why she sticks by my side.

Because when I'm not easy for people, when I'm not a
convenient version of me, I always manage to lose them.

* * *

THE NEXT MORNING WHEN I walk Elyse out, I force a bright smile and wave, telling her to call me when she makes it home.

And when I turn back to the dilapidated building and see my *husband* sipping coffee on the balcony, I'm reminded of the second item I spied on the little task list he'd begun to draw out. The one that comes right after Permit Application.

I roll my shoulders and crack my neck, decide to chant it to myself like a mantra because it is definitely one thing I am dying to get to at some point in the near future: demo.

When I get inside, he's got another stupid printed shirt thrown on—this one covered in little Airstream trailers—and is lacing up his boots.

"I'll be at the campground if you need me," he says.

"Oh—you're already headed out?" I ask.

"Worried you'll miss me?" He grins sideways up at me, laces snicking together with a whoosh before he stands. I spare him a bored look in response.

"I figure I'll stay out of your way as much as I can." He shrugs. "Once the check gets here, we can work on a budget and get some stuff demo'd and cleared, but until then. . . ." He shrugs some more. "And then the permits . . ."

I mimic the same motion, tossing my shoulders. "Perfect," I say flatly. "Works for me. I'll mail the marriage certificate today."

His eyes roll. "Yeah, yeah. I figured." He slaps a note on the counter. "See you soon, Larry."

"Later, *Deac*." I let my accent slip through so it sounds like Dick. I doubt he misses it.

SIX

LARYNN

I think there's really only so much walking one can do on the beach.

I walk and run daily. Sometimes I carry my no-cooking-required breakfast of the day with me before I sit on a bench to watch the sunrise, hoping maybe *this* will be the one. The one sunrise that brings a new dawn, a new perspective on my life.

I think it might be making me worse. Like, maybe physically reminding myself everyday how insignificant my little life is in comparison to this great big ocean is making me retreat further inward, making me more frustrated with myself.

Today's sunrise is shaping up to be another glorious one, and just as I'm about to get up and head back home, my phone vibrates in my pocket.

Mom flashes across the top of the screen, the second time she's called in the last two weeks. So strange that she keeps trying. I'd normally have caved by now, would have called her back so she could tell me about her *wonderful new flat* with her *gorgeous new husband Liam* and their *yummy goldendoodle Fitz*. Or I would tell her some detail about my life that she'd respond to with a story that is supposed to illustrate just how much she can relate, but in fact achieves the opposite.

I should get it over with soon. On one hand, she's at least putting forth an effort to have a relationship with me whereas Dad won't and would prefer me not to try, either. Not since I veered away from his path.

"You have no follow-through," he'd said. *"You are careless and lazy and spoiled. You are throwing away a great deal of my time, and my money. . . ."*

I suppose I should call and give my mom what she needs. The reminder that I'm alive and fine and therefore she managed to succeed as a mother, despite the Thing we never ever should mention. I'm her little triumph.

And my father's greatest failure.

No . . . I don't think I'm in the right headspace to make idle chat with Mom, yet. Maybe it's the salty wind and the general abrasiveness of this new environment rubbing off on me, but I feel worn down and scraped away. One wrong remark and I won't be able to hold back the tide.

I briefly checked out the note Deacon left on the counter—five days ago now. It only contained specific instructions regarding the plumbing and what to do if things go awry. He also left his number "in case of emergency," which I took to mean not to contact him otherwise. As if I would.

On the bright side, I've managed to pick up shifts at the coffee shop every day since I was hired. June's warm, quiet presence is a balm to my nerves. She doesn't try to make small talk with me, hasn't asked me to update her on my life (or lack thereof) since I last saw her eight years ago.

We were summer pals who met when we were twelve and had a friendship that existed solely within the confines of this town during those months, so it's not as if we were inseparable to begin with. But I *could* see us being friends again. For someone who doles out caffeine in droves she is disturbingly serene.

I'll have to work on a way to ask her out on a friend date of sorts, even if it's hard to picture. Elyse planted herself in my life and didn't give me a say otherwise, so making new friends as an adult is not something I'm familiar with, and it sounds daunting as hell.

Still, I generally enjoy being in that space, and I think it'll help the friend stuff get easier over time. The customers have quickly started to greet me like they know me, sans the trepidatious looks. It's oddly . . . lovely. Serving people. Offering someone some small comfort. It's a nice change, bringing someone some joy.

It's also been nice that I've been able to work so consistently with the busy season. Especially since I don't know when my check from the trust will show and I'm down to the last $137 in my account from selling my car. I'd texted June to let her know I was available today, but no such luck.

Blame it on the stupid sunrise, but a flash of something desperate courses through me, something that doesn't want to feel small or lonely or useless. I hit call on Elyse's name.

"Hey!" she whispers into the phone.

"Oh shit, I'm sorry," I say when I realize the day and time. "You're in class, aren't you?"

"Yeah just give me one sec though—"

"No, no, I'm sorry . . ."

"—stop, I'm here. This professor won't even notice I'm gone, too caught up in hearing himself speak," she says, normal volume now.

"I'm sorry, I wasn't even thinking about class."

"Stop apologizing. How are you?"

"I'm"—*lost, more anxious than ever, dying to get out of my own head*—"I really like the job." I settle on a truth.

"I kinda thought you might." I can feel her grinning into the phone. "How's Deacon?"

"Gone, thankfully. He's been staying over at the campground. Left the same day as you. Can't start much until we get the check, anyway."

"You still sleeping on the couch?"

"Of course. Where else would I sleep?" I almost verbalize an LOL to emphasize the ridiculousness of that question.

"Hmm."

"Hmm?"

"I mean, you haven't slept under the same roof without a chaperone there yet. Just an observation." I hear the innocent shrug implied through the phone.

"A very astute one."

"Well," she sings, *"I think you might as well start making yourself comfortable, LaRynn. It sounds like it's gonna take a while."*

"Yeah, yeah. I will, alright. Don't worry about me."

"Miss you."

"Miss you, too."

There's a small silent pause before she says, "Rynn?"

"Yeah?"

"Just *try*, okay? Try to open up a bit and *try* to be nice. If anything it'll throw him off his game, but more likely it'll make working together that much easier."

I sigh, and it comes out more weary than I'd intended. "Okay."

"Love you," she says.

"Talk soon," I say.

I MAKE MY WAY BACK up the hill and unlatch the gate. It's surprisingly sturdy and fluid, the bougainvillea vines draped over the pergola mendaciously lush given the state of the place they're welcoming.

And when I get inside I stealthily climb upstairs, careful to avoid drawing Sally out from her unit.

I know I need to visit her soon. She was *Aunt* Sally to me growing up. It's just . . . I think seeing her here and in this place makes the contrast of my grandma not being here so much more stark. My plate feels precariously full as it is and I just need a little longer, I think.

The sound of running water hits me from somewhere when I walk through the doorway, and a cursory glance around leads me to believe that Deacon's here—showering. A pair of unlaced boots sits haphazardly flung in the middle of the walkway, a ring of keys lay just as sloppily on the would-be countertop.

One of the few walls that does currently stand fully intact, is the one that leads to "his" room—formerly the guest suite that served as my quarters every past summer stay. But there's still no door to close it off entirely and the idea of being in the house alone with him—naked— throws me into an immediate state. I have exactly zero right to be flustered and just as little right to be annoyed, but . . .

Laundry. I'll go do laundry. I have clothes. Plenty of them. I'll wash and dry them thrice if necessary.

I grab my phone, headphones, and everything from my designated hamper-corner and bolt.

I'VE ALREADY GOT ONE LOAD going and have begun spot-treating a coffee stain on my favorite white tee when I think I hear a thump above the din of my music. I don't hear it again when I remove one of the earbuds, though, so I carry on.

But then I think I *feel* another thump. I take them both out this time and I *definitely* hear banging coming from above me, followed by a few muffled expletives.

"Shit."

Shit. Shit. Shit. He's banging on the floor.

Deacon's water forebodings.

The sloppily scratched out letters jumble together in my brain but I remember that there was something along the lines of DO NOT USE WASHING MACHINE AT THE SAME TIME AS SHOWER written the loudest on the page.

I fling open the lid before I slam it shut again and try to find the stop button, but it's an old machine and in my ruffled state I struggle to decipher them all.

"*LARRY!*" I make out Deacon's roar from upstairs.

"Fuck," I hiss under my breath before I call out, "I know I know, I'm sorry! I forgot and I don't know how to get it to stop now! How do I get it to stop?!"

I hear his feet slap the stairs and start slamming buttons in a panic.

Oh Jesus. His body is a blot in my peripheral vision, but he's definitely in a towel, *only*. I continue my manic button-whacking as he shoves a paper in my face.

"I wrote it down, Larry. I wrote it down."

"Just tell me how to get it to stop, okay?!" I yell, my voice high and tight.

"Read it. You need to remember this and know how to do it. We can't fucking afford water damage and mold on top of everything else," he says.

I rear on him. "Don't you dare parent me," I spit, my finger jabbing into a very wet and impossibly firm pec. His chin dips to look at it before he deigns to look back at me. He's flushed, panting, and there's a mix of bubbles and something chunky and gray splattered across his . . . *very* developed chest and abs. Real-life abs stacked on top of each other. *Jesus.* I blink, blood rushing to my face, my ears and neck going swollen and hot. I speak again before he says something I can't respond productively to. "Just. Show me."

He looks me over for a moment that stretches and rounds, like he's lost his train of thought and is searching for it on my face. I track a droplet of water as it slides down a curl of hair and splatters against my wrist.

Suddenly, the smell hits me.

"Oh my god. What is that *smell?!*" I cup my hand over my face, but it already feels like the stench has adhered to the inside of my brain. "It's like . . . like mildew that's grown inside of someone's fetid gym bag, and then also somehow gone stale."

"It's what happens when you don't heed the warnings about the water. If you can't be courteous, Princess, next time I'll make sure this is all over you." He gestures to his body, and it takes my brain a humiliatingly long moment to determine that he was referring to the gray gunk and *not* his body.

He catches me leering and narrows his eyes with a cocky grin. "Don't get any ideas, Larry."

"Oh, *fuck you.*" Not my best line.

"Nope, not that either."

I nearly stamp my foot in agitation, my now-crossed fists grinding against my ribs. He stretches past me, holding his towel with one hand as he reaches behind the washing machine and cranks a knob.

"If it ever happens that you *forget* again," he says, brows raised and blinking stupidly at me like he suspects I did this on purpose, "just turn the water off altogether. This knob here."

Another thought occurs to me, then. "How'd you know it wasn't Sal?"

"Because he texted me beforehand," Sal says from her open doorway, sipping something that looks like a cosmopolitan from a martini glass, an oxygen tank at her feet. "I text now, you know. And *I* know not to run any of the water when the shower goes. Multi-sink usage seems to be fine so far, only the occasional hiccup." She takes another sip from a straw. "And hello, my girl. It's good to finally see you."

I swallow and let my eyes drift over her. She's even tinier and frailer than I recall, but somehow undiminished. Emotions collide behind my ribs and wind up my throat.

"H-hi, Sally," I say, my eyes settling on my feet next to Deacon's bare ones. I scoot them away, not liking how small mine look beside his.

"It's still Aunt to you, if you like," she says with a sigh. "Come here. And Deacon, go away and take that stench with you."

"Yes, Ma'am."

I wait until he disappears around the corner before I stiffly make my way to Sal. She guides me inside her apartment and shuts the door behind us.

Her eyes look me over, head to toe. "It's been a long time," is all she says. Simply, and kindly.

And when my arms wrap around her knobby body, I break. "I'm s-sorry," I say, wailing like I'm eight again and just broke her glass dolphin sculpture. Years of regret burst up from my chest. I should have been here.

She sighs. "Nothing to apologize for. You're here now."

She shushes and holds me, lets me cry it out, soothes me until I eventually settle. When I lean back from her embrace, she reaches up to dab my face with a tissue. Something she must keep in a pocket handy somewhere.

"You have time for a visit?" she asks.

"Yes," I choke out before I awkwardly sink into the old sofa and look around the place.

So much is the same—the same round table we'd all play Yahtzee and Dominoes at. The same photographs. I avoid looking too closely for fear of losing the leash on my emotions again.

The Price is Right plays lowly in the background while we make polite small talk for a quick moment. Until she straightens, visibly gearing up for the harder stuff.

"So." She lets out a ragged breath like it pains her to ask. "How are your parents?"

My sigh is similarly worn. "Dad's still angry with me for dropping out. And then he found out grandma left the property to me not long after, so . . . he was pretty unhappy." I blow out a breath. "We haven't spoken since."

She shakes her head with a chuckle. "He hated when she moved here, anyway. And hated it more when she found Helena. Not sure what he expected."

"Dad hates a lot of things. I still don't understand how he came from her." I snort.

She tilts her head as she considers me. "Being old allows you an inordinate amount of time to consider the things you never understood, so it got a little philosophical at times. . . ." She mimes smoking a joint and a wet laugh bubbles out of me. "But Cece blamed herself a lot." She sighs. "I think our kids develop little resentments, small things at first, things they think their parents do wrong or traits they have that *are* wrong, and therefore cost *them* something. If those small things fester they end up dedicating all their energy into not being that thing, I think. Drink?" She nods to the one on her end table as she pushes up from her chair.

"It's 8 A.M.," I say. She cocks an eyebrow and waits. "Oh— um, sure. Let me, though." I move to get up.

"Sit your ass back down LaRynn Cecelia," she barks. "I'm not yet an invalid."

"Yes, Ma'am."

Using her walker, she wheels over to the kitchen and opens the fridge, a near-full pitcher of cosmos already prepared, as it always was. She pours me a glass as she continues. "Do you know why your grandma immigrated here in the first place?"

"No." I frown. I realize I'd simply made the very American assumption that she just *wanted* to, that this country was some dream realized.

Sal nods. "Cece left Quebec when Max was six. His father was never in the picture. She modeled, which you know, and I guess that made life a little unstable and chaotic for the first few years they were here. And I'm not sure if you knew this part, but she married the first man who could provide any kind of comfort, was able to secure citizenship for her and for Max." She sighs a rattled sound as she returns the pitcher to the fridge.

And I can't help but think: another marriage born out of necessity, and look how that ended up.

"That man was a lawyer," she continues, "and was the first father figure that showed your dad any kind of love. Gave them security and a pretty cushy life. But, when they divorced, that same man wanted nothing to do with Max anymore, either."

An image of my dad surfaces in my mind: his stern, stubborn face. I try to imagine a younger, sadder version of him. One lonely and struggling. I can't conjure it against the picture of him standing over me and berating me as I struggled to read through tears. The man whose insistence that I be excellent at everything left me perpetually exhausted and disappointed in myself. Sal hands me the drink and labors back to her chair.

"Cece thinks he equated stability with love, since his only example of a marriage was one that was . . . utilitarian in nature. Devoid of much love or affection. And she'd been denying who she was for years, was unhappy herself, which didn't make anything easier. Anyway, all just theoretical. But my guess is Max is the way he is and tried to force it on you because he always wanted you to have stability, too."

A bitter laugh tumbles free. I suppose it makes sense, then, his anger toward me. A dyslexic, emotional little girl whose favorite pastimes included art and music and daydreaming. And then my mom . . .

"I don't get how he ever ended up with my mom, though," I say. Can't imagine how they ever thought they were right for each other.

Sal swallows back another breath. "I suppose love brings out the best in us at first, makes you want to be what the other person sees in you. Maybe your mother brought that out in him, in the beginning . . . before."

Before me, she doesn't say. Before they fell apart and she left him, left me in the same process. Signed away her rights when I was five, until she came back when I was eight.

"Sometimes I think my mother only came back so she could feel better about herself," I say, staring at the screen as someone hits a number on a wheel and begins jumping frantically, celebrating some great win. "It's not like it was some happy reunion. She was miserable. All I knew was their misery."

"I think they tried. Max tried to be more romantic, to take her around the world."

Which is how I ended up here every summer.

So I guess something good still came from it. The memories I was able to make in this place.

"Anyway," she continues, brushing her hand through the air like she can swipe away the mood. "Tell me how it's going upstairs." She smiles conspiratorially and I tilt a brow her way.

"*Nothing* is going quite yet, but we'll get there."

I don't bring up the sale. Don't tell her about the trust or the marriage either because I'm not sure what she already knows or what Deacon's already apprised her of, and for some reason it feels like he should get to be the one to do that.

I do end up buzzed and oversharing pieces of my dismal dating history before noon, though.

And when I trip out of her doorway later that afternoon, some optimistic kernel in me prompts me to check the mailbox. . . .

WHEN I SKIP UPSTAIRS, EXCITED to show Deacon the check in spite of myself, he and his things are gone again.

SEVEN

DEACON

It shouldn't offend me, seeing LaRynn in her nice clothes, sleeping on my favorite bench by the beach. Confuse me, sure. Annoy me, undoubtedly, since that seems to be par for the course when it comes to LaRynn. But offend?

I haven't seen her since our water fiasco three days ago. Figured it was in our best interest to go back to giving each other a wide berth.

There was something so uncertain that passed over her expression when she saw Sal that day. Almost like she was afraid. Didn't know what to do with someone's genuine care. . . .

I have *got* to shake that kind of thinking, though, which is precisely why I went back to my perimeter.

She's just . . . She was always way too sharp for the likes of me, so I guess I'm having a hard time letting that wariness go.

Still . . . I shouldn't be having such a *visceral* reaction to this. To her. There are plenty of open benches nearby. But some part of my brain sees this as a sort of smug foreshadowing for my life. Everything of mine gets overtaken by her. Every summer she still takes over my mind.

The princess turns newborn vampire, her eyes blasting open as she rears up with a violent gasp. "What the—" she says when she registers me hovering. "*Jesus,* Deacon, can I help you?" she barks. Dark brows dart down over those green, wide set eyes. I feel my face frown in response at the same time something squeezes in my ribs.

"Why are you sleeping on a bench?" I ask, curiosity being the winner out of warring sensations.

"Why is it any of your business?" she snipes.

"Because it's not exactly safe. Or remotely smart."

"Oh, thank you. I *love* having the dangers of being a woman mansplained to me first thing in the morning." She rolls her eyes. "If you must know, I did not fall asleep here on purpose. I must've just—dozed off. And I happen to sleep like the dead."

"I remember," I say, and her nostrils flare. "And I don't think that makes it any better."

"*Oh no.*" She clutches her chest in mock-horror. "But I simply *live* for your approval."

"Look Princess, I'm just saying, maybe have some more regard for your own safety."

She jerks up, the long legs that were neatly tucked beneath her unfurling with precision. The look on her face says she's done humoring me.

"I went for a run," she says, "and was having a rest before I needed to get ready for work." She sighs and crosses her arms, her gaze drifting up the incline toward the house. I scratch a spot on my jaw and shift on my feet.

"June says things are going well?" I try, thinking this is a safe subject. She frowns quizzically in response, but before she can reply, a guy on an electric bike speeds past, close enough to blow her hair from her shoulders. Instead of moving, she scowls at his retreating back before eyeing the rest of the bike lane goers like a dare, and then proceeds to turn that glare on me. I physically have to move her to the interior side of the sidewalk, and I immediately brace myself for the barrage that's headed my way when Jensen ambles up, his own coffee in hand and a sly grin on his face. LaRynn follows my line of sight and turns to face him.

"Rynn?!" he shouts, his steps stuttering.

One side of her mouth lifts politely. "Jensen. Hey."

He wraps her in a hug and she pats him on the back once. "Great to have you back. You playing today?" he asks.

"Playing?"

"Volleyball." He laughs. "We play at least three or four days a week, but I've been on night rotations at the hospital for the last month." I'm irrationally irritated at the open friendliness there.

"Oh." She breathes out a small laugh. "No, no. I'm just here in town to take care of—" She stabs a thumb toward the house. "And hospital, huh? Guess you stuck with the doctor plan then?"

"Sure did. And nice about the old house! Hopefully that frees this guy up for a break, finally."

"A break?" She snorts. "From what?" The tone implies how unimpressed she is with what I've managed to triage on my own so far.

Fine, I can play rough, too. "Alright, *dear*," I seethe, "don't you have to go get ready for work?"

"*Dear?*" Jensen asks.

Her mouth hangs open and her eyes widen, searing into me.

"Yep. Larry and I have some happy news to share," I declare brightly.

Jensen searches between us as I tuck her into my side—a lapse in judgment on my part because I fucking forgot that scent of hers. Like burnt sugar, something like cotton candy but richer. It's like an immediate, dirty slideshow via olfactory. I recall running my tongue along her neck, wanting to see if she'd taste like it, too.

I blink away the thoughts. "Say hello to the new wifey, Jay." His face falls open before he clutches his side in a laugh.

She swipes the coffee from my hand and starts toward the crosswalk. "I'll let you explain the *rest* of the story to him, *mon petit puce*." She blows me a kiss that turns into the middle finger before she struts off, sipping my coffee as she goes.

"Explain," Jensen demands.

I sigh and sit down on the bench—nicely warmed from its former occupant—and break down the story.

WHEN I FINISH, JENSEN'S STILL standing, still sporting a bag of volleyballs slung over his shoulder and his typical shit-eating grin.

"Sounds like kismet to me. You guys always did make a good team when you actually worked together," he says casually, patting me on the shoulder before he trots down the cement stairs onto the sand.

Easy for him to say. The man could get his foot run over by a car and respond with a pithy tale about a distant relative's injury and the newfound perspective he gained from it. His relentless positivity used to exhaust me. Now that I know how genuine it is, I usually can't help but appreciate the guy. It's probably an ideal trait for someone who wants to be a pediatrician.

The next hour passes in traditional fashion: doubles matches in the sand against other regulars, occasional shit-talking and catching up. I wonder how LaRynn's been filling her time these last days. Wonder if she's liking the shop.

"I guess you didn't hear that she's working at June's, then?" I ask Jensen.

Jensen looks up from his crouched position with a squint. "Huh? Who is?"

Oh. I realize I haven't been talking about LaRynn out loud. I dig a foot into the sand and watch it disappear, wipe the sweat off my face with a forearm. "Larry. June gave her a job."

"Nice. I'll go visit after."

"Why?"

"Why . . . not?"

"Just don't go getting attached to her, alright?" I tell him.

"If you need to keep saying things out loud to me that you should be saying to the mirror that's fine, my friend, but I knew LaRynn even before I knew you. I'll do as I damn well please," he says with a laugh.

I roll my eyes and shake my head, but he presses on. "So, if you don't mind me asking, what's the, uh, bedroom arrangement? She free to see other people? Since, according to you, it's 'on paper only'?" I stare at his smiling face before it splits into another laugh. "Don't tell me you guys didn't discuss this?" he says.

I walk toward the sideline and grab my shirt.

"Can't wait to hear how that goes!" he calls, and I fruitlessly try to dust the sand off my limbs before I start the march up the hill. I end up sloughing off a layer of skin and barely any of the sand, instead.

There's nothing more humbling than trying to stomp up

both a hill and stairs in flip-flops, but after a few years living here I gave up and sold part of my Easterner soul to wearing sandals—to and from the beach only. I kick them off as soon as I get inside and snort out a breath. I swear her scent followed me from the courtyard and up these stairs and has already invaded every inch of space here.

And then I freeze as I start to take in everything around me.

There are six—*six!*—new pillows on my couch. A new coffee table with a candle the size of my face on it next to a stack of books. A weird, overlong chair thing that doesn't fucking fit stuffed in the corner next to another new stool thing—one that looks like a stump she hauled up from the beach, another candle on top of it. Some modern-looking record player of some kind on top of a small bookcase. I whirl around and see that there's even a bunch of new shit added to the kitchen, too. There are no doors on the cabinets that are left, but there are now little wire shelves stacked full of shit in them. Clear containers holding various nuts, pastas . . . bags of chips arranged by color. It's like peeking into the mind of a serial killer. *Another* candle. Some dish towels rolled up in a basket next to the sink, a toaster oven on the counter, a copper kettle on one of the burners, a rug on the floor, *another* candle, and . . . *a fucking new refrigerator?!!*

Oh my god. There are curtains. *CURTAINS* on the windows.

Christ. We don't even have real cabinets and the countertops are plywood and plumbing is still testy and this woman is spending money on fucking curtains.

I scramble to my bathroom next, and groan.

"What the fuck?!"

New pink bath towels sit rolled up in a basket on the ground under more pink towels that are hung on a towel rack. A tan shower curtain with a matching pink stripe at the bottom (and fucking tassels) has replaced my old one, and—you guessed it—there's another candle on the counter.

I vaguely register what looks like four new pillows on my bed but choose not to count. Instead, I sink onto the six inches of couch that remain pillow free and rock back and forth a bit.

She did this to show me something, didn't she? This is a power move to get the upper hand, to make me scared of what she'll do with the money. *She* has rich parents and friends in other places to fall back on. She doesn't need me to do this even if I do it for free. Her father is a fucking lawyer for God's sake. They could take it all away in a heartbeat.

But . . . no. She's also got a job here now, she's *here*, she's in this . . . She doesn't have a car, and something tells me that means she's on her own. . . .

Still. Our budget is tight, to say the least. And *we're* in this together.

I grab a plushy pillow and clutch it to my chest, leaning back into the couch with a groan.

There's got to be a good way to approach a money conversation that doesn't end in my castration, but fuck if I know what that is, or what that looks like.

I'm not sure how long I stare up at the ceiling trying to find the answer in my brain, but it's long enough that she finishes her shift and walks through the doorway.

My face must give something away, sitting here clinging to a ridiculously soft plaid pillow, because she walks in look-ing . . . relaxed. Happy. But that look rapidly falls when our eyes meet and she tosses her bag on the counter before fold-ing her arms. It's like I can visibly see her building up for a fight, brick by brick. Shoulders stiffening, chin lifting.

"What? What is it? You wanted a wife, Deacon. You got a wife."

I remember as a kid my dad coming home most nights and pulling my mom into a dance. She'd playfully try to toss him off so she could finish her task, but he'd coax her away and send her through a twirl and a dip anyway. I realized later in life that she'd worked just as many hours as he had, but would still be the one to prepare a meal every night. She'd still be the one doing the clean up afterwards, too, so maybe she just wanted to finish so *she* could unwind.

He'd make plans for vacations and dates and would bring home flowers. He'd fix things around the house and make sure we had the most immaculate lawn in the neighborhood. He even coached me and my brother in Little League until he had an affair with one of the other player's moms.

The first affair.

He begged and pleaded and promised his way back into Mom's trust. And then he got sick. I watched her give him a shot in the ass every night for months on end. Watched her plaster on a smile and shield us from his mood swings. I was convinced that she single-handedly healed the man when he went into remission when I was fourteen.

Mom found out about the *second* affair when I was seventeen.

Two months later we found out the cancer had come back and spread, right after she'd put a deposit down on an apartment for us.

We moved back in with my father, and she proceeded to care for him with the same unending patience until he died six months later on Thanksgiving Day.

She was lonely and lost, and my nana told her about a job that came with housing, out here at a campground in Santa

Cruz. I'd blown out my shoulder earlier that fall and had been skipping most of my classes at junior college, aimlessly drifting. So when she'd looked at me with her tired eyes and asked me if I'd be up for a fresh start, I said yes, and came with her.

She didn't talk about the affairs much. Still won't. But sometimes, typically around the holidays or his birthday, she'll let something slip. I've heard her cry and seen her clutch cards that he'd written to her and ask "How? How could he write these things to me at the same time he was sleeping with them?"

So, even though my gut reaction is to stay suspicious, to err on the side of judgment, to remind myself that someone can always be more duplicitous than they seem . . . I look at LaRynn now, and maybe it's those same tired eyes that make me wonder if this is *her* fresh start. I decide to give her the benefit of the doubt, and to consider that she was trying to do something nice, maybe. Something to make her comfortable and, though it's hard to believe, maybe add some comfort for me, too.

"I fucking love these pillows," is all I say. Maybe if I show her she can count on me to have her back, she'll open up and have mine, too. Maybe I'm an absolute sucker and I'll get left at the end of this a lot more broken and minus a house.

She blinks a few times in surprise. Shifts uncomfortably on her feet. "I—um. I tried not to go overboard, I know that we'll have to move a lot of these things around during different phases and I probably should've asked if the fridge was fine, but it was actually a good deal and I just figured we could be more comfortable in the meantime, you know? The pantry stuff just helps it all stay organized instead of piling up on the counters, too."

And there it is. A glimpse at LaRynn when she opens up.

Maybe . . . maybe we can be friends. Something we never got to be. Not really.

"I'm headed out with the twins tonight . . . if you want to join us?" I ask.

She unties her apron and my eyes flick to her chest as it presses against the v of her shirt. I blink back down to the pillow in my lap, turn my palm to study it instead.

"I worked with June for the last five hours. I think if she'd wanted to include me she would have. Thanks, though," she responds quietly.

I make a tired noise. "We *just* made these plans, Lar. Seriously, in the last five minutes." I hold up my cell phone for emphasis.

She looks like she wants to say something snippy back at me, but shuts her eyes and rocks back on her feet instead. "Fine. Okay. Give me ten minutes. I'll go change over there."

When I get up, I steal a glance through the doorway to look across the landing where she pointed, catalog the make-shift room she's set up for herself. There's the edge of what appears to be a cot behind one of those folding divider things, plus a few more baskets on the ground. *Jesus, she's clearly got a thing for baskets and goddamn candles.* Her shoes are neatly lined up at the base of the divider, an upright dresser floating in the room nearby, next to a rolling rack of clothes and a standing full-length mirror.

It's . . . weird.

Weird that she bought enough pillows to build her own bed but didn't buy a real one for herself. But whatever, I guess. To each their own.

"Could you *not* stare over here while I change?" she asks, and I only just notice her standing at the edge of the frame.

I make a noncommittal noise and head to my room, wishing I had a door to shut behind me. Instead, my line of sight through the open doorway leads straight through the entry and onward, right to her area.

My body goes tight when I look over my shoulder as she slings her bra over the top of the divider, right before I spot a kneecap as she bends a leg—presumably to step in or out of something. I turn away to smother a groan before something else catches the corner of my eye—a tag on one of the new pillows on my bed. Why did she get me new pillows anyway, dammit?

I hesitate for only a moment before I decide to look. It'll be fine. Maybe I'll be happily surprised.

I AM NOT HAPPILY SURPRISED.

$94.99.

It's a $95 fucking. PILLOW.

IT IS A SINGLE PILLOW. My vision goes blurry. I'm—is this what pillows cost? Am I having a stroke? I'm not even twenty-seven but crazier things have happened. Like pillows being $100.

I'm moving before I'm even cognizant of it. "Hey!" barks out of me before I feel the impending meltdown unspool. "Heyheyheyheyhey—what in good *fuck*—" I round the divider and walk straight into the sight of her thonged ass bent over, jean shorts pooled at her feet before she jerks them up and whirls on me.

Fucking Christ, I forgot about that birthmark on her ass— dark pink. Like the curve of a palm swept across it with paint.

"What the HELL, Deacon?"

I turn the other way. "I'm sorry, okay?" *No I'm not.* "But a hundred dollars for a fucking pillow?!" I shake it in the air despite not facing her. "How much have you spent already?!"

She's completely silent behind me. There's only the whir of her zipper and a huffy breath that puffs out of her.

"I'm not obligated to answer that," she says, low and dangerous.

I can hear my heart in my ears, feel my blood thud against my temples. I will myself to turn around slowly.

"Like *hell* you're not."

Her cheeks redden and her nose scrunches in fury. "Funny, that check was addressed to *me,* they let *me* cash it. Neither your presence nor your approval were required."

"How. Much."

"I'm not sure. Guess I'll go add up all my receipts." She feigns indifference but there's a challenge behind those words, I'm sure of it.

"Ballpark number, Larry. Give it to me."

"Like five grand, give or take." She says this like she has no idea how monumental it is.

I . . .

I need to sit.

I sit—no. My ass *falls* onto her cot.

And then I lie on it and put the hundred dollar pillow over my face in case I scream into it. What I actually need is to take a deep inhale, but I'm currently suffocating myself instead.

When I end up throwing it off in a move that I'm certain is tantrum-adjacent, she's scowling down at me, hands bracketing her hips, and I can't seem to hold it in anymore. "You spent FIVE GRAND IN THREE DAYS?!"

"I bought a refrigerator," she says, tone peaking at the end.

"And—like—fucking—eighty-eight—pillows—and—twenty-seven—fucking—baskets!" I bark back. It's like the words are too thick with agitation, they have to force their way out of me.

She makes an unflattering sound and rolls her eyes before she turns away. "Obviously, you can go out without me. I'm not going to subject anyone else to this." She gestures between us.

"SOUNDS GOOD." It feels like a vein is popping out of my forehead as she bends over me with a sneer. I can make out every shade of green in her eyes this close, even when they're as slitted as they are.

"Get off my bed," she says, quiet and sinister.

I get up and snatch the pillow from the ground. Use it to point at her on my way out.

"*That* isn't a bed. *That* is a COT you *COMPLETELY INSANE WOMAN*."

"GET. OUT!" It shouldn't satisfy me that she finally matches my volume, but it does.

I toss the pillow across the landing and back into my half. "BYE!"

Dammit. I'm certain that just set us back even more and it feels stupidly anticlimactic to schlep down these steps in my rage right now. "IF YOU WANT TO JOIN US WE'LL BE AT THE HARD WATER BAR!" I yell up the stairs, like an idiot.

"NOT LIKELY!"

Never mind. "EVEN BETTER!" And at last, I have a door to slam as I step out into the courtyard.

MY FRIENDS ARE LAUGHING AT me. Swiping away tears from the corners of their eyes, leaning back on their barstools.

"It was three days since I was last there. *Five grand* in three days, you guys. Permits alone are over twenty."

They exchange looks with one another in their merriment, have one of those twin-telepathy episodes.

"Care to share with the class?" I ask flatly.

"It's just that history has a way of repeating itself," June says. "Remember the planter boxes your grans had you guys make?"

"Yeah, I also recall LaRynn getting just as much credit despite the fact that *I* built them."

June sighs as Jensen lets out another laugh. "Deacon," Jensen says, "she stained the boxes, put plants in them that *she* proceeded to care for while she was here. She researched what kinds of things would do well together, paid attention to the sun exposure they got, had a watering schedule."

"Exactly! They asked us to build them planter *boxes*. The rest was overboard!"

"And she made them even better. Completed them. She felt she was helping. And if all she cared about was the credit she would not have bothered doing all that extra stuff because they weren't even hers. She made it nice for *them*. Maybe she was trying to do the same for you?"

It's a struggle not to roll my eyes, because clearly they don't get it. I had a moment where I forgot, earlier, when I'd let myself consider that, too. But then I saw that $95 price tag and knew she'd been trying to be malicious. LaRynn would never try to do something nice for me. Not after what I did.

I don't think.

Fuck, I feel eighteen again, discombobulated and confused and completely mystified by her.

I heave a sigh before June continues.

"LaRynn acted like she had to prove herself to everyone. And sure, if she wasn't good at something, she'd quit and act too good for it. But when she *tries*, when she cares . . . I don't know, but to me it always seemed like if she gave a shit about you, she'd go above and beyond." She winces and takes another sip of her drink. "I always got the sense that no one did that for her. People change, and I barely know her anymore. But—from what I've seen at work . . . a lot stays the same, too."

EIGHT

LARYNN

I catch myself muttering in French, a string of expletives that would've made even my curse-happy grandmother threaten me with soap. But I've also been looking for an extension cord for the last three fucking hours.

I can feel myself spiraling, my metaphorical heels digging into the hill I'm apparently choosing to die on right now. But I got my area set up. I gave him back his stupid couch. I even found a refrigerator with same-day delivery.

I can't cook to save my life, but I spent the remaining money in my personal account on groceries—snagging things that would make easy meals. Mostly just boxed pastas and jarred sauces, but still. I started a separate account for the trust money that I planned to give him access to as well, but I'm pretty damn certain I will no longer be doing that.

I set out with a positive attitude—planned to be the bigger, unaffected person in this. *Look at me, I'm ready to tackle this with maturity and consideration and I am an excellent, contributing member of this team. I am completely indifferent to the fact that once upon a time I gave you my body over and over (and over) again and then served up my heart on a platter, plated with*

*accoutrements and expert-level presentation, before you promptly
threw it in the trash in front of my family and friends. All good,
bro.*

But no, he belittles me instead, throws a full-blown, man-
sized fit. And *fine*, perhaps I went the tiniest bit overboard
with some of the comfort items. But I figured it was all stuff
I'd be able to use to help stage the place when it's time to sell,
and, like I told him, we could at least be comfortable in the
meantime. I tried to be considerate of him, too. To make sure
I got things he would also use. I haven't had my own space in
so long that maybe I just got a little overexcited. I did stop
myself from buying a bed for myself, at least, when I saw how
things were adding up. Embarrassment zaps through me, and
I try to bury it back down under my justifications. I'm twenty-
six and still have a limited concept when it comes to money.
I was never allowed to work growing up, all my extracurricu-
lar time spent with tutors.

Another stab of shame pierces me when I pause in my
rifling and think over the past few hours, finally coming
down from my anger spiral . . .

I paced and stomped around after he left, unable to calm,
growing angrier and angrier until I worked myself up into a
fit of my own. Threw myself into his bathroom in my rebel-
lion, grabbed his toothbrush and pumped the air in glee
before I dropped to my knees in front of the toilet. This is
also when my reflection and I made eye contact in the mirror.
I looked at her and she at me; she of the bloodshot eyes and
the mouth set in a hard line. And then "we" shrugged in
unison before I scrubbed the toilet good and hard with his
toothbrush because *fuck him*, that's why.

*I think I'll draw the outline of a middle finger using my hair
on the shower wall*, I thought. *Maybe I'll take a butcher knife to*

every pillow in this place and let him enjoy the mess. Put the toilet paper roll on backwards. Maybe I'll go spend another five grand on bobby pins and a leaf blower and spread them across his entire half of the floor, Rambo-style.

I eventually tired myself out with the scheming and tried to settle into my newly assembled quarters. Which is also when I realized that there isn't a reachable outlet to charge my phone.

I need the alarm on my phone to go off so I can wake up on the (especially early) mornings I'm scheduled to open up the shop. I like to have audiobooks or sleep noises at night, too, but I also need it to be within arm's reach so I can turn it off whenever I do manage to unwind. I just—I need *something* to go right.

I refuse to move all that shit again or admit further defeat, and I also refuse to bother Sal, especially now when it's past 1 A.M. There has *got* to be an extension cord somewhere in this goddamn shitting place.

I tear into a box that has more records, but I pull too hard and they slip out, clattering to the ground. *"Merde!"* I hiss before I start picking up the pieces of a broken one.

The Drifters. I drag another container over to sag down onto, the plastic bottom chafing against the cement floor.

The sight of that album calls up the sound of my grandmother's voice. "Under the Boardwalk" rang behind her words as she said to me, *"When you have a bad day, ma fille, think about it from beginning to end. Walk your way through it. Was it really a bad day, or was it a few bad moments? What part of your day would you like to hold on to before you close your eyes? Find that good bit, and let it be the thing you fall asleep to."*

Her pieces of advice carried me through so many lonely, dark days, and at the thought of her, my chest feels instantly tight. Like my heart is wrapped in thorns and vines, like too deep a breath would leave me punctured all over. I inhale shallowly through my nose and try to follow her words again as I close my eyes, rewinding to the beginning of the day in my mind. . . .

WHEN I OPENED THE COFFEE shop this morning, it was quiet and clean. I flipped on the lights and pushed down on the steam wands an extra time for good measure, even though I knew they were cleared during closing the evening before. That whooshing noise tickles some part of my brain, so I like to indulge myself with it regularly. I took all the cute woven stools off of the counter and lined them up along the breakfast bar. Did the same to the tables and chairs before I spotted June's note on the counter with what she had planned for today's drink special. A frozen blended matcha drink with toasted coconut on top. After I filled the pastry case, I decided to draw out the sidewalk sign for her since I had the time before we opened, anyway. And it was such a small thing, but even creating a welcoming picture and coloring it in . . . It was ridiculous how it made me smile to think someone might walk past and think "Wow, that looks good, I want one," or even just the first part, that small bit of admiration for something *I'd* done. I could practically hear Elyse's voice quipping about me *healing my inner child.*

In any case, it led to me rewriting all the little signs for the pastry display to match, which then led to me straightening up the menu board, and checking our stock on cups, napkins, utensils, and cleaning supplies everywhere else. I found an empty clipboard by the walk-in fridge and created a checklist and made a mental note to see if June wanted me to create a formal template later. When I finished with that and still had twenty minutes to spare, I hopped over to the corner market and bought chamomile flowers to put in all the old antique tins around the place—on the counters and tables next to the napkin holders and small baskets with individual jams. The tins were decorative on their own, but now they felt purposeful and cheery.

It never even occurred to me that I might've been going overboard until the bell chimed over the door and June herself walked in. She paused and looked around, her hands stilling in the air for a moment.

"I'm sorry," I blurted out. "I should've asked before I drew out things, right? I totally should have. I'm sorry. And don't worry about the flowers. I bought them myself, I just thought they were really cute, but again, I absolutely should have asked first—"

"LaRynn," she cut me off as she put a palm to her chest. "I'm having a hard time not tearing up and dramatically blubbering all over you because this is the *nicest* my shop has looked in a year. Thank you for this." She smiled and continued looking at everything. "I like what you did with the mugs, too."

I'd still felt strangely shy about it all for a bit, but she complimented every small touch and asked me about my ideas—like why I'd moved the toaster oven. I explained my thought process on the efficiency of its location and how the crumbs would mix with the inevitable liquid spill area before. I offered to create stock sheet lists and she was incredibly grateful for that—said she would love it.

"I just set out to have a place with good, local coffee and good, local bites. The jams, the pastries, even the mugs are all made locally. But these little things will not only help it run more smoothly . . . they just make it feel so much better, LaRynn. Thank you."

I tried . . . I truly gave it a Herculean effort to keep the whole thing in perspective. It's probably a job any sixteen-year-old off the street could do, with no education and hardly any specialty skills. But to me . . . to me, her gratitude felt like I'd been handed a plaque with my name on it.

Every customer that came in that morning seemed to smile, even when it was wall-to-wall busy, doors propped open so the line could continue out onto the street. Some of the locals started to introduce themselves to me, like I was one of them. I met Glenda, a bike taxi driver that runs a street vendor cart during the day.

"What do you sell?" I'd asked.

"Oh, this and that. I try not to get too attached to a brand. I don't know that I'll ever want to stick to one thing in life to define myself by, you know?" she said with a smile. She had red, crimped hair, wore glitter up to her eyebrows, and it was impossible not to smile back. "Last month I went through a jewelry-making phase. This week I'm selling sage bundles and crystals. Next weekend I'll be visiting my brother Abel down in southern California and will be bringing back apples from his orchard, so I'll be at the farmer's market the following week."

"Oh! I'll make sure I come buy a few," I told her.

It was even fairly easy to let it roll off my back when a customer annoyed me.

"I take it you're new here?" one guy had replied when I asked for his drink order.

"I am, yes," I said, hoping my smile wasn't a grimace.

His own grin turned smug. I suppose he could've been considered good-looking. Looked like a quintessential surfer man-boy. Dirty blonde hair that looked grungy and a little sun-bleached. A tan that was more of a sunburnt red. Bright, teal-blue eyes that I'm sure most people would truckle over, but made me wonder if he blinked less than normal humans.

"I'm Rafe," he said with a toothy grin.

"What can I get you, Rake?" I'd asked, mimicking his expression.

His smile faltered, but he ordered and snagged a seat at the bar.

"Don't worry, he doesn't stay long," June said conspiratorially, before she adjusted her voice into a Spicoli parody. "He'll need to go catch some gnar-gnar waves, bruh."

The impression made me laugh so hard the steam wand blew hot bubbles all over my apron.

THE GARAGE SHRIEKS OPEN AND I startle back into the present, the noise shocking me out of my incoherent muttering. I feel like a rat caught in a sticky trap, frozen in the moonlight that silhouettes what can only be Deacon's looming figure.

"I got you something," is his chosen greeting.

Huh? "Why?" Guilt burns up my throat like acid reflux.

"'S a bike."

Oh lovely, 's drunk. "Again, *why*?"

"To get places. Like work."

"Work is like, three blocks away."

"There's a steep"—*hiccup*—"hill."

"As opposed to the lesser known, *flat* hill?"

"Dammit, LaRynn, d'ya want the bike or not?!" The "not" comes out as a fluid "nhwat" and I hate that I like it.

"That depends. Did you *steal* it?!"

Hiccup. "Did not steal it."

"Then where'd you get a bike at 1 A.M.?"

"*Obviously,* I ac—ac. *Ac*—quired it earlier in the day." *Hiccup.*

"'Acquired' is a specifically vague term."

"I've had some beers, but I think *that's*"—he points a finger at me—"an oxymoron." The triumphant look on his face should not be cute. Flushed cheeks, the flash of straight white teeth against sweat-beaded skin. It is *not* cute.

"Big man know big word, huh?"

"A few. I'm more than just a pretty face."

We stare at one another, his eyes hooked onto mine despite the slight swaying of his body.

"Could we—could we talk in th'morning?" he asks, expression grooving itself into a frown.

I nod.

He walks forward, but stops when he's in line with me, his damp arm brushing against mine, and I stiffen. His head tilts slightly with an inhale before he lets out the same breath, ghosting against my neck.

"I'm sorry," he says, his voice a low, grating rumble that tugs something deep inside me. *Fuck him for that, too.* For having so much pull over me, for making me feel so out of control.

When I get upstairs after giving up on the cord search, Deacon is snoring in my cot, holding on to one pillow, another tucked between his knees. I discreetly rip off the $94.99 tag before I go flop down in his bed and plug my phone into his charger.

I'm asleep within seconds.

IT TAKES LONGER THAN NORMAL for me to get my bearings in the morning. When my eyes open, they're staring out through open French doors—one missing multiple panes and half-covered in a tarp—over the small balcony beyond. I can make out the tower of the old mission-style church and see a slice of the pier to the right of it, palm trees framing the entire picture. There are already faint screams from people on the rides, sea lions barking from their posts.

I'm in my old room, but . . .

The day before filters in through the fog, just as Deacon steps around the broken door and lays his hands on the frame, obscuring the view.

"Coffee?" he asks. And maybe it's the stillness of the morning, or the fact that despite drinking yesterday he is up and looks perfectly fine . . . unbothered. As unaffected as ever. So unassuming in some tank top and shorts, with his bicep-bunching and stubble-scratching. Maybe this is why I want to tell him. To *affect* him. The words want to pour out of me. *You broke my heart and you took something from me and I hate that I have to share even more with you now.*

I can't, though. I can't allow myself to give him that. It'll leave me blown wide open and even more scattered while he remains stoic and steady, shrugging carelessly at the pieces of me around him.

I choke on the words instead and nod, my head still against the pillow.

I get up and use the bathroom, that prickle of guilt zipping through me again when I spot his toothbrush.

When I make my way onto the balcony, he's set up a camp chair next to his, two coffees placed next to each other on a stool between. We sit in silence for a few minutes and I'm unsure if it's just to give the other the floor first, or if it's to prep for battle again. I have the oddest sense that he doesn't know, either.

"I didn't mean to get so upset," he begins, squinting into the sun. "It's just that—well—five grand out of a hundred, when it didn't touch any of the structural issues, is a lot." He sips his coffee stiffly.

So we are going to try for a discussion. Okay. I can do this. "I—"

"Did you do it on purpose, though?" he cuts me off.

"Do what on purpose, Deacon?"

"Spend a ridiculous amount of money just to get back at me."

"You know what would help here?" I gesture to the space between us. "If you didn't automatically refer to me as ridiculous."

"Just answer the question."

"No, Deacon. Not everything is about *you*," I spit.

"Then why?"

"I'm not—" Oh my god, this is my nightmare right now. Having to explain or justify myself to him. "I just wanted to be comfortable, alright? I didn't—" I adjust in my seat. "I didn't set out to piss you off, believe it or not."

He searches me for too long to be comfortable, then comes to some internal decision. "Do you have time to go over a budget for things this morning?"

A hollow laugh tumbles out of me. "You don't think we should have a lawyer present?" I ask.

He laughs back before running a palm down his face. His legs sprawl wider and straighten, his entire body relaxing visibly with that shared laugh, his bare foot sweeping up against my own. "Sorry," he mutters. And this balcony is almost too small for the amount of leg between the two of us. "I'd like to think we're capable on our own, yeah?" he says. "Let's just go over a general estimate for things, what we need to allocate for and when, and try to figure it out."

He leans his head back in his chair and looks at me, waiting. It's such a casual pose, but the way his eyes track mine feels anything but. As if what I say next is so much more important than he's letting on.

I settle on, "Alright. How?"

The grin spreads across his face like butter in a hot pan. "I know where to start."

NINE

"Okay, but why not? Why couldn't I get my own bathroom first?" she asks. And I have to take a beat and remind myself that her tone is simply curious, so I don't need to automatically jump down her throat about it. She's not asking in order to whine or to imply that she thinks I'm wrong. She's merely inquiring.

"Well *first,* because we have to figure out what's actually wrong with the plumbing before we add anything in that department. And tile and all the finishing things need to come *later* or they'll inevitably get damaged by all the other stuff we gotta do along the way."

She turns in her seat and bends a long leg, bringing a knee up to rest her chin on it. I can just make out the edge of the birthmark peeking out from her tiny shorts. Heat creeps up my neck.

"Speaking of bathrooms," she says, "I've been thinking about it a lot, and there are no bathtubs in this place. People love baths."

"If by *people* you mean small children or short people, maybe."

"No. *People* love baths. Adult people. Trust me. I love a good bath. And plenty of tubs are big enough for tall people like us now. I think if we reworked the bathroom—" She starts drawing on the paper we've been using to list out our project to-do's.

"Hold on," I have to say. "We've already agreed that the budget is likely to run out, right? And that's with fixing up and working with what's already here. You're telling me you want to try and rework the layout and add new stuff?"

Her face falls an inch before she tries to cover it by turning up her nose. And I'm worried I just tossed aside the shred of camaraderie we'd barely established, so I add, "Because that's fine. If you want a bathtub, I'll give you a bathtub. I just want to know because then we have to reexamine the budget and timeline a bit closer."

She blinks, and her full upper lip twitches. It's almost as if she wants to smile, like that *pleased* her. The rest of her face lights up when she looks back to the paper and starts again.

"Okay, well, here's what I've been thinking. And keep in mind that I don't know anything about load-bearing walls or any of that, so some of this might not work anyway, but here are my ideas . . ."

MOST OF HER IDEAS ARE doable, actually. And they're—*good*.

And every single one of them will be expensive.

AFTER WE COME TO TERMS with what things are just entirely out of our price range and settle on the priorities, I lean back and scratch my neck.

"I'm uh . . . I'm gonna have to stay here more. Like, full time," I warn her.

She frowns, but makes a good show of smoothing it away. Progress is progress, I suppose. "Why?" she asks.

"Well, realistically I'll need to rent out my place on the campground because we'll need the money," I explain, which has her folding her arms and looking away again.

"I'm not a complete tyrant, Deacon, I'm not asking you to do that. If any of this isn't feasible, I'm not going to make both our lives miserable over it."

"I wasn't saying that, really." I hold my hands up in surrender. "I stand to gain something here, too. Your ideas are good." I leave it at that.

Her gaze lingers, trying to suss something out. "I'll try to stick to the . . . budget."

I try to give her my most charming smile in return. She only rolls her lips and lifts a brow.

I should probably quit while we're ahead, but—"Since we're both sufficiently uncomfortable now, we have to talk about something else," I say.

Her entire body goes rigid as her gaze cuts over to mine.

"It was Jensen who brought it up," I add, like a complete knob. "But, we probably need to have a discussion about . . ." I nod my head toward the bedroom.

Both brows lift in confusion. "The—doors?"

"Behind those."

"The walls? Obviously we need them. And I'm thinking a warm white."

"White? No. How boring. But past that."

"White is classic and it makes everything feel bigger and brighter."

"I'm talking about the *bedroom,* Larry. You and me in a bed in the bedroom." *Oh Jesus, that was not—*

"What about it?" She enunciates each syllable, eyes growing bigger with each one.

"I mean, obviously we *are* married."

"AND?!" Oh, God, she's turning red before my eyes. I'm not sure if I'm afraid or if I like it. Or both.

"I'm not—" A laugh whistles up from my throat. "Jesus, this is coming out badly."

"Clearly."

"I'm just saying that despite the whole marriage thing, you're free to see who you want."

Her eyes narrow to slits. "Oh, *am* I? Well, thank you. I assumed you already were, but if you need my permission in return then there it is." She snorts.

I sigh. "I'm just trying to make sure you know you have your freedom."

She looks me up and down again, a muscle twitching in her jaw, until she sighs in return. "I appreciate it. And I meant it, so do you."

I'm not sure why that doesn't make me feel any better.

"So . . ." I try to pivot. "Any plans today?"

She tucks both knees to her chest, now. "Apparently I have a new bike to break in?"

I look away. "Yeah, that's—uh, Jensen's. He's not using it while he's on nights, so I thought I'd see if you could. He said you're welcome to it."

She scrunches her nose like an offensive odor found it. "That was—thoughtful of you . . . both."

"You always did like your toys."

She scoffs and moves to get up as the playback hits me.

"You know, you managed to take a nice thing and make it sound dirty," she whines.

There's no venom in it, though, and I keep laughing when she heads inside.

"LaRynn," I call after her, following behind. She primly starts making my bed. "I promise I wasn't trying to be slick."

"No, I'm certain that just comes naturally to you," she coos. "You just love to get a reaction out of me and you know it."

"I was referring to all your nice—*things*. Your nice car, nice headphones, nice clothes. You had the nicest, newest phone. Twenty-five pairs of shoes for one summer. Don't think you wore the same swimsuit twice."

"Well, I don't have nice shit anymore, Deacon. This"—she makes a circle with her finger—"is all I have."

I feel my expression tighten, debating if I want to press on that little fissure or not.

"But, regardless," she says as she karate chops a pillow down the middle, "it was nice of him to let me borrow the bike."

I guess I won't push it for now.

"It's electric. I have one, too." I shrug and try the same pillow maneuver on my side. Her lips twist down at my efforts. "I could show you how it works and all that. Thinking about going for a ride and grabbing some lunch, anyway, if you want to join."

She bends and stretches her long, lean body across the bed to fix the pillow, and I have to stifle a snort because *of course* I did it wrong. When she stands up, she looks past me, out over the balcony, and gives a quick, limp toss of her shoulders. "Okay."

* * *

WE STUMBLE AROUND EACH OTHER a bit, separate, and change,
then go about our morning.

I haven't lived with anyone since I was eighteen. And I've
never lived with a woman other than my mother. So it's a
strange, charged feeling, orbiting around a person.

When we eventually make our way downstairs, I hold the
bike and start to show her the different levers and how to
change gears, to switch from manual to the electric mode,
until she sigh-groans over me.

"As much as I appreciate this, I think I've got it." She
grins, quirking an eyebrow at me. *"I know my way around my
toys."*

She takes off at full speed and I'm left wondering, for
what feels like the millionth time in under a few weeks, what
the hell I've gotten myself into.

TEN

LARYNN

It's just a lunch.

It doesn't have the power to undo all the hard-learned lessons.

It's just that . . . somewhere between sharing a platter of bone-meltingly spicy wings and him spinning his hat around backwards, I catch myself forgetting.

"So what is this? Is this bonding? Are we bonding?" I spurt out. Because he gave me all the flats and took all the drumsticks and despite the fact that we've talked about nothing of real consequence, I find myself wanting to ask about his tattoo and his job, and for some reason that feels like conceding. Feels like *losing*.

His hand pauses midway before he brings his beer to his lips and takes a hefty gulp. The curls of his hair wrap around the tops of his ears and escape through the hole in the front of his hat, something so boyish juxtaposed against the rest of him.

"I think a more palatable term to use here would be 'team-building'?"

I blink at him. "Okay?"

"Think about it," he says. "People that work together and don't particularly care for each other still have to go to company retreats or team-building activity things all the time." He studies a thumb before sucking some sauce from it, letting it slip out of his mouth with a *pop*.

"How often do you suggest we—*team-build*?" I ask warily.

He juts out a glistening lip and flings a single shoulder. "Once a week oughta be enough, I'd think?"

"Once a *week*?! We're already about to be living together full time. Sharing a *toilet*. You don't think that'd be overkill?"

"I think the purpose of the team-building is that it's cooperative and everyone approaches it with an open mind and a good outlook, thereby keeping up morale," he says meaningfully, dipping his chin and lifting his brows. "I suppose we could take turns picking said activity if that would help? I'd be happy to visit your coven, stand outside of kindergarten classrooms with signs telling them that Santa's a hoax and your mom decapitated your Elf on the Shelf . . . throw M&M's at them while they cry. You know, whatever it is that you like to do for fun."

"Joke's on you, I'd never waste M&M's like that, and my next coven meeting involves a sacrificial ceremony, so . . ." I scrunch my nose apologetically.

"In need of a virile man, huh?" He bites his lip in a grin.

"More specifically one that no one will *miss*."

"Oh sugar, you and I both know I *never* miss."

"*That doesn't even*—"

"Every other week."

"*What?!*"

"Give me every other week," he says, placing his veiny forearms on the table and leaning toward me. "For team-building.

I think it's the only way we remind one another that we're *on* the same team."

Damn if this isn't an upgraded version of the charming asshole that had me canceling plans with friends, my grandmothers, and sneaking off to a plethora of unsavory locations all so he could twist me up like a pretzel. Who had me whipped up into a lust-crazed, angst-laden, love-struck idiot. . . .

"Come on, Lar. It's just a lunch here and there."

It's just a lunch.

It's just a piece of paper.

It's just sex.

It's just that I couldn't keep it straight back then and I can't afford to get it mixed up now.

"Every other week."

"Deal."

His tattooed hand shakes mine, and I know it's only in my head, but I swear I feel the creature wrap itself around me, too.

ELEVEN

LARYNN

It only takes a week before he starts walking around naked.

To be fair, it might be my fault. The first time was, at least.

But he started it when he bitched at me after finding out that I got rid of his bleach-stained, raggedy, threadbare towels. Tie those things to some golf clubs and they could've been used as international flags for bachelordom.

"You don't *throw away* towels, Larry," he'd said. "You keep them for things. Like car-washing rags or—I don't know, but you *keep* them! Now all we have is your pink foo-foo bullshit!"

"Where?! *Where* was I supposed to store your beloved towels? I had no idea that they were so cherished. Was it the holes or the frayed edges that made them the ideal jerk-off rags?"

He put his hand to his chest with a theatrical gasp. "How *dare* you! I am feeling extremely objectified. You keep my self-care out of your filthy mind, you Jezebel."

I made a noise akin to a pirate suffering a surprise anal probe. I was suddenly regretting the extremely thorough wash I'd given his toothbrush in my previous guilt.

He laughed in my face, clutching one of my towels around his trim hips. Then he rubbed a big palm across his arrogant chest, scratching at some invisible itch.

"Do you have an allergy you need to address? You're constantly scratching yourself," I snapped.

He fluttered his lashes and I swallowed back a growl. "Watching me rather closely, aren't you?" he said, before he turned and strutted off to shower.

SO, *YES*: I, A TWENTY-SIX-YEAR-OLD adult woman, snuck into the bathroom and took all of my towels. If he's going to complain, then he doesn't deserve to use them.

I'd already begun going through my grandmother's records in the garage since, during my splurge, I'd purchased a combination record player/Bluetooth speaker. That day I went with *Redbone*, turning up the volume until it reached full blast and effectively drowned out his terrible singing.

This also allowed me the luxury of pretending I didn't hear him hollering at me when he was done.

I was cheerfully flipping through a home magazine in my chaise, feeling pretty proud of myself when a wet, irritated, and *very* naked Deacon came bounding into the living room.

I suppose there aren't actual degrees of nakedness, but if there are, he was on the extreme end of that spectrum. Miles of suntanned skin dusted in dark hair. Thick, hard limbs stacked in slippery strength. My eyes abandoned my brain and moved from his bare feet to the muscles shifting in his thighs as he stomped my way, and up to—*God*, everything else—before I threw the magazine at him in my panic and screwed my eyes shut with a screech. I scrambled out of the chair blindly and ended up sprawled on the floor and crawling . . . somewhere. Anywhere. Until he snatched the hem of my maxi dress and dragged me back, where he proceeded to dry himself off with it.

I cracked an eye open to the sight of him looming and dripping over me with a cruel smirk.

"Thanks, *wife*. Think you're right, after all. This was much nicer than those old rags," he sneered and shook his hair like a dog.

I gave up the battle with my eyes and let them watch his bare ass march away—my consolation prize, I guess—while he casually continued humming along to "Come and Get Your Love."

TWO DAYS AFTER THAT INCIDENT, and because we are clearly killing it here as it is, I find myself halfway up the stairs "hauling" my end of a mattress, with Deacon barking at me from below.

"*Jesus* do you even have any of the weight on your end up there?!" he whines.

I insert as much strain as I can into my voice. "Yeah, do you?" I reply, dancing my fingertips on the edges of it. Just enough to maintain some control, to get it past another step while keeping the entirety of the load distributed on him.

The thrill of seeing his face in its red and haggard glory will sustain me for at least another week, I decide.

But then he has to pause for a rest and a guttural groan rasps out of him. Something so masculine and damn near pornographic that I'm pulled into the mental fantasy of being under him. Of being overwhelmed by him, lost in sensation, that sound spilling out of him like he can't help himself, brows furrowed, head tossed back . . .

I'm immediately changing my mind and would like to get it up and over with, after all.

I don't know what it says about me that I feel the need to remind him when we're almost to the top, "I didn't ask you to do this, by the way. I just want to reiterate that."

"Yeah, yeah, I get it, Lar—*you don't need me.* You were fine on your cot." We reach the landing, and his face lights up with a grin. I also don't know what it says about me that I know exactly what he's going to say next.

"Don't be that guy," I say before he can. "Don't say the thing that every person who's ever moved furniture since 1999 has said. I'm begging you. It was really before our time, man."

He ignores me. "PIVOT."

AFTER WE RETRIEVE THE BOX spring and set everything up with the freshly washed linens he's also brought with him, something in me relents. A bit of ice chips off and falls away.

"Thank you, Deacon," I tell him. "This is . . . nice. Of you. This is *nice*."

He frowns and studies the bed for a moment before skimming a palm along it, swinging a hooded gaze my way. "I might have selfish motivations."

I have no idea what my face is doing while I try to decipher that statement. He traces the entire outline of me with his eyes, smiling so suggestively that he may as well be caressing me with a finger, instead. His tongue darts out to swipe across his lip. "I've got our next *team-building* exercise picked out and I want your back feeling good and strong for it." He steps close enough that I catch the faint scent of him—some brand of deodorant or soap that has to be the same one he used when we were younger. Something about that smell, that fine layer of *him* just under it, calls up the mental image of his palm slipping up my thigh, pushing my skirt up with it, his thumb as it tucked aside my underwear in a darkened theater. My heart thundering in my throat because we weren't alone and it felt like a dare.

And suddenly, the devil on my shoulder gasps like she's been bound and gagged, because some part of me recognizes that I *expect* this of him. I expect him to turn everything into some game. He's a bird with a worm, one that enjoys watching me squirm and writhe. But . . .

But I don't think he could actually handle it if I responded in kind. If I flirted right back and didn't let him throw me off. *He's* nothing if not predictable. I, however, am not eighteen nor inexperienced anymore and I am done being toyed with. If he wants to play games then *fine*, I'll play willingly, but I don't like to lose and I certainly won't make it easy for him.

I school my face into a bored expression. "Oh yeah? Planning to put me to work?" I ask, teeth sinking into my lower lip demurely.

The quick double-blink of his eyelids gives it all away, the way his expression pulls wider and a muscle ticks in his jaw. He'll be rendered useless if I truly dish it back. If I lean into the innuendos and double down on the double entendres every time he feigns being scandalized.

He clears his throat, Adam's apple bouncing. "We have to start demoing some stuff this week, is all," he says. And it's clipped on the edges, like he never got that full breath back. "And I have a maintenance day at the campground planned." He shrugs before he turns on his heel and leaves.

It feels like a retreat.

The rest of that ice in me remains, but it feels fucking buoyant now.

TWELVE

DEACON

The majority of June slips away in what feels like a montage of labor with very little gain. I'm sure it's typical for this phase—at least when it comes to DIY.

Since I went ahead and rented out my place for the rest of the summer, I decided to grab my mattress and set LaRynn up with it. I'd feel guilty with her using that damn cot anyway and the guilt would be . . . distracting. When it was clear she was *shocked* to find out that I am, in fact, a decent guy, it was too tempting not to try and needle her. May as well act for the role she's cast me in, right?

Plus, the masochist in me loves the way one side of her nose scrunches up when I piss her off.

What I did not expect, however, was to be teased back. I'm certain there's a game in the works and I'll be damned if I blink first. I have a feeling this part of the process would get incredibly boring without it, anyway.

EARLIER IN THE WEEK, I showed her how to properly and safely tackle some demo, after she came home from her shift. I'll have to be back at the campground during the days over the next two weeks while my mom takes her annual trip with some of her girlfriends back east, so I figured she'd be fine with a bit of homework. I quickly learned that one should not hand their cohabitant a tool and ask them to work when they get home from . . . *work*. Especially when said tool qualifies as a weapon. She tore down more than her half of a wall, but I won't deny being afraid while she did it. There was a very particular intensity there.

The only other progress we've made on that front is ripping up the remaining carpet, which I got around to today, and now on the monetary side, which is kicking off to an awkward start to say the least. LaRynn's just told me she added me to the account that the trust funds are in, tossing the packet with my info onto the counter in a huff.

"Permits were approved, too," she grumbles. "Twenty-one-and-something grand came out of the account."

"You knew it was coming out, though," I say warily, setting down a load of debris. "You wrote the check."

She swings her eyes my way. "Doesn't mean it was fun to *see* it come out."

I chuckle lightly, but am not afforded another response.

"Hey, Lar?" I say to her back, since she's already sifting through her records. I've begun to notice that one of the first things she does when she gets home is play music. Today she settles on "Suspicious Minds".

"Hmm?" she responds, back still turned.

"What would you think about just pooling our money together and using the same account? Since we've got so much mixed in anyway, now that I'm living here full time too, and we're going to end up eating each other's food—"

"No, *you* end up eating *my* food."

"It was *one* apple," I reply. Then, under my breath, "Jesus you can hold a grudge."

"It was *three* days ago!" Her face pulls up in that scrunch thing before she starts muttering in French. "And why would you do that anyway? You make more money than me." Her eyes cut away when she says it, like she's ashamed of that for some incomprehensible reason.

"We'll have to pay the subs out of the same funds, and I don't know," I say shrugging. "I'm not exactly experienced with sharing a space with someone. I might stumble upon a banana and eat it. Maybe I'm hoping that contributing to the overall grocery fund will buy me forgiveness occasionally."

"So you're trying to *buy* my compliance?" She lifts a brow slowly.

"I—" I look away and kick out a boot. Was I? I didn't think I was, but, shit.

"I guess if we pooled money together for groceries and utilities it *would* make it simpler to pay for things instead of going over percentages and arguing about usage, weighing every cost against the hefty food tab you *surely* hike up," she says, cocking her head and looking me up and down.

"Takes a lot to maintain all this," I say.

"Yes, yes, you're a god amongst men and all that," she monotones with a sigh, but it's more worn than biting. "If you really don't mind then I'm fine with that. I just . . ." She inhales deeply through her nose before she turns rigidly to me. "I just ask that I can use your car occasionally for grocery shopping."

Surprise unfurls in my chest, but I cover the feeling with a cough. The way she asked made it sound like she's been *looking* for an opening. "Alright. Um, yeah. That's fine with me," I say.

"Obviously, that would be beneficial for us both, here. I'd be able to get whatever you need, too," she adds, like she's still trying to convince me.

"Totally, yeah," I add, voice picking up at the end. And then I hold very still while she regards me.

When she seems satisfied on that matter she does another uncomfortable fidget. "I also—and feel free to say no to this—it's really not a big deal. I just know it will cost a lot on my own and thought it might be easier if I went through you . . . but . . . Would it—would it be difficult or costly to add me to your health insurance?"

"It won't cost a thing. I have it through the union," I answer right away. *But you mean to tell me she's been riding around town on an electric bike and I showed her how to use a nail gun and she hasn't had medical insurance?!* I shrug, even though I'm biting my tongue. I have a feeling that the last thing she needs is a lecture.

"Thank you," she says warily.

She's never been especially easy to read, but I get the sense that she's trying to find a catch. The self-conscious way she looks at her feet when she comes up empty makes me miss her glare, though.

"What's wrong?" I ask, and the glare roars back.

"Nothing." She taps a foot and scoffs from her sinuses, arms swinging open in frustration. "I snapped at a customer today, okay?"

She shifts to her other hip and shakes her head at herself, arms refolding across her chest.

She's stronger than she was when we were teens—with a body that's only grown more . . . dramatic. Everything about her is. Long, slender throat, wide-set shoulders above a steeply curved waist. The kind of lengthy, powerful thighs and rounded ass that make you think there's definitely a god and he's *definitely* a mean bastard who lives to see his creations make fools of themselves drooling over his finer ones. The capped muscles atop her arms shift and tense now, working beneath her skin, thighs flexing below her miniskirt. A ridiculous scrap of fabric.

"And you feel—bad?" I ask, genuinely. I deduce that if I just come out and ask her exactly *what* happened she'll shut down.

"Not for the *customer*," she says. Like it should be obvious. "June said she wasn't upset with me about it, but he's a regular, so . . ."

"He make a pass at you or something?" I laugh. Her expression sours further.

"Glad that's such a truly *laughable* thought." Her eyes roll. "He didn't hit on me, he just pissed me off. Repeatedly."

"An equally *laughable* thought."

A twitch. I swear the corner of her mouth twitched at that one.

"So," I say, eager to keep this going for some reason I'm not yet in touch with. "A regular, huh? What's his name?"

"Some moronic name. Roofie, or Raid, or—"

"Rafe?" I snort.

"Yep." She walks over to the couch and collapses onto it. "Know him?"

I nod. "What'd he do?"

"Just—the normal. Misogynistic, entitled bullshit. Calls me sweetheart condescendingly, called me bright eyes one of the times . . . today he got on my last nerve," she says, sighing. "I was talking with another regular, Glenda, and he took it upon himself to shout—from all the way at the end of the breakfast bar in front of a crowd—and tell me that I should *smile more*. And when I asked him why, he said, 'Because you're nice to look at from a distance without it, but with it, you demand to be approached.'" She gags and I have to swallow a pop of laughter. "He thought it was *elite,* too, my *god.* He really felt he was owed a favorable response to that." She chews her lip to cover a cruel smirk.

"I take it your response was less than?"

"I told him if we were both lucky then all my expressions would be from a distance, and he'd do well not confuse any of them with an invitation, let alone a demand. And then I drew a dick in his latte art."

"Atta girl." I smile her way, and her expression shifts into something owlish. "Doesn't sound so bad. Sounds to me like you went easy on the guy."

She eyes me suspiciously again. "Somehow, I think my carefully executed restraint was lost on him."

I reach down and start gathering up debris. "Well, if June wasn't mad then I wouldn't worry about it. Here, help me drag this?"

She rocks up from the couch with a beleaguered sound, but shuffles over and grabs an end of the roll I'm working on.

"I just think—I don't know." She looks behind her to find the stairs. "I don't know if the place is doing great. Not sure if scaring off regulars is a great move right now. I saw her looking at listings for new spots the other day. And she's mentioned how expensive the retail space is here."

I pause and she gives the load an annoyed tug. "What do you mean? It looks busy in there all the time," I say.

"I'm not sure. I just know she's been waiting until the last minute to do stock orders, and has mentioned a few things, that's all. Now can we finish this? I told Jensen I'd meet him and be his second for a few pick-up matches tonight."

"What?! He didn't ask me!"

She huffs out a groan and drops her end. "What is so unfathomable about the words coming out of my mouth right now? Did I slip into French at some point?!"

"Why would he ask you?!"

"Maybe because I'm GOOD? Perhaps because I played indoor in *college*? Also, it's CO-ED."

"Oh."

"*Oh*," she mimics, unflatteringly. "Do you want my help or not?" She gestures to the rolled-up carpet and I nod, and we make our way down to the dumpster I've got in Sal's side of the courtyard.

"I'm coming too," I announce dumbly. "To play." We toss the bundle into the dumpster, dust and debris puffing up into the air.

"It's a free world, Deacon. And it's a public beach." She shrugs sideways at me before her face arranges itself into something smug. "But look who doesn't like sharing his friends and his spaces and places now. At *twenty-six* versus eighteen, no less." She dusts off her hands, clapping them together. "How the turn tables."

I can't help it, a laugh bursts free. "Look at *you* making a joke." She rolls her eyes, so I press on. "You know, you're not as mean as you think you are," I say, leaning back as I open the door for her. She moves to walk past me and I attempt to follow behind, but she stops short, our thighs bumping into each other.

"Sorry," she mutters, twisting toward me, "you just— *here*—" She reaches up and I flinch back. Her eyes narrow to slits. "What do you think I'm going to do to you? Pull your precious hair? *Bébé géant.* Hold still, I'm trying to *help* you." She mumbles more under her breath in French.

It's the first time I've been this close to her since she came back, face-to-face this way. She steps even closer and I suck in a breath, the moment settling like we're sinking under a wave. I note that little freckle on her chin that I remember with disturbing clarity, next to the corner of her lip there. The other two that dot her cheek beside her nose on the same side, a small constellation I used to skate my thumb along. The dark lashes that nearly touch her brows—when her eyes *aren't* narrowed in irritation, that is. Clear green irises. I feel the puff of her breath on the center of my throat.

Her eyes meet mine before I watch her mouth gently open, the tiniest peek of her pink tongue as it darts out across her lip, her teeth biting down into it . . . until it slips back out with a little flick.

"*Deacon,*" she says huskily, and I love how she holds onto the N just a little longer, like a breathy hum.

Something starts to whirr in my chest—spinning and filling up my head with cotton candy, with that scent on her I want to press my nose into, like some sugar-hungry bloodhound.

"Yeah?" grates out of me. *How did we get here? Is she about to kiss me? Fuck, I think I'll let her—*

Her teeth flash in a cruel smile. "You have about a hundred of these in that mop on your head," she says, waving a thread of carpet in my face and curling a brow. "And you're not as smooth as you think *you* are."

She sways past and struts up the stairs, and I blow out that breath. Let my skull thud against the door.

She might be right, I think with a wry laugh. Either way, game on.

THIRTEEN

DEACON

She wins round one.

She handily wins *match* one almost entirely on her own, but she's figuratively killing me, too. She and Jensen teamed up against June and I, who I convinced to play. And LaRynn apparently thinks that the best attire for sand volleyball is a thong bikini. The woman is *not* precious about it, either. She's diving, sprinting, powering through the sand without restraint. Jensen wears a delighted expression when he and I face off at the net, but the rest of the time he looks a bit afraid—like he's working that much harder to avoid being yelled at by his teammate.

They switch when it's his serve, and now it's LaRynn and I closest to each other across the divide. She bends and rests her hands on her knees and I see a guy take a ball to the temple on the court behind her. His partner is equally slack-jawed and staring, so he proceeds to trip over him, face first in the sand.

"*Jesus*, you should come with a liability waiver," I tell her, shaking my head.

"Huh?"

"Nothing," I mutter.

She easily slips back into ignoring me, wholly focused on the task at hand. We rally back and forth countless times, a crowd gathering around us as the hits get harder, save after save. Until Jensen sets her a perfect ball and she makes an equally perfect approach. I time it out, meet her at the net just as she slams her hand into the ball, spiking it with all her might—directly into my outstretched palms. The ball ricochets off the block and she scrambles, immediately laying out behind her to try and reach it, but coming up short.

She gets up and slowly turns to me, a vicious look blinking across her face before she tips her chin and tucks it away. Sand coats half her body, from her hair to her toes, stuck in the places she's sweatiest.

"You've got something"—I gesture to my head and down the length of my body—"here." I smile.

She turns and bends to pick up the ball, swiping her palms across her ass to dust off the sand, the motion a bit slower and more drawn out than I think is necessary. I struggle to swallow, my vision pulsing.

"Your serve, Deacon," Jensen says, and I realize I now have the ball in hand and don't know when I got it. *Christ.*

JUNE AND I END UP narrowly winning the second and third match, victorious for the evening. And LaRynn surprises me by telling me *good game,* clasping my forearm at the end. She acts . . . entirely unbothered. When we say our farewells, she even gives Jensen a pat on the back that makes my lip curl.

The last time I beat her here she tripped me and pretended it was an accident. Then I *know* she bought out all of my favorite gum from the corner liquor store so that there would be none in stock for me for the next week. She never admitted to the second thing, but I know it's true. Every time I tasted her mouth that following week there was a hint of it on her tongue. The LaRynn I know is *not* a good sport, and my hackles are definitely raised now.

"Want to grab tacos at the stand? On me," I say to her and June, determined to push on this new development a bit more.

June checks her watch. "Yeah, I've got a bit of time."

LaRynn gives a stilted nod. "Sure. Sounds good."

We make it the whole meal though, and she remains completely collected, the facade never cracking. They talk about ideas for the shop, banter about certain customers. There's *friendly* conversation over carnitas and margaritas . . .

. . . and an underlying sense that I have no fucking clue what's going on, that maybe I am completely wrong, that maybe I always was. It's a jarring sensation, to say the least.

When we return home, her eyes brighten a bit when she turns to look at me. "You've got some cilantro in your teeth, by the way. Make sure you brush them extra," she says in a sing-song voice before putting some modern tune on the record player and heading over to her area. Some song I don't recognize.

I don't see what she was talking about, but I do brush them a little bit harder than normal that night.

FOURTEEN

A better woman wouldn't enjoy Deacon's obvious discomfort. A *better* woman would probably push an adult conversation and use the opportunity to tell him, *"Hey, I'm not eighteen anymore and I know how to play a casual game and still have fun. Let's not continue to assume the worst of one another."* Even though I am competitive, I'm not always petty or childish about it. Anymore. When it comes to him beating me on the beach, I could also remind him that he plays multiple times a week whereas I haven't in multiple years, but I don't, so . . . obvious growth there, at least.

But, here's the thing. Self-awareness does not equate to self-control.

Instead, I'm enjoying the side-eyeing and odd flinch here and there. The little tilt of his head like some silly, confused pup when I respond to his flirting in an unexpected way. I've been leaving bobby pins in unexpected places, tossing them on his bed, or leaving some in the coffee mug he refuses to put *in* the cupboard. Hair ties in his car or in the tool belt he leaves lying around every day. After he left his beard trimmings in the sink again, I put the toilet paper roll on backwards—three times in a row. He came stomping out of the bathroom the last time and I'm certain he was about to break, but I was splayed out on the chaise in my favorite silk robe and, before he could speak, I told him, "Oh, by the way, I grabbed you your favorite sub from the cold case at the end of my shift. It's in the fridge next to some pie."

"You—a *pie?*" He blinked stupidly, a roll of toilet paper in his hand.

"Mm-hmm. Cherry." I bought it pre-made from the store and just baked it here, even messed up the crust a little to look a bit more rugged. Then I threw the box away in the neighbor's dumpster to hide the evidence, but he didn't need to know any of that.

I moved the vinyl record I was studying away and watched every inch of his face as I crossed my legs, smoothing them over one another, the robe riding up just slightly. He fumbled the roll and bent clumsily to pick it up, rubbed a palm over his brow and down the rest of his face.

"Did you need anything else?" I asked coyly.

"What?" he barked. "No, I—no. Uh, thanks. For the sandwich." His eyes bounced between my face and the hem of my robe. And then, because once again, I am not a better woman, I kept my knees together and brought them up, let them fall to the side, let one of my hips be utterly exposed, my ass hidden behind my tucked feet.

"Sweet cream," I said.

He fully swayed on his feet. "W-what?"

"The ice cream I got to go with the pie. It's called sweet cream. It's just French vanilla, really."

"I—um—" he stammered as he shook his head, cheeks and ears crimson. "I have to go. Skunk."

"I'm sorry?"

"Mrs. Gold."

"You're not making any sense, Deacon. You feeling okay?"

He half-turned his body to look out the doorway. "Mrs. Gold is a yearly regular at the campground. She stays in one of the semi-permanent Airstreams there, and she thinks a skunk is living under her deck." He darted his eyes my way before they went back to the open door frame. "Really, her idiot grandson and his cousin have been smoking weed and throwing their roaches under it. None of my business, but I have to at least reassure her there are no skunk—shenanigans."

"Right . . ."

"Well . . ." His expression cycled from want to irritation to confusion again. "I'll uh, see you later." He then grabbed his keys from the basket and fled out the doorway, toilet paper still in hand.

I find ways to justify all this to myself.

It's all just to pass the time. It's not serious. I'm certainly not *hurting* the man. He dishes it right back, believe me. This morning he strolled into the kitchen, fresh from the shower, holding only a hand towel over himself. He grabbed an apple and crunched into it loudly, chewing over the sound of the coffee brewing. When I turned to glare at him I asked with a saccharine grin, "Enjoying your breakfast?

He replied by lifting that towel and wiping his mouth delicately, eyes on me to see if I'd succumb to sneaking a peek. As if my pride would've allowed that.

In addition to these more obvious little stunts, he's got the art of the subtle seduction down to a science, too. I'll come home to him in one of his stupid unbuttoned shirts, bare-chested underneath. He'll be on all fours and sanding a spot of hardwood we agreed to try and restore. Something twangy like Rufus on the record player, something that toys and plays with my libido like a string instrument. The giant fan will be blowing and he'll stand up, safety glasses on, his bronzed skin glistening, and *God* I'll want to laugh or tell him he looks ridiculous, the fan making his shirt billow around him like some dirtbag, male Beyoncé . . . but the effect is like dropping ink in a tub of liquid—heat bleeds and spreads and curls through me.

It's a nonstarter, though. And if he calls my bluff I don't know what I'll do, because I simply can't—won't—act on desire again. I'm mature enough to know that I can't handle that, at least. We only have to be a functional enough team to make this thing—the renovation—happen.

And it *is* happening. The back-and-forth isn't detracting from our progress. We're less than a month in and nearly all of the demo is done, with the plumber on schedule for right after the Fourth of July. We know where the things should end up and overall it's going to be a great layout for a single family home upstairs, with a second unit below.

And . . . maybe all of this makes me a terrible person. It undoubtedly highlights just how dysfunctional I am but I also think this is the most fun I've had in years.

Most of the time.

Some of the time I end up frustrated, twisting the night away in my sheets and spending the next day on the edge. Short and irritable and in need of relief. I can attend to myself, but typically won't. The absence of a door makes it feel too close to him when he's in the house.

But then there are days like today, where I'm off and he's gone. I decided I couldn't take not having *any* sort of barrier, so I bought one extra curtain and a shower rod to rig in the doorway, so at least I have that in addition to my divider. And

Deacon let me know he'd be staying over at Santa Sea tonight—something about the same Mrs. Gold wanting him to set poles to hang string lights from and to go over the Fourth of July barbecue menu and festivities. I heard that he'd be gone all night and had to suppress the urge to cheer.

The moment I registered the sound of the door shutting downstairs I charged up the only toy I own and tidied around the house so there would be no other distractions in my way. An hour or so later, an audiobook is primed and ready, and I've even lit a candle for myself to set the mood.

It does briefly cross my mind that I should consider using this time to find a hobby, but it's simply not on my hierarchy of needs at the moment. I just need to take the edge off, then I'll worry about other shit, later.

I settle down into my bed and put my headphones on, shimmying under the cool sheet, practically giddy with anticipation. I push play on the book, adjust the volume so that it's loud enough to drown out the buzzing of my—assistant—and close my eyes. . . .

The narrator describes the way he's kissing down the length of the heroine's spine, she on her knees in front of a mirror. His rough hands skim her skin, curling around her hips and between her thighs. She leans up and back and he's talking to her from their reflection, and . . .

. . . and, dammit, it's Deacon's face in the mirror next to me, chin at my neck, mouth beside my ear, his dark eyes meeting mine. I'm watching his fingers working between my legs, the bones in his hand shifting. The tattoo as his other palms a breast. I can practically feel his hair in between my fingers when I reach up and grab at the pillows with one arm above me. I toss my head, desperately searching for someone else to fill the picture, needing to replace him with someone—anyone.

But then the words *God, you feel like mine. You've always felt like mine,* are whispered in my ear and the vibrations take over, reverberating throughout my entire system. Up my fingertips through my thighs and down to the very soles of my feet and back, rushing and drumming in my core, bright spots behind my eyelids and ecstasy crashing through my system in waves. I press the button to stop and pull away, beads of sweat trickling from the creases of my knees down the backs of my calves. I immediately feel high, drunk on the feeling . . . I laugh with sheer, bone-melting relief.

One more wouldn't hurt.

I'M NOT SURE HOW MUCH time goes by, but a while later sweat slicks my hair to my temples, so I throw on my robe and venture out into the kitchen for some water and a light meal.

And find Deacon.

Setting a sizzling cast iron skillet down onto a potholder on the table. He doesn't even look my way when he asks, "Fajitas?"

"Oh!" The sound tumbles out of me, three octaves higher than normal, and I gulp. "Sure, that sounds good." He couldn't have been here long or heard anything because there is zero doubt in my mind he'd be giving me shit if he had. I try to steady my breathing and grab both a water bottle and a beer from the fridge.

"Here, let me," he says, taking my drink from my hand. He proceeds to tear the cap off with his teeth, something I *hate* but am too shaken to acknowledge. Hands me a wedge of lime.

"Th-thanks."

We settle at the table and assemble our plates. I'm about

to take my first bite when he pops up out of his seat. *"Oh! Music.* Want to listen to some music?" he asks cheerfully.

"Sure," I say back lightly. Surprised at this good mood. Normally he comes back from seeing Mrs. Gold, grabs a tool, and starts breaking or taking apart something.

He sifts through the music until he finds what he's looking for, then comes back to join me at the table. "Cheers." He holds up his own beer in salute.

"Cheers." I clink my drink to his.

The food and tune flood my system, some happy oldie I can't help but nod along to.

And then I notice him not eating.

I look up to his face—red. Laughing silently. A vein pulsing in his forehead at the effort.

And then the song's lyrics hit me.

". . . he's giving me the excitations
I'm pickin' up good vibrations . . ."

"Good Vibrations".

No. *No, no, no, no.* An embarrassing gurgle of sound escapes me as I try not to choke. I groan around the mouthful of food, heat flooding my cheeks.

God dammit. He *heard* me. I turn my face away toward the window and swallow painfully. I remember those Greek mythology stories of women walking into the sea and suddenly see the allure.

He's now clutching his chest, laughing heartily, head tossed back and wiping tears from his eyes.

"I thought you were gone for the night!" I scream.

"Oh, believe me, I *know.* I thought you were gonna take all night, too. I tried to make a bunch of noise in here to let you know. Banged around pots and pans and everything."

"You did *not.*"

"Oh, sugar, but I did." He chuckles, shaking his head, his eyes watering further. Gasping for air.

I groan and push away from the table, ready to hide for the rest of the evening. Perhaps forever. At the minimum, I'll leave the country. I'm bilingual, there are options for me.

"Wait, Lar—" he says between chortling, grabbing my wrist to stop me. "Don't be embarrassed. You were just having a wank. A *few*, it sounded like. We all do it. I'm impressed by the stamina, actually."

I snatch my wrist from his grip and stomp to my room-that's-not-a-room and throw myself back under my sheet.

I don't often cry when I'm sad, rarely do when I'm angry. It takes a high amount of physical pain to pull the tears from me, but . . . but I almost always cry when I'm embarrassed. The emotion clogs my throat now.

So much for the confident siren I tried to embody. Back to the emotionally and sexually stunted angry bitch I go.

"LAR—LARYNN," COMES HIS VOICE. I feel the bed dip when he sits at the foot and I pull the sheet tighter around my head.

"LaRynn. I didn't mean to embarrass you. I just—" He sighs. "I just thought we could have a laugh, that's all. I shouldn't have, though." He finds my ankle and squeezes. "Maybe I should've known that you wouldn't like to be laughed at when it comes to that kind of thing. I'm sorry."

He *did* know that once. About the younger me, at least. Learned it from experience, which in itself is its own sort of chagrin, despite how long ago our sexual history took place. He was endlessly patient and kind in private back then. Never made me feel dumb when I got shy. I think it was part of what made me think we were more than we were. . . .

But, I haven't exactly been giving off the same inexperienced, curious-yet-clumsy impression I did when we were teens. Have been *trying* to act far above it, in fact.

He gets up to leave, and I make out his silhouette through the sheet as he pauses in the doorway, palms braced on the frame. A frustrated sigh gusts out of him.

"And if it makes you feel any better," he says, voice scraping like sand on the Boardwalk planks, "the last time I saw you in that robe—that day on the long-chair—"

"The chaise?"

"The *chaise*, yeah . . ." He drums his fingers along the wood to some short, internal debate. "Well, that day, I had to jerk off twice in the campground shower just to calm myself down. And it wasn't some audio-porn or something that had that power over me, either, LaRynn."

I know he means it as a concession. This is him handing over a piece to even up the scoreboard, to ease my humiliation, to settle me.

Somehow, the effect is the opposite. Even more disorienting.

FIFTEEN

DEACON

Had a dream about LaRynn, her hair spread across the sheets, hand between her thighs. Woke up with my own hand in my briefs, tugging and squeezing. Wrestled enough control over myself to take a cold shower.

That buzz replays in my brain no matter what I try to replace it with, but it's not irritating in the slightest. It's worse. It's a hum in my bloodstream, set to the percussion of her strangled moans. I've been playing the same songs on repeat in the hopes that one of them would dig in and take over, but no such luck.

I miss the days when I thought that her wrath would be the most agonizing part of this arrangement.

SIXTEEN

LARYNN

Things have shifted since our "Good Vibrations" dinner. There's not been another incident of nude breakfast or naked lunch. There's zero flirting. He rarely calls me Larry. Rarely says my name at all, if he can avoid it. I think he's just avoiding *me* in general. He's back to being at the campground more of the time than here.

All of which should be fine. *Is* fine. Really.

I just hate feeling like it's because I've done something wrong. He laughed it off, paid me his small admission. But now he's retreated, and that *should* be a relief, but instead it grates on my nerves like nettles against my skin. And now we're stuck in this awkward limbo and I'm itching to burst free of it, in any direction, but I don't know how.

We cross paths in the stairwell after my shift this morning as he's on his way out (*again*), and I swear the man is trying to plaster himself to the opposite wall to avoid skimming me. The same man whose direct and consistent eye contact used to unnerve me keeps looking down the steps toward the door, like he's desperate to make his escape.

"Headed out?" I ask, dully.

"Yeah. I've got a few small projects over at Santa and one of the rental RVs is open, so I'll probably stay there for a few days," he replies, before looking at something on his boot. "For real this time."

Is he *blushing?* "Okay," I say with a shrug, trying to convey apathy.

"To keep up momentum, you could start looking at some of the finishes and getting prices on things so that we'll be able to move quickly after the plumbing gets done. If you want," he adds, his eyes barely flicking my way. "Like countertops, tile, floors, hardware for cabinets. The small decisions can get to be a time-suck if we drag our feet on them."

"Got it," I reply. And he immediately begins dropping down the stairs, two steps in one stride. "Wait," I call, before I'm even cognizant of why I want him to slow down. A perturbed sigh rolls out of him before he looks back up at me.

"When are we supposed to—" I roll my eyes at myself. "You said something about a campground maintenance day. When is that happening?" Maybe the team-building could help us before we utterly fail one another and our grandmothers and this building.

"July third."

"Okay. And you'll be back before then?"

"It's four days from now."

"Okay? So, yes?"

"Yeah, I'll be back before then." He frowns. "Why?"

"The—car," I say, inwardly groaning at being so helpless. "I'd need it to go into town to look at things."

"Oh," he mutters. "That's right." Scratches the back of his neck.

"And," I huff back, relenting, "I don't know how to drive

a stick. That's why I've still been walking to the market or taking the bike."

My phone starts ringing from my apron pocket, then. *Mom.* I ignore it as Deacon steps back up the stairs.

"I was hoping you could teach me," I blurt.

Nothing. Not a quip about teaching me to drive a stick? The jokes are writing themselves and all I'm getting is a stupid blink.

"Or not. It's fine, actually. I'd rather not anyway, I'll—"

"I'll teach you. Tomorrow. Gotta take Sal to an appointment so we can just all go together if that works. You scheduled?"

"No, I'm off." My phone rings again. Deacon lifts a leg onto my step and leans a forearm on it.

"You can get that, you know," he says with a nod. "I've seen you ignore your mom's calls at least six times in the last week."

I inhale deeply through my nose, that previous unsteady feeling screeching into irritation.

"Actually, I can't. How's *your* mom, by the way?"

That has him stepping back with a mild roll of his own eyes. "See ya, Larry." He opens the door and pauses. "I'll be back in the morning. I'll, uh, make sure I text you when I'm on my way," he adds awkwardly.

Oh Jesus, he's worried he'll interrupt me again. "It's *fine*, Deacon." Then, feeling reckless, I say, "I'm not really a morning-mood kinda gal, anyway."

He snorts a laugh, but leaves without another word.

I STARE AT MY PHONE in my hand when I get inside. That small, desperate feeling sneaks through me. I hit call on *Mom* before I let myself reconsider.

"LaRynn?" she says in greeting.

"Hi, Mom."

A blown out breath. Like I've already managed to wear on her with my *hello*. "I'm glad you finally saw fit to return my calls."

I'm glad you saw fit to suddenly start giving a shit about being my mother. "I've been fairly busy."

"So I hear. I was forced to recruit your father into my efforts because I was concerned that you might be a missing person."

Such simple language, and yet so many layers.

She's angry and expects me to feel sorry that she was forced to interact with my father. A nice little callback to me being the only thing leashing her to him in the first place.

"You . . . What?"

"He's assured me that you're living in Santa Cruz at Cece's old place." She lets out another ragged sound. "I don't appreciate that I have to get this news from him, by the way."

Dad has *assured* her? The last time I spoke to him was almost a full year ago now, when he told me he *would not support me or make it easier for me to throw my future away.* When he removed me from his health insurance and phone plan and signed over my car to me like I was an employee receiving a severance. It probably chafed him raw that I just said thank you. That I refused to afford him a bigger reaction then, and that I haven't come crawling back since. That would be the only reason he'd have any interest in what I'm doing or where I am—the fact that he's no longer in control of my life. I wouldn't put it past him to pay a hired hand to come investigate. He had to have known I'd come here eventually.

"You are careless and lazy and spoiled."

I don't mourn his absence, at all. I don't feel badly for leaving. But this thing with my mom is different . . . This pretending and this resentment is almost worse.

"Well, Mom," I say. "I didn't appreciate when you left me to fend for myself against him for three years. Or when you returned and still may as well have been a ghost for how present *either* of you were."

My eyes widen when it leaves my lips, shocked by my own insolence.

But once it's out there, something like solace washes over me.

Relief at letting go of a piece of my rage.

She lets out an indignant sound. *"What*?! What did you just say to me?! Do you know what I sacrificed for you? What I put up with? LaRynn, you had the best of *everything*. Private school, private tutors. The most expensive sports programs in the state. I—" Another choked wail. "I came back for *you*. I sacrificed my own happiness for *you*. Your father—"

"Was a miserable bastard, Mom. I know he was. And I don't know what it was like to try and fix a marriage and be a parent in those conditions, I really don't." A hysterical noise tumbles out from her end. "But I'm so tired of pretending that just because you weren't the one screaming at me, terrifying me, calling me *débile* . . . that you weren't in the background, allowing it. I'm sick of acting like just because you want to have a relationship now, it makes up for everything back then."

She gasps softly. And it's then that I instantly panic. I panic like I did the first year after she came back and I got suspended from school for beating up Peter Gillespie in the cafeteria. He'd been ruthlessly picking on the girl I sat next to for weeks, but it didn't matter. I lived in a constant state of fear—one more toe out of line, one grade below par, and maybe that'd be the time he'd graduate from the yelling and he'd actually hit me . . . But almost worse, if I added any difficulty to their lives, then maybe *she'd* leave again.

"Mom, I . . . I just wish you would've taken me with you," I admit. And even in my fear, it's like the muscles loosen in my jaw with the *honesty*. That small, desperate feeling abates and hope sneaks in. Maybe we can have an honest conversation.

She snorts ruefully. "I don't know where this is coming from, LaRynn. This is completely out of nowhere. I don't know what you've immersed yourself in to build such a melodramatic view of your childhood, but yours was a walk in the park compared to mine. Compared to most."

I've tried. I've tried to understand my dad, tried to understand her. Tried to fill in the gaps where their love should have been with excuses. But God, I'm tired.

And it's something that I started when I dropped out of school, but it's in this moment when I start to realize that being honest feels so much better than being easy. Even if it leaves me feeling stripped bare.

"I have to go, Mom. I'm sorry you feel that way."

And I hang up the phone.

SEVENTEEN

DEACON

"Nope. Stop the car," I say after I'm whipped forward for the umpteenth time. At this rate Sal's bound to get her neck broken before we even get her to her appointment.

"Fine," LaRynn says haughtily, her lips pinching as she pulls forward in the empty parking lot.

I blow out a breath. "You'll get the hang of it. I just think we should practice when there's maybe *not* a frail old lady in the car."

"Kindly eat glass," Sal replies from the backseat. "But I do have to agree, dear."

"It's *fine*. Really. Do they even make cars that aren't automatic anymore?" LaRynn huffs, not waiting for a reply before she puts on the brake and gets out. I meet her at the trunk, expecting her to step around me. She surprises me by pausing, the toes of our shoes nearly touching.

"You'll get it," I say again, quieter and more gruff than I intend.

"I know," she says, one shoulder lifting half-heartedly. "It's not . . . I'm really not concerned about that part." She sighs and meets my eyes. "Honestly, it's just the dynamic here that's difficult for me. This—" She gestures between us, her hand hitting my chest before pointing to hers and continuing, "—doesn't come naturally to me. My own dad paid an instructor to teach me to drive in the first place." She looks off to the side. "I don't always know how not to be . . . *abrupt* about things. But I do recognize that you're doing something nice for me. Spending any of your time to teach me something and also letting me use your car. I *do* know that, alright?" And then she walks around me and slides into the passenger seat before I can respond.

I'm left a little dumbfounded as I finish the drive to Sal's doctor's office. That was . . . a surprisingly forward response from LaRynn. Vulnerable, even.

But . . . her own dad didn't want to teach her to drive? And I know—I remember some of the other things she'd let slip about her parents before, though it wasn't much back then. Remember the general impression I got from my Nana, based on what she knew from Cece. From the bits and pieces I've gathered overall, I know that LaRynn's mom left for a time, and then left again. Moved out by the time LaRynn went to college after that last summer she spent here.

I like to keep people where I understand them. I typically choose to do that through charm. Keep them happy with you, but keep it surface level. Keep them just far enough so they stay in focus and I can see every move before it comes. Too close and they blur, too many things are easy to miss. When someone's arms are wrapped around you it's easy to miss the knife in their hands.

So, maybe LaRynn is more like me than I ever realized. Her methods are just different. She'd rather keep people away altogether. I guess when the ones who are supposed to love you the most never made you feel safe or important, I'd probably assume the worst of people, too.

WE PULL INTO SAL'S DOCTOR'S office and the same jittery feeling I get every time starts shaking its way through me.

"You'll have to keep an eye on him, LaRynn," Sal says with a nod my way. I roll my eyes.

"Why?" LaRynn asks.

"You'll see."

"Doctors make me nervous, alright?" I say.

"That's all well and good, dear, but keep your nerves to yourself. You make everyone else around you anxious with the squirming and the pacing and the knocking old ladies out."

"I did not—well, okay I did, but it wasn't—"

"Explain. Immediately," LaRynn tells Sally.

"The man can't keep still and has to touch everything. His grandma used to tell me that even when he was little you could look at him and say, *Deacon don't touch that, it will burn you. It's hot.* And he'd look you dead in the eyes and touch it anyway. He spent months figuring out a mystery light switch at my house because it *bothered* him. Put holes in my walls." She glares at me and I put my hands in my pockets as we stroll through the automatic doors. "When I left him alone in the waiting room for fifteen minutes the first time, he took it upon himself to repair a shelf."

"It was already leaning. I was actually trying to prevent an accident!" I say, trying to defend myself.

"Someone wheeled in poor old Ruby Chester at the same time the whole thing collapsed. Knocked her clean out."

LaRynn looks back at me with her lips pressing together. "I hope she made a full recovery?"

Sally laughs. "Oh yes, and then some. Deacon took Ruby and I both to bingo once a month for about three years after," she says before she heaves a sigh. "She passed away a year ago now."

LaRynn's smirk falls. "Oh no, I'm s-sorry."

"Don't be!" Sally replies brightly. "She was ninety-eight and ready—quite literally begging to go. And that hag won every time she came to the hall anyway."

LaRynn and I both fail to suppress a small laugh.

We check Sal in, and the receptionist takes her usual jab at me and asks me to limit myself to the magazines available. But then we sit and my palms start to sweat. *What if this is the appointment they tell Sal something terrible? Who else is here in this place, maybe just a few rooms down, getting the worst news of their life?*

Sal is called back quickly and LaRynn's watchful eyes only add to my nerves.

"I'm going to go look for a vending machine," I blurt, unfolding from my chair.

"Sounds good," she replies, standing to join me.

"You don't have to."

"I don't love doctor's offices either," she says flatly.

We make our way down the hall, past other practitioners' offices and the pharmacy, before stepping onto an escalator that I know leads down to the cafeteria.

"So, is it a fear of needles then?" she asks from the step above me. "Whatever gets you nervous about these places."

"My dad." I sigh. No use tiptoeing around the point. "Not sure how much you remember of what I told you about him, but he died of colon cancer."

She frowns, a little line forming between her brows. Her hair's down today—something rare since she almost exclusively wears it up for work or for working at the house. "I *remember,* Deacon," she says. And her tone is frustrated, like it upsets her that I think she forgot.

I nod and we step down onto the floor. "I was home from school when he went in for a routine appointment, so he brought me with him. He wanted to go for ice cream after or something . . . my dad was like that. Wanted to make a big deal out of everything. Now I know he was most likely just overcompensating." I shove a hand through my hair. "Anyway. He was telling the doc some things that'd been coming up. He was playing it off like he thought they were no big deal. Part of aging, yada-yada. But the doctor's face got rightfully more concerned, and he ordered a gamut of tests." We turn into the cafeteria now, so I try to push the rest out quickly. "And yeah. It all went to shit from there."

"I'm sorry, Deacon."

I shrug. "It was worse for my mom. Twice."

"Doesn't mean it wasn't painful for you, too."

We study one another for a moment, and something about the honest sympathy in her gaze—so different from her typically fierce one—makes me feel like voicing the rest of my thoughts.

"I still don't understand why, after getting a second chance at life, after we'd forgiven him and were the ones there while he was sick that first time . . . I still don't get why we weren't enough." It's the thing you're not supposed to say. The man is dead, it's not as if he "got away" with it. But it's also the thing I've felt like saying out loud for so many years, and simply verbalizing it makes it feel like my chest is lighter, like I can gulp down a full breath.

It occurs to me that LaRynn and I keep wading through the ugly. Between revealing all these less-desirable parts of ourselves, and constantly falling back to the uglier versions with one another in that torn-apart house, we still keep going. Me with my phony charm and bad temper and her with her worse temper and cruel-toned apathy. I wonder if there's some comfort to be had in being able to show those sides to someone and have them still stick around the way that we are, even if it's out of obligation.

I also wonder what it'd be like if we ever got to the good. If we ever defaulted to the good versions of ourselves. If we didn't keep expecting the worst from one another.

WE PICK OUT A FEW snacks and set them on our trays before we slide into a booth.

"Did you—did you talk to him about the affairs before he passed? Did he apologize?" she asks. "I don't think you ever told me—before."

"Nah, we were usually too preoccupied to spend much time on the shitty stuff, I guess."

She tilts her head and levels me with A Look, but there's no ire in it. And I actually appreciate that she doesn't shower me with sympathetic words. Her gaze simply remains softer than normal, and so I decide I'll stay chattier than normal in return. Each anecdote feels as satisfying as ripping down a literal wall, anyway.

I elaborate as I tear into my chips. "My mom is the type of person who desperately wants to hold on to all the good. I figured it was already heavier on her, so I didn't need to add to it."

"He never tried to bring it up when you were alone or anything?"

I shake my head. "In a weird way, I bet he thought he was

doing that for us. We'd already grieved—*differently,* sure, but we still grieved two other times and would be grieving a third in that way." Her brows twitch, something like anger passing over her face. It warms something in my chest to have her be anything on my behalf at all.

"And sometimes . . . sometimes I don't know *what* I feel about it. It just—*was.* I get angry for my mom. Mostly I'm just confused. But then you start looking through all your memories and wondering what you were missing. *Oh, that time at that tournament when he left the hotel room for a few hours. Was he off meeting someone?* That sort of thing. And *that's* when the anger shows up. I get angry at all the questions I'll never have answered.

"And . . . I'm angry at all the parts of him I'll never get. Then I'm angry that I even *had* to be angry at him when he was weak and dying. That I'm left with this guilt that'll never resolve, because I never even gave him the chance to apologize."

"Deacon, *you* didn't do anything to feel guilty about. He should've been using his remaining time apologizing, I don't care if he had to use every breath," she says sternly, the fine muscles in her jaw working. And I'm struck anew with how fierce and formidable she is. Bits and pieces of smaller memories slip through the cracks. All the verbal dressing-downs she dealt out on other people's behalves, or the time she threw some sleazy guy's surfboard off the pier for bothering June. I wonder if she's quick to want justice for other people because no one ever did that for her.

"Thank you," I say, before we eat quietly.

Sal texts us soon after and tells us she's done, that everything went well.

We park the car in the garage when we get home but

decide to walk to the taco stand for dinner. We laugh and eat greasy food while the sun sets, and Sal treats us to story after story of her and our grandmothers.

And when we get home and bid her goodnight, we take the stairs together, my knuckles accidentally brushing hers when we reach the landing.

"Sorry," I mutter.

"It's okay," she replies.

I study my foot. "Uhh, so . . ."

"So."

I let out an agitated breath. "So, maybe tomorrow we could start looking at countertop slabs and tile? You could practice driving again?"

"Okay." She nods with a small smile before she turns to head to her "room."

"Goodnight, Lar."

"Sweet dreams, Deacon."

Let's hope.

EIGHTEEN

TWO DAYS LATER

LARYNN

"It's the land of your people!" I declare, proudly sweeping an arm toward the aisle.

He doesn't spare me a scoff, only side-eyes me. Deeply exasperated, it would seem.

"You said you wanted to continue to be more involved from now on, *mon amour*," I remind him in the face of his glare. "And since you spend so much time on them, I figured you'd be the expert opinion on the commode." I flutter my lashes his way.

"You nearly used up our entire exterior budget yesterday on countertops. I feel I need to be involved so that I have the right to complain later when the walls cave in," he grumbles.

"It was not the entire budget."

"You hardly even cook!"

"I might cook more when my kitchen serves my needs." I try for a light tone, but it tumbles out shrill instead. "For the time it's ours, at least." I sigh wearily. "And we did not end up going with them, anyway, so drop it."

"Only because I stepped in."

"One: you also almost knocked over an entire display shelf of sample tiles because you can't keep your hands off of things." I swipe a paintbrush out of his hand and push a drawer of knobs closed that he'd immediately opened. "And two: don't give yourself that much credit. You were also under the marble's spell briefly. I seem to recall the word 'beautiful' even being thrown around." I halt and turn back to him again. "Three: you sure like to talk a big game as far as the budget goes, but don't think I don't see you stealing my pillows, Deacon Leeds. Buying your fancy overpriced socks every other day. That blanket you like to drape yourself in whenever you watch whatever you're watching on your laptop was a very *spendy* blanket—"

"*Don't* tell me how much. Please."

"My point is," I say, lifting a lid on one of the toilets, "you like luxury and your creature comforts. As long as they're *yours,* or *you* get to use them."

The corners of his eyes crinkle and relax before he gives me a sidelong grin. "Alright, Lar. Let's pick out a shitter."

I make a very French-sounding, disgusted noise as he proceeds to step up onto the display shelf and sit his big body on the first option.

"*Deacon,*" I hiss.

"What?" he asks innocently, pulling out his phone and pretending to scroll. He leans back and forward again.

"*Get off that,*" I implore again.

"You're right. This one doesn't mold to my ass quite right."

"*Deacon—*"

"Wait, I know." He points a finger in the air like he's had a revelation. "Silly me. I can't get an accurate read this way. Need to make it more true to life to get a good sense." He lifts the hem of his shirt, exposing a sliver of tanned skin, a peek at a dark trail of hair. I've seen him nude or shirtless numerous times in the last month—could probably identify him by the path of one particular vein that trails down a section of his lower abs alone—but something about that little gesture, the way he unhooks his belt, the zip of his jeans . . . it slips a knot in my core and tugs, heat pooling behind it. His jeans hit the ground with a small clink as he dashes a crooked smile at me.

My face feels tight with the effort not to smile back. "You're going to get us kicked out and banned from this store."

One shoulder kicks up in a shrug. "Eh, there's another one a few miles away." And then he sits. "Come on, Larry, live a little. Try the toilets with me."

I turn away on a laugh, pathetically happy to have this playful version of him back. Enough that I'm going to indulge him. "My leggings are staying on."

"They're so thin and adhered to you I imagine the difference won't be noticeable," he mutters. I have to smother another grin.

We sit in mock-contemplation, adjusting ourselves and snickering like kids. I catch a glimpse of him shuffling over to the next one in the row, the one right beside mine, his pants still around his ankles.

"You know this is ridiculous, right?" I ask him.

"Having a toilet-fitting for a house we don't actually intend to live in? No. Seems like a vital use of our time." He smiles, but I notice that it's weaker and falls more quickly than normal. Like he's reaching for that former edge we had, just as unfamiliar with this filed-down feeling between us.

I think about him the other day—that sad look in his eyes

when he told me about his dad, when he said *I'm angry at the parts of him I'll never get.*

"Did I . . ." It feels only fair to show him a piece of me. A piece for a piece. "I'm not sure if I ever told you, but I've sort of done this whole thing before."

"Marriage?!" he blurts.

I bark out a laugh. Only *he* could think sitting on toilets together at a big box store was related to marriage more than home renovation. "No. Not marriage. This house stuff, kind of. Picking out things for a house you won't even live in long." I look down at my toes. "I don't think I ever told you, but we moved every two years, from when I was eight years old on. Almost like clockwork, while I was growing up. Usually just far enough that I'd have to switch schools, but not every time." I take a deep breath and find him watching me closely. "I don't even know why, because I rarely showed strong emotions as a kid. But I'd thrown a fit the first time—I'm talking screaming, crying, trying to stage a sit-in in my own room. The next house was nicer or maybe it was bigger, I don't even remember." I look down and away, remembering. "And it's not like I had many friends, so I don't *really* know why I cared . . . but . . . I accepted that the tantrums wouldn't work after that, and my parents would pacify me by letting me pick whatever I wanted for a new room." I sigh. "I knew it was a pay-off, but eventually, when no one listens to you or considers you, you just . . . take what you can get." I force a hollow laugh. "They didn't even care when the requests got ridiculous. When I wanted a hand-painted mural wall or a built-in bunk system. And believe me, I know how spoiled and privileged I sound, okay? You don't have to tell me."

"I wasn't going to," he says. Too gently. The corners of his mouth downturned.

"Don't do that," I say, looking away again.

"Do what?"

"Don't pity me. I'm not trying to make you *pity* me," I say, more venomous than I intend.

"There's a difference between feeling sorry for someone and being angry for someone, LaRynn. You should know," he replies firmly.

Emotion twists in my throat and I pick at some invisible lint on my leggings until I can swallow it down. "I just—I just wanted you to understand why maybe it's easy for me to get carried away with this. Why I end up accidentally going with things that I'd choose for my home, or if I take it too seriously. I know it's not—I know it won't be *mine*. I've *always* known that for every place, but I've always tried to make it feel like mine . . . for a little while. And maybe I want to do this right, for my grandma. For Helena, too." I meet his eyes. "They always talked about the house like it was something magic that brought them together, you know? And it felt like that for me when I was younger, too."

Deacon searches my face for longer than is comfortable, sitting here on the display shelf toilets. "That's why everything at Cece's—everything *here*—was so important to you, why you were so annoyed by me back then."

I feel my brows pinch together and shake my head. I immediately want to deny it, don't want to be entirely too transparent. Not to him. Don't want to be seen so clearly only to be rejected again.

"And you think I ruined it for you," he adds quietly.

You did ruin it for me, I almost say. Almost hand him my humiliation on one of those silver platters again. *I let you ruin it for me because I tricked myself into believing it was my favorite place and that I belonged here more than anywhere, then.* Where not just my grandmothers and Sally—people that loved me—lived, but where someone else cared for me when they didn't have to, without familial ties, and despite being difficult to love. Cared for me in such a way that he snuck in every free minute he could with me, sex or not. Because I'd believed that being horny teenagers was never what we were about—at least not *all* that we were about. He'd made me laugh, made me want to try things. He'd seemed like he wanted to try with me.

The trying was what it was really about. I'd begun to believe that trying was its own love language. Trying to understand a person, trying to make them happy, trying to make yourself happy, too. My relationship with him is what made me believe that.

And he'd proven that I still didn't know *anything,* really.

After that summer, all I could think about was another home that went on without me, another place that wouldn't miss me. Where a happier family could exist, with people who were less damaged.

"For the second time today, don't give yourself that much credit, Deacon." I huff out a sigh. "I should've visited more, regardless. I was fine after everything." I get up and step down.

This suddenly doesn't feel fun or nice or like a game I stand a chance at winning anymore. It feels like I've handed him my last little puzzle piece. Like he's got me solved and could promptly crumple me up and shove me away again. "We were young and dumb—*especially* me—and it meant nothing."

"LaRynn, wait—"

"Sir, you need to get down from there," a woman in a bright orange apron says, her hands balled at her sides.

"Yeah, okay I'm—" His belt clangs against the shelf as he stumbles up and nearly trips.

"*Sir,* you need to pull up your pants, immediately!"

"Alright, *alright.*" He gets up but looks to me and doesn't rush to scoop up his pants.

The woman stamps a foot. "I'm going to ask you to leave the store."

"Happily," I reply on his behalf. And then I head out to the parking lot, jogging through the doors when they part.

But I find out when I get to the car that it's locked, and I'm forced to stand by stupidly and wait for him to follow. I pace alongside it like I'm caged.

"Here," he suddenly says to my left. "You drive." And then he throws me the keys, which I catch on instinct.

And maybe it's just because I want to prove I'm fine, not sure whether to him or to me, but I squeeze them in my fist and walk around to the driver's side.

"Don't even put your foot on the gas right away at first," he directs me when I hurl myself in. "After you start it and put it in reverse, just slowly let off the clutch so that you can get a feel for when it grabs." He nods. "It'll start to roll."

I do as he says and feel what he describes. But when I try to put on the gas and let off the clutch all the way at the same time, I end up stalling out.

"It's alright, just start it again. Don't try to let off so fast at the same time. Smooth and slow and steady," he says patiently.

This time I get it, and I pull out of the space smoothly before flipping it back into first.

I go at a snail's pace, but I make it out onto the street, downshifting and shifting accordingly. I stall out again when we get to a stop sign, but restart and pick it back up.

My focus begins to divide and sharpen between the driving and his presence. I flick my eyes his way to find his inky gaze spilling over me, bleeding through everywhere it lands. I can practically feel the blots of color left in its wake. Everything behind that knot from earlier surges, and occupying my hands and mind with the drive becomes paramount. His eyes never waver, his chest rising and falling steadily in my peripheral, my own matching the rhythm after a bit.

I'd rather he *fight* with me than give me this space, rather he give me an excuse to fight back. I don't want to be the one who cares more, who's hung up enough on some fling to drag it all out into the open.

We're even right now, matched up in terms of the vulnerabilities we've conceded, and I am terrified to be the one to give up more ground.

I don't know how to do this, how to have a discussion where feelings are involved. All I know is fighting and retreating, passion eclipsed by resentment. I saw Grandma and Helena and their healthy relationship, but that always felt like looking at a snow globe: something lovely to enjoy through the glass for a short period every year, before it was stuffed away in the garage for the remainder.

I'm trembling by the time we pull into the garage. My clammy hands leave damp spots on the steering wheel.

I slam the car door and quickly bolt inside, him at my heels.

My steps fly up the stairs in rapid succession, my breath juddering in and out of me like I've run a marathon. My foot slips on the final ledge and his hands are there, steadying me from my ribs. He lifts me up to the landing and steps in front of me in a singular, smooth movement. His hands find my waist as my back gently presses into the framing.

"It *meant* something," grinds deeply out of him, sending shivers up my arms and heat to my ears. His breath gusts a strand of hair from my face as I study the skin fluttering rapidly at the base of his throat. At the same time my eyes finally clamber their way up to his, my chest presses against him on a pant.

"It meant something," he says again, this time nearly a whisper. And I don't know if it's because I needed to hear that or if it's because I want to stop him from saying more . . . but I press my mouth to his and kiss him either way.

NINETEEN

DEACON

A noise hums out of LaRynn from somewhere high in the back of her throat. Her scent in my nose, her full upper lip between mine. And my body reacts on instinct; relief, confusion, and desperation mixing a cocktail in my bloodstream. I taste the air between us and her tongue slips into my mouth, her head tipping back for more access. Her teeth sink into my lip and I groan, change the angle to taste her again. Her cool palms glide under my shirt and she scratches my skin with her nails. I press our hips together and she whimpers, the sound like a pull cord to every nerve ending in my body. One hand slaps into the wall beside her head, the other skates up her ribs, calluses scraping against her smooth skin.

The hand on the wall finds the strands of her ponytail and I lightly tug, expose her neck for me to lick and nip and kiss.

Something thumps on my mind's door, some warning knock I go on ignoring.

More of that cotton candy smell. I'm floating on a cloud of that scent, sugar and salt, and my eyes roll back behind my lids when she tangles her fingers in my hair.

A distant alarm rings in my brain, something that calls up the memory of the last night we kissed like this all those years ago, as a tsunami warning rang through the trees. *We can't, we can't do this.* This is going to end up worse for us both if we don't fix things first.

But then she glides the heel of a palm up the swelling part of my jeans and I groan before I push myself away, our lips peeling apart with the lightest smack. She frowns at me, swollen lips and mussed hair and *Jesus* no one should be that painfully beautiful. It's like taking in a lightning strike as it cracks across the sky; that little shocked, awed pause before thunder rumbles through you. Something equal parts scary and mesmerizing.

"Go," shreds through my chest. "I think we need to go to bed. This—this shouldn't happen like this." I'm a husk, barely another touch and I'll get swept away. And I may not know much, may feel shaken and rattled, but I know this can't be about sex this time. We can't let sex get in the way, can't use it as a Band-Aid for the past either, and it's clear neither of us can handle it on its own with any emotional intelligence.

I watch the expressions roll across her features: Confusion, disbelief, frustration, before landing on pure, unadulterated, seething rage. She snorts and shoulders past me, clipping my still-hard erection with her hip and pulling a grunt out of me.

"Wait—" I barely choke out.

"*No,*" she bites back.

There's no door to slam, but the jerk she gives on the curtains has the sharpness of a knife slicing across me.

I rub my palm up and down my face, adjust my pants as I make my way to my room. Why didn't I *think*? Why couldn't

I just speak? Just say *Wait, we need to slow down, we need to have a conversation.*

Because I'm scared that conversation might only make things worse. Make it harder to work with one another. We still have this fucking house to fix. Because as little as she trusts me, I think I panicked about trusting her, too.

I TOSS THE NIGHT AWAY, eventually calming down enough to know that we have to have some semblance of a conversation. I try to play it out in my mind, try to memorize what I want to say.

When I shuffle out to the kitchen in the morning, LaRynn is frying something on the stove, a pot of coffee dripping and gurgling in the background. She's already dressed for the day in the same leggings—the kind with the seam up the middle of her rear, emphasizing every curve. Some tank top with a flannel half hanging off one shoulder. Her hair in two long braids down her back.

"Good morning," she says without turning to me. Overly sunny, at least for her.

"M-morning," I say groggily. "LaRynn, I—"

"Beignet?" she asks cheerfully, turning to show me the contents of a plate. Something dusted in powdered sugar.

"What?"

"Would you like a beignet? Essentially a donut. The only breakfast pastry I know how to make." She lifts her brows in offering.

"You made me breakfast?" I ask, unable to mask the wariness in my tone. Something's not right.

I swear I see one of her eyes twitch, but she simply replies, "I made enough for the both of us, yeah." She starts plating a few. "And I wanted to thank you for last night. Clearly, we need to get out and get laid. This forced proximity has our heads all muddled up and it was easy to get carried away."

"Wait. *What?*"

She gives me an innocent look. "Listen, I'm not mad at all. I'm just saying it's clear that our signals are getting crossed. What with your eavesdropping on my private time and constant leering—"

"Hold on a damn minute—"

"—mauling me the instant my lips came near yours."

I narrow my eyes at her. "You damn well know *you* kissed *me.*"

"I was merely thanking you for the driving lesson. You're the one who started practically humping me up a wall."

"And I suppose it was my own hand clutching at my cock then, too?"

"Must've been."

"You don't get to do this." I shake my head in disbelief. "Look, I'm sorry if I made you feel—*rejected* last night."

"Nothing to reject but bad judgment. Truly, thank you, Deacon."

"*Stop it.*"

"No, really. You told me in the beginning that I was free to see other people and *yeesh,* clearly I should, right? We both should. You even more so. A man like you must be very—" She eyes me up and down and scrunches her nose. "—*needy.*"

She starts tearing apart her beignet and popping pieces of it into her mouth. The circles under her eyes tell me she didn't rest well, either.

"Fine," I say, before shoving an entire one into my mouth. When I eventually swallow it, I add, "You want to hurt me back? That make you feel better?" I watch her nostrils flare as she tears into a bite. "You're acting like a child."

Shit. It was the wrong thing to say. She pauses in her chewing, her eyes lifting back to me in slow, deadly motion. It's like watching someone crank back on a catapult. She swallows and licks away some powdered sugar from the corner of her mouth, and I hate that I imagine I can taste it, too. "Is this not what you wanted? *You* wanted to stop. You said this shouldn't happen. I'm merely making it easier on us."

"Because it *shouldn't* happen until we talk about some shit, LaRynn." I toss down the beignet. "And *you* and *easy* don't belong in the same fucking sentence."

She bares her teeth at me in a phony grin. "Truly, I can't begin to express my gratitude. Would've been such a colossal mistake. It was a moment of weakness."

My gut rolls with shame and hurt, the feeling like an echo from the past as she sits there and rips into another bite without a care. I catch the clock on the wall behind her. *Is this how real couples have to function? Continue on with their obligations while they fester?* All my longer-term relationships were too casual to ever encounter this. "I guess you're right, if that's how you really feel," I say.

"It is."

"Whatever you say."

I CLEAN UP THE KITCHEN after we eat, earning myself a bitter-sounding "thank you" before we meet at the landing to head out.

She turns up the volume on the music the moment we get in the car, and it's probably for the best, because I'm still fuming and anything I want to say will inevitably come out wrong. It always comes out wrong, anyway. I flick my eyes her way to find her leaning against the window, her hand balled in a fist.

It's the sight of that fist, knuckles nearly white, that makes the anger evaporate into something . . . worse. Something like hopelessness.

We can't ever seem to get on the same page, the right foot, or build a good foundation no matter how hard we try. And we can't seem to escape each other, either. Not really.

She straightens in her seat when I make the sharp turn into the campground.

"It looks so—*different*," she says. I simply nod but she doesn't catch it. "When did they add those?" She points to the pairs of Airstreams that don either side of the little camp store. They have decks and plants, and per Mrs. Gold's incessant badgering, poles set with string lights.

"I finished restoring those and building the decks about four years ago now," I say.

"You?!"

I sneer at her on instinct, the words "colossal mistake" replaying in my mind. "Yes, *me*, no matter how unbelievable you find it. I own this place, after all."

"Own it?"

"My mom and I used my dad's life insurance funds to buy it when the former owners wanted to sell. Two years after we moved here," I tell her. "Ramsey's more of a silent partner, but he also owns a third."

"Ramsey? As in your brother?"

"That'd be the one."

She shifts in her seat. "I saw that he made it to pro-ball a few years back. He still playing in Georgia?"

"Ah, yes. If only you'd met the perfect prodigal son, instead of me."

Her head rears back. *"Jesus.* Now who's acting like a child?"

I grip the wheel tighter and don't reply. I shouldn't talk about Ramsey when I'm already feeling this way. My brother escaped the hardest period in our home since he was away at school—off succeeding, off doing big and great things. Unlike me. We talk and do just fine during the holidays, but . . . we're just not close and I don't know if we ever will be. We were pitted against each other too much while we were growing up to start feeling like we're on the same team now.

I pull into my parking spot and see Jensen already here, rakes and garbage bags in hand. A few of the campers signed up to join in, too.

I get out and wait for the group to gather before I brief everyone on tool usage and our plan. Refreshing gravel and bark, pulling any weeds, replacing campsite numbers, etcetera, before we set up for the party. I pair off with Jensen and LaRynn separates with some of the other campers.

So much for a team-building day.

JENSEN'S BEEN PUSHING ME FOR constant updates since this whole thing began and is rapidly turning into a monster. I feel like a middle school girl with the repetitive *and then I said, and then she saids* I've recounted over the last month.

"She said that?!" he says, wincing at me when I update him on the *kiss* to *LaRynn saying we should go out and get laid by other people* transition.

"Yes. Why do you look like that makes you nervous?"

"Because it does. It makes me *very* nervous."

"I'll be fine, Jay. I know better than to get this thing mixed up with her."

"It's not that. Though, believe me, I think you two parading other people around each other has the potential to be a truly categorical disaster. But . . ." He takes a pull off his water bottle. "It's just—wouldn't you risk your community property in cases of infidelity?"

"It's not infidelity if we've had this discussion? Which we did. And it's not like I have actual plans to." My rake scrapes through the ground aggressively. "*And* we have a prenup."

"For the trust money. But not for property. You guys getting hitched made that community property—I think? Doesn't it? Despite the fact that it was already shared. She could technically win it over if it all blew up, couldn't she? I just wonder if maybe she's trying to bait you into something."

"*Jesus Christ*, Jensen, you think *I* know?! You're telling me this now?! After you're the one who told me to bring up this conversation to begin with?!"

"I think I saw it going differently in my mind."

"No shit." I dig into the ground again moodily. "You think she's trying to set me up?"

He slaps his forehead with a groan and drags the hand down his face. "Let's not jump to conclusions."

"Yes, let's *not*. Especially when a very simple Google search would clear all of this up for you," comes LaRynn's voice from behind us.

I close my eyes and exhale through my nose before I turn to face her. She's breathing heavily, her flannel now tied around her waist, red-cheeked . . . and fucking *pissed*.

"LaRynn—"

She tosses down the wheelbarrow and pulls her phone out of her back pocket.

"Here. Multiple articles on how in California, since infidelity is not actually illegal, it would not affect property division in divorce proceedings. Here's another result saved on how we are both additionally protected since this was left to us in both of our names."

"Rynn—"

She cuts me off with a cruel laugh. "You really didn't think to research that beforehand? Glad one measly little kiss has you falling over yourself so much that you think I'm really trying to lay out some nefarious plan to *trap* you. Maybe I called it Operation Blue Balls. Maybe I planned to call Elyse and have her seduce you. Is *that* it? That's really what you think?" She turns her glare on Jensen and he slinks away.

I toss the rake aside. "LaRynn, I *can't* think half the time I'm around you because I'm too busy trying to figure you out."

"Well, fucking stop, then! I'm not some *project*, Deacon. I'm not some car, or some trailer, or some house you can take apart and figure out before you restore it into something shiny and new, alright?!"

TWENTY

LARYNN

I whip around and start marching away before he can respond, my palms itching to hit something, my throat pulling tight.

He's hot on my heels and I try to think of something to make him go away.

"I'm not broken," is what I hiss instead, my traitorous voice catching

I head toward a building on the opposite end of the campground, closest to the turnout that heads out onto a collection of alcoves above the beach. I don't recall what that building is, but I'm determined to keep my focus on it. And the bastard just keeps following me, so I try again to fling something else his way. "If you need a project so badly why don't you work on yourself, huh? Figure your own shit out." He doesn't react, just continues to keep pace.

I finally get to the building—the camp laundry room, I see now—and wrench open the door. It must've swelled from the damp air because it gets partially stuck, and when I fling it back I stumble off the concrete step before I haul myself through it. I rear on him from the doorway and look him dead in the eyes.

"I don't *want* you." I try to shut the door and he blocks it, crowds into my space as I back away. His eyes are black, his curls wilder here, where the air is thicker with mist and salt.

He shakes his head and clenches his jaw. "You're a lot of things, LaRynn, but you're not usually such a *liar*." And *God* I hate that he's right. I hate that even now, after he turned me away again, all I want is to sink my teeth around his Adam's apple and bite him just so I can taste him.

"You tell me to go and I'll go, right back out that door. But you want to know what I really think?" he asks, his voice hoarse.

"Not really."

"I think I hurt you last night even though I didn't mean to, and I'm *sorry*. I also think you *meant* to hurt me back with that bullshit this morning, and it worked." He takes another step. "I think I want you against my better judgment and I think you *hate* how much you want me."

My ass hits one of the machines and I brace my palms against it as he stalks closer.

"I think you're dying for me to kiss you right now," he says quietly, dark eyes dipping to my mouth. "To touch you. To wind you up higher and tighter until everything snaps."

This drumming thing in me hardens into determination. "I think it's *you* who's aching for that," I say back. I will *not* be the one to close the distance this time. "Dying to feel me again." A bead of sweat cools a path between my breasts.

"How about I start and we'll see who's begging by the end?"

"We both know it'll be you and you're going to *love* it

because you're such"—I drag finger down his heaving chest—"a *good*"—I drag it further, toying with his waistband—"boy."

And it's like a cord is snapped, the way his expression unravels. I'm not sure whose hands are where but his shorts slip to his ankles at the same time the strap of my tank top is yanked down and our mouths gasp, open against each other.

"*LaRynn,*" he rasps, forehead pressing into mine, body rocking forward. My breath hitches when I feel him, hard against my stomach.

"Just—" *Just don't talk*, I want to say. *Just put your hands and your mouth on me and chase this with me. Please.* I'll let him be right this time. I'll beg.

"*Excuse me!*" A shrill voice pierces our bubble, and both our heads whip that way. The swift movement tilts our balance and our cheeks graze, his rough scraping against my smooth. I want to curl back against it like a cat.

"Mrs. Gold," Deacon says, forcing a breathy laugh. His shorts remain on the ground, body still angled toward me in an attempt to hide his—*acute*—condition.

"This is a *campground*, Deacon. There are *families*," she sputters.

"We're sorry, Ma'am," I say, giving her my sweetest grin, whatever that may be. "We just got carried away. We're uh—" I look back up at him briefly before I turn to her. "We're newlyweds."

The change is so instantaneous it's comical. Her downturned mouth relaxes into a knowing smile. "Oh, well . . ." She sighs merrily. "I suppose I remember those days. And it's about time someone snapped this one up." She gestures toward Deacon with her basket. "I'm Cheryl Gold. I'm sure Deacon's told you all about us. We come here every year for the Fourth."

A sound warbles out of me before I manage to come up with, "Yeah."

"When did you get married?" she asks casually, so very unable to read the room.

"Married?!" comes a voice from behind Mrs. Gold, and Deacon's head falls to my shoulder on a groan while I start shaking in laughter.

"Deacon?!" the new voice says again and *oh God*. The laughter dies.

His head snaps back up. *"MOM?!"*

"LaRynn?!" cries Macy Leeds.

"H—Hi, Mrs. Leeds," I murmur, putting a palm up in a stupid wave while her son still has a half-mast boner pressed against me.

"*Oooh,* I bet you'll have grandbabies in no time!" Mrs. Gold prattles on, shoulders bouncing in moronic glee.

"You came back early?!" Deacon asks, and *heaven above, he is still in his fucking underwear.*

"Apparently not early enough if I missed you two getting engaged," Macy replies, looking between us in shock. "Let alone *married*." My gaze falls to my feet.

"Can we just have a moment?" Deacon asks the women. "Mom, we'll come meet you at your place?"

Macy only nods, sparing me a shaky half-smile before she turns and walks away.

"I hope we'll get to see you at the barbecue, Lauren—she did say Lauren, didn't she? I'd love to hear all about your whirlwind romance," Mrs. Gold coos.

"She'll be there, Mrs. Gold. Thank you," Deacon replies with a curt nod.

"Oh! Right. Okay. Buh-bye now," she says, finally stepping back out of the laundry room.

The moment the door clicks shut he yanks up his shorts and paces a few steps.

He's pale, running a palm over his mouth nervously. "I can't have my mom know that this isn't—" His eyes dart up to mine. "I don't want her to think that I don't take marriage seriously. That it's less than serious. I don't want her to think it doesn't mean anything to me."

"Deacon, just explain *why* we are and what happened just now, your mom will understand."

"LaRynn. *Please*," he says urgently, his voice strained and breaking.

"*Why?*" I ask, taking in the tense lines of him.

"I don't want her to think I'd do this out of some obligation, alright? That it wouldn't be for . . . love," he says, hands clutching his hips. "I know she wouldn't admit it, but she'd think I put some lesser value on marriage and she'd think it was her fault, that I didn't see it as something you do exclusively when you *love* someone." His throat works. "Please."

Our eyes search one another, his as dark and difficult to decipher as always. But there was something desperate and bleak in the way he said "please."

"Okay," I whisper.

His eyes shut in relief. "Thank you." And he wraps me in a hug so abruptly that my chin glides against the crook of his neck, the tip of my nose behind it.

I fit perfectly here, my face pressed into the place where his collarbone meets his throat. That salt and soap scent of him makes me want to rest, and it hits me that this is the first time we've hugged since I came back. It might be the first time we've *ever* just hugged, I realize. We've been wrapped and bound so tightly there was no endpoint to us, but I don't know that I've ever just been held by him this way, with his arm banded across my spine and his other palm cradling the back of my head. I bring my still-trembling hands up the broad muscles on the backs of his ribs, press them into his shoulder blades.

We peel apart shakily and awkwardly move around each other and out the door. He's far twitchier than even myself, despite the whiplash of the last fifteen minutes.

And as we walk in the direction to his mom's, the meanest part of my brain sees him wiping his palms on his jeans and raking his fingers through his hair and realizes that it would be easy to tip him over a barrel now. For some reason *this* has him so anxious that I bet I could garner whatever promises I wanted at this moment.

Stop leaving your socks in the living room.

Close the goddamn cereal box before you put it away.

If I have to see another half-drunk glass of water on your nightstand even though it shouldn't concern me, I think I will have an aneurysm, so stop that.

Stop leaving your tools strewn about.

But then I recall how I've constantly aggravated him right back. How I'm just as responsible for this state of irritated need. How . . . *God, this thought fills me with embarrassment and worry for myself . . .* but how sometimes it makes me truly *laugh* when I leave my hair on the shower wall or when I light every candle throughout the house, thinking about how he'll shake his head or mutter indignantly under his breath. And how laughing at that has also felt *fun*.

Maybe I really am just rotten inside, wrong or backwards in that way. Because I've also laughed while shaking my head when I've come across those things that he does that annoy me so thoroughly. When I've found his stupid socks again or collected his water glasses because I couldn't stand even walking past them another time.

Maybe as crazy as he makes me, it still feels good to share something with someone . . . most of the time. Stale cereal is a shit way to start a day, though.

Even if I am wrong or backwards and have too many mean and angry parts inside, I can't seem to summon them into action while I watch him panic.

"Would you like to hold my hand?" I ask, my tone thick with feigned annoyance. "If you want this to look real for her, I mean," I add gently.

His face softens, unsure. "I think that would be good, yeah?" he says.

I lift my brows and a hand his way.

TWENTY-ONE

LARYNN

His mom's place ends up being in the same spot I recall it being before, but the shabby manufactured house has been entirely replaced by a cute bungalow, painted to match the same deep green as the camp store building. Out front, posted against a small picket fence made of driftwood, sits a sign that says Camp Host.

As we come in through the gate and approach the porch, the grip on my hand gets tighter. He squeezes one extra time when he knocks on the door, though he decides not to wait at all as he opens it and calls out for her.

"I thought you'd value the concept of a door a little bit more," I mutter to him.

One side of his mouth ticks up before he frowns and looks down the hallway.

"Mom?"

Macy comes bounding for us in excited, long strides, with her face scrunched up in a sob. "Mom, *why* are you crying?" Deacon asks, horrified.

"I'm just happy, that's all," she replies, a mewl escaping

her when she hugs each of us tightly. I stand stiffly and try to keep the smile plastered to my face.

"I just thought," she wails, "I just thought that after your dad—I thought you resented the idea of ever being bound to someone that way. You were so *angry* and you just hated that I went back or stayed or—" She swipes her hands in the air like whiteboard erasers. "Or whatever it was. I think I thought you didn't believe in it after that—*I'm sorry I'm snotting all over you.*" She brushes off his shirt after hugging me again. "I was always worried you'd never see the merit in finding a real *partner,* even. Let alone marriage. I just—I'm just so happy for you, baby."

Deacon swallows. A muscle jumps along his jaw. And then his face cracks into a faint smile before he looks back at me, pleading in his eyes. He hugs her again and keeps his gaze on me. "Thank you," he says. And I know it's meant for me.

"Come in, come in. Let's have lunch. They've got it handled out there," she urges.

"Mom, we have to get finished and set things up for the barbecue."

"Deacon James, you were about to get busy in the camp laundry room. You can afford the time with your mother," she states firmly. "And I have chili."

Deacon and I both look at our shoes and I snort out a laugh again. "I'm sorry," I try to recover.

"Don't be. It's not like I don't know what it's like, you know," she replies, hands going to her hips.

"*Jesus,*" Deacon groans.

"And," she continues, leveling him with a look, "it's not like I didn't know what you two were doing when you were *younger* either. Anyone camping here knew. Despite your insistence that you were just buddies, you weren't exactly discreet."

"Mom—"

"The shocks on the Bronco and those old trailers weren't great back then. Anyone passing by could see those things rockin'!" she laughs.

I hope she poisoned the chili. I'd like to die a swift death straightaway.

We slump into a small built-in dinette in her kitchen, and Deacon takes his hand back to bury his face in his palms. I fold and focus on my own in my lap.

"Hold on, let me get us some lunch and then I want to hear everything!" she chimes before she starts collecting dishes and stirring a pot on the stove. Deacon nudges me with an elbow and mouths *I'm so sorry,* silently. I have to stifle another laugh. *It's okay,* I mime back.

Macy slides chili in front of us and a tray of cornbread muffins before she sits down with a flourish. She's got the same hair as him, streaked with gray, and something does a flip inside me when I imagine Deacon's ever going that direction, with strands of silver. Macy's eyes are lighter, though, and wrinkled in a way that lets you know she doesn't shy away from a laugh.

"Thank you, this looks delicious." I nod down to the chili.

"Eat, *eat.* But talk at the same time. Tell me everything," she coaxes. "God, you're gorgeous," she says to me when I've taken a bite. She backhands Deacon across the bicep. "Deacon, isn't she stunning?"

"Ma, *please.* I'm genuinely begging you, calm down," Deacon pleads. "And yes, I know she is." He keeps his focus on his bowl.

Warmth floods my system, pooling in my cheeks.

Because here's the thing: I do know that I'm attractive. I always have. But . . . men are always saying things to me like that Rafe idiot did. Some version of "smile more" and "lighten up," or "be shorter."

Well, not that last one in exact words, but being six foot is always remarked upon with a little shrug, like they could "deal" with my height but it doesn't please them. So something about that simple acknowledgment makes me feel almost bashful, in a way.

"Maybe she can get you to cut your hair," Macy replies. "He needs it cleaned up doesn't he?" She directs the question at me.

I swallow and look back at him. "Maybe a little?" I shrug and he narrows his eyes and shakes his head. "But not too much. I like it this way," I relent. My fingertips ache with wanting to feel it.

He pauses and grins crookedly. "Thanks, Larry."

Macy slaps him across the back of the head. "You cannot still call her *Larry*. You can't call *your wife* Larry. It's a terrible nickname and I don't even know how you came up with it."

"First of all, *ow*. Secondly, maybe what I call her at home isn't appropriate for your ears."

She slaps him again and I shove an elbow into his ribs. He rubs at his side and sucks his teeth. "Don't bully me."

"Wouldn't dream of it," I say flatly with a smirk. "Do you even remember when you gave me that nickname?"

"Of course I do," he says. "I remember everything."

And that simplicity again makes me lightheaded. I wonder if he remembers the first time, when I lost a tear despite myself and he kissed it away. The time we left a window open in the Bronco and a seagull few in. How he batted it away with panicking hands while we both screamed. How hard we laughed afterward, naked in the backseat together. I wonder if he remembers me telling him I loved him.

He grabs a corn muffin and butters it generously before he continues. "Nana and Cece asked us to work on their planter project, and I was still trying to recover from the volleyball incident," he says, and Macy winces with a laugh. "So I was just trying to charm her."

I flick back to the memory as he tells the story.

"So," he'd said as I tried to flip through a magazine. The headache that showed up every day since he broke my nose had already begun, and his incessant drilling was only making things worse. *"LaRynn is a different name. Pretty. What does everyone call you for short?"*

I looked up at him from the pages, and he had the decency to look back down. I felt grotesque, the bruises under my eyes fading to a sickly yellow. *"It's two syllables,* Deac. *Most people can handle it."*

He cracked his neck with an over dramatic sigh, but didn't give up. *"Rynn, maybe?"*

"Rynn's fine."

"But what do you like?"

"I like not having my nose broken by morons and then being obligated to work with them."

"I meant in terms of the nickname, but that doesn't sound like much fun either," he'd replied. I went back to my gardening magazine.

"Frenchie? Like that chick from Grease, *and since you're French?"* he pestered.

I spared him a glare.

"LaRynn Lavigne, LaRynn Lavigne," he repeated to himself. *"What about LaLa?"*

I glared again, anger throbbing in my temples. *"Do I look anything like a 'LaLa' to you?"* I barked at him.

He cocked his head to the side. I should've acted less

perturbed because it was clear it was only encouraging him. *"I've got it,"* he said with a delighted smile. *"I'll call you Larry."*

"IT STARTED AS A JOKE, but once it irritated her enough I just sorta ran with it back then," he's telling his mom now. He slants a glance my way. "But I suppose you're right, probably shouldn't call my wife Larry." He searches my face, the words *my wife* bouncing through the caverns of my brain. Warmth unfurls in my chest.

I look away and search for a subject change before Macy saves me the task. "So, tell me how this"—she points between the two of us—"transpired. *This* time, I mean."

"Well, she came back for the First Street house, and—"

"Let LaRynn tell it. We women know how to tell a story better," Macy cuts him off. He lets out a weary sound.

"Um. Well," I begin, and try to piece it together quickly, to speak it even faster. "It's like he said. I came back to . . . help. With the house. And, uh . . ." I look back at him, suddenly a little angry to be in this position because I hate and am terrible with elaborate lies. "We just—clicked. We butted heads at first, but I guess whatever we had when we were younger turned into that plus some and . . . and I, um—we fell hard. We got married on a whim and it's my fault he didn't tell you, Macy, I asked him not to. I haven't—I haven't told my parents yet. Things have been strained between us and I don't think they'd understand, plus I think I should tell them in person. *And* I at least wanted to see you again before we told you. I also worried you might be upset that we didn't do a big wedding or something." Guilt crawls up my already tightened throat, imagining her sadness when Deacon tells her it's over.

"Oh, I couldn't care less about the wedding. Those things always become a production for everyone else instead of *you,* anyway." She beams at us both, eyes filling again.

"Mom," Deacon chides when a tear bubbles over, and she shrugs.

"I'm just happy. I can't help it. Mom always said that house was something magic. How it brought her to Cece and brought them together. I guess she was right." She sighs mistily. "And don't worry, I know better than to start asking about grandbabies." A pause. Then, "Do you *want* babies, though? I'm merely curious." She holds her hands out in surrender.

"Alright, that's *enough,* Ma. We need to get out there and help now." He starts shoving himself down the seat, nudging his mom out with him.

"Fine, fine, *fine.* I get it. *I get it.*" We all make our way to the hall.

A knock comes on the door then, followed by what sounds like Cheryl Gold's voice. "Macy! I found a little someone over in my site-neighbor's tent!"

"Why was she *in* her site-neighbor's tent?" I whisper.

"Happens more than you'd think," Deacon whispers back.

But something scurries in from the dog door I've only just noticed and he fully hip-checks his mother and me out of the way. "Baby V!" he coos at a pitch I would not have believed he was capable of, before the tiny creature leaps into his open arms.

"Oh, shoot. In all my excitement I forgot I'd been out there looking for the little shit!" Macy exclaims. "Before we caught you stripping over the fabric softener, that is."

"Don't you speak about her that way," Deacon says, ignoring the last bit. He goes back to letting the dog frantically lick every inch of his face.

"She a wiener dog?" I ask. "She's cute."

"She prefers the terms dachshund and *beautiful,* but yes." He ruffles her long, dappled hair. "My wittle Vienna-sausage."

O-kay, then. "Should we give you two a moment?" I laugh.

"Probably best," Macy says. "She's *my* dog, but she forgets that fact the moment he comes around."

"Nah, let's go get this place set up for a party!" Deacon cheers, holding Vienna's paw up in salute. She darts her blue eyes over to me and her little dog-lips curl up in a happy, mischievous grin.

MACY USHERS ME ALONG AT her side as we get things set up, asking me questions about the house and how I'm enjoying working at Spill the Beans. In our sharing I learn that it was Deacon who built her entire new house. He, along with his brother Ramsey.

"It started with him building furniture, really," she tells me. "That bed of his—well, the bed that belongs to you both, now, I suppose . . . He built that when he was nineteen or so. Built all the picnic tables here sometime after that. And soon enough he was digging into more mechanical things. Electrocuted himself too many times for comfort until I convinced him to find an apprenticeship and get a damn license."

I try to volley back questions as much as possible to keep the pressure off of me and minimize the risk of me slipping up in our fib, to which she continues to reply warmly, without a hint of suspicion or resentment.

If I told my mom I had eloped it would be a *very* different response, that's for sure. But Macy's just genuinely happy that her son's found partnership it seems, and that only makes me feel sicker.

"How's your mom doing, by the way? I know you said you haven't told her about Deacon yet and that's fine, I get it. But . . . I remember Mom saying she remarried?"

I sigh through my nose. "Yeah, she did. She, uh . . . lives in New York now." And now that she's happy in her life, she wants me in hers. But only on her terms. I'm not sure what else to say because I'm not sure where we stand or where we'll end up.

"Sweetheart?" Macy's hand falls to mine, and I pause rolling up the plastic silverware in the patriotic paper napkins. Her expression pinches in concern. "I asked when you last spoke to her?"

"Oh!" I feign a laugh. But then . . . maybe it's that I've already reached my limit on lies today. I let the smile die, and land on the truth. "It's been a few days since I last spoke to her. I think we went about four months before that, though. We don't—we don't have the closest relationship."

She nods with a frown. "If you'll permit me, I'll try to tell you something that I've occasionally tried to explain to Deacon when it comes to his father, too?" The question is genuine, and I feel like I could quite easily tell her "No thank you" and she would go on without judging me for it. But, maybe I do want the insight.

"Yeah, of course," I say.

She inhales wearily. "The messes and mistakes we make as parents are more about *us*, than our children." She looks at me softly. "I think when you remind yourself that their choices were more about them than you, you can get to a place where you're open to forgiveness. Or at least, not punishing yourself anymore over it. Because sometimes that's all that forgiveness accomplishes. Setting *yourself* free of it." She sets down the napkins and holds up her hands. "And please don't misunderstand me here: you don't owe anyone anything. But if you want her to know how you feel, you have to tell her, honey. And you might have to keep telling her. If Deacon's father were alive I'd tell him the same thing. I regret not pushing it at the time, but . . ." She blows out a shaky breath. "But I wanted to only focus on the good bits there at the end, and by doing that, I fear I did my sons a disservice." She goes back to her task. "Deacon, more so."

Maybe Mom thought coming back meant we could put enough pretty things on the shelves so we could forget about all the messy corners, the overflowing closets and broken things hidden behind new ones. Maybe she never realized that I was one of the broken things, too. Maybe that's why it was so liberating to speak up for once.

Because there's power in that. In saying, look; I was damaged, and you played a role. But I'm repairing myself. Not you, and no one else. If you can accept and love this version of me, chipped bits and all, acknowledge your part in that, then maybe we can have something real.

I look up across the blacktop dance floor and see Deacon looking this way, his brow creased in concern, Jensen unloading a bale of hay beside him with Vienna panting at his heels. I try to rearrange my face into something reassuring. He smiles a small smile back before he winks—obnoxiously and terribly. Even as something like static fills my chest, I shake my head and laugh through my nose.

"Then again, I think he's doing just fine," Macy adds, following my line of sight. "Seems to me you both are, even with all the messes left on you."

God I wish she was right. I want her to be right.

TWENTY-TWO

DEACON

It's past dark by the time we finish the campground clean-up and get set up for the barbecue. The holiday celebrations seem like they get bigger every year, but I pity anyone that tries to tell my mother to dial it back. I should've figured she'd end this year's trip early when she realized it fell over the Fourth.

There's a dunk tank, a popcorn machine, bottle toss and ring toss, plus a dance floor that will no doubt see much more action than anyone thinks, what with June in charge of creating a playlist.

"You ready?" I ask LaRynn after she's set down a bucket full of sparklers. Her hair has mostly escaped her braids, wispy pieces in every direction.

"Yeah, I'm beat."

We load up in the Bronco woodenly, shutting ourselves into the cocoon of the car, and head home.

There's no smooth way to bring up everything from earlier, so the energy grows stiffer and more awkward with each passing second. We've already sat in strained silence for twenty-eight minutes of the thirty-minute drive when she redirects her air vent, and I turn it off altogether.

"It's alright, you don't—"

"No, it's okay, it was getting chilly in here anyway."

There's another brief pause before she asks, "Can I?" and points to the volume dial.

"Yeah, sure." I go to turn it up at the same time and our hands clash.

"Sorry," we say in unison.

Christ.

"Hey!" she says so loud that I flinch. "Sorry!" She starts laughing. "This is fucking awkward, huh?"

"Truly, only getting worse by the second." I laugh back.

A sigh spins out of her. "Anyway, what I was going to say is, *hey,* I know we need to talk about earlier."

I pull into the garage and turn off the ignition before she continues. "I know we need to talk about a lot of things," she adds quietly.

I catch sight of her palms dragging up and down her thighs anxiously, and I can tell this is hard for her. "We don't have to get into it tonight, LaRynn. I know you're exhausted. I am, too." I flick on the interior light so we're not blanketed in total darkness. "Thank you for what you did for me with my mom. You don't have to come tomorrow if it'll be too . . . difficult to do again," I tell her.

"Do you . . . Would you like me to come?" she asks.

"Yeah, I want you to come," I say before I can overthink it.

She catches a smile with her teeth and I nearly groan because I want her to let it go so damn badly. *Let yourself smile, dammit.*

"I could use a drink," she declares.

"Same."

We get out of the car and head into the house, past the laundry area and to the stairs.

"I'm impressed you resisted the joke, by the way," she says.

"Oh, the one about you *coming*? Trust me, it's killing me." And that *finally* pulls a full laugh out of her. A quick toss back of her head, her long throat exposed, her hand splayed against her chest. I pause on the step next to her, try to make the moment freeze. I'm smiling like an idiot when she looks back at me.

Light blares down from above us, suddenly. "There you are!" a shadow calls from the landing. "I've been calling you both for hours!"

"Elyse?!" LaRynn says.

"Surprise!" she calls back.

WE GET UPSTAIRS AND THE girls hug while Elyse excitedly tells LaRynn that she came out for the holiday. "I figured there'd be fireworks or something happening over at the park!" she exclaims.

"Oh, we're actually going to a barbecue over at the campground," LaRynn tells her, her eyes cutting back and forth between us. "It's Deacon's campground, so he kinda has to go."

"Oh!" Elyse looks at us sideways. "That sounds fun, too."

"I'll let you guys get caught up." I make to bow out of the room.

"You don't want a drink?" LaRynn asks. And it's the way the question lifts at the end, the slight shift on her feet, the way she turns her shoulders toward me, that makes my stomach jump. I think she wants me to stay.

"Yeah," I say. "Sure, I'll have a drink."

* * *

WE EACH END UP HAVING about four while we get Elyse up to speed on what we've accomplished on the house, along with the impression we've given my mom. She agrees to play along but doesn't press us about why. I have a feeling LaRynn will cover that later, when I'm not around.

We make plans to split up and head out in the morning, since I'll have to get there early and they can take Elyse's car now, plus give Sal a ride.

"Alright, I'll head to bed," Elyse announces, jumping up from her seat on the couch.

"Oh, uh. Okay," LaRynn replies. "I'll be right in."

"Take your time, I won't wait up," she replies, and LaRynn throws her an annoyed look. She hums her way across the landing to LaRynn's room.

"HEY, WE'LL HAVE TO UPDATE Sal, too," LaRynn says quietly when Elyse is gone.

"Yeah, she'll be fine. She was pretty . . . *unstirred* by the whole thing to begin with when I told her."

She laughs through her nose.

"So," I say, filling the pause in her wake.

"So," she says back through a yawn. "So, about . . . this morning. Today. All of it, I guess."

"LaRynn—"

She cuts me off before I can tell her not to worry. "I promise to stop being on the verge of ripping into you all the time," she says. "That's how I've felt, I guess. Like I'm waiting to either tear into you, or—"

"Tear clothes off?" I say with a laugh. "Because, same. I know the feeling."

She looks down at her lap, lashes fanning against her

cheeks. "I want to be a good *team member,* here. I want to—I want to do right by this place, too. I don't want to fuck this up. It's a good opportunity for me to start—*something* for myself," she tells me.

I exhale tiredly. "I don't, either. That money could help me hire a crew, get some new tools, equipment . . . and could go far over at Santa Sea, too."

Her eyes find their way back to me. "So, maybe it's not about fixing what's broken—not this time. Maybe it's about starting something new together? Like we are with this place in a way, too?"

I hesitate because I know that you *can't* do anything new if you don't repair what's broken. You can always bandage up the problems, but one way or another they eventually spring a leak if you don't do it properly. But I know she means it more about us, and I want to believe she's right.

Maybe I simply feel like holding on to this peace for now.

"Yeah, I'm sure you're right," I agree, nodding.

She gets up and I follow, and we both stall for a moment longer.

"Shake on it?" she asks.

I take her slender hand in mine, soft and cool against me. My fingers slide from the underside of her wrist to curl their way around hers.

"Goodnight, LaRynn," I say, voice hoarse. "Thank you again."

She lets her hand fall away, her fingertips sliding in stripes along my palm.

"Goodnight, Deacon," she says. "And thank you, too."

TWENTY-THREE

THE FOURTH OF JULY

DEACON

I roll out of bed and make my way to the kitchen, try to start coffee and go about breakfast as quietly as possible so I don't wake the girls, but LaRynn emerges shortly after me, bleary-eyed and bed-headed.

"Morning," she croaks, one eye squinted my way. "Did Elyse get up already?"

"Must have. I haven't seen her," I reply, voice too loud for the quiet this early, when it's still dark and the marine layer makes everything feel more still.

She frowns and scurries back to her room before she returns with her phone in hand. "She got up early to go to a CrossFit gym and is 'chatting with some people from the class.'" She shakes her head. "Freak. You couldn't pay me to be social with strangers this early."

I chuckle. "You seem to do just fine at the shop."

She grunts and reaches for the coffee pot. She's cute in the morning, with everything a little puffier . . . even if she's pouting. There's less threat in it.

"The shop's different. I like feeling useful. And I like . . ."

She sips her coffee. "Customers come in happy for their caffeine, and I guess I like being a good part of someone's day." She rolls her neck and her lips curl down, like the remark escaped her, but left a strange aftertaste on her tongue. It's soft and sweet and so simple it makes something in me twinge, her wanting to be any good part of anyone's day. "I just mean June runs a good business, and people appreciate it," she explains. "She uses as much locally as she can, including the roasters and the bakery items and everything." I nod in response, since I already know this but don't want to cut her off. "Have you talked to her about how things are going business-wise, by chance?"

I shake my head. "No, but I can if you want me to?" I say. We settle across from one another at the table.

"I don't want her to think I'm nosy. I've only been there a little over a month, but . . . Wait, are you in a hurry or anything?" she asks.

"No, I'm good on time. Tell me." I probably sound too eager, but fuck it. I remember this feeling. Being starved for these open, vulnerable pieces of her.

She blinks rapidly, sitting forward in her chair. It reminds me of when we talked about tweaking the layout and how excited she'd been to have her ideas heard.

"Well, the little touristy shop next door is shutting down next spring, apparently. The owner is retiring. And I can't help but notice . . ." She puffs out a breath. "I think the coffee shop closing over lunch but opening up for dinner service is where she loses the most money. The park doesn't even open until eleven on most days, and we close at eleven after the morning shift. There are—" She starts counting on her fingers, then says, "—*six* other dinner options with a full bar between the pier and this section of Front Street. *We* only have beer and wine for dinner service. I think . . . I think she's missing out on *lunch*. Every single day that I'm there, someone tries to open the doors when they've already been locked for the afternoon. Not everyone wants the park food; some people want to grab a sandwich or a salad or something and hop down to the beach. If she expanded into the next door, even if she still only wanted to have deli options and not a full kitchen, I think she'd kill it. There isn't any plain, simple, semi-healthy lunch option within walking distance." Her excitement gathers with each point. "And the tourist shop has a much bigger sidewalk section out front. I measured it the other day, and we could easily continue our outdoor space over there. From what I understood on the county's website, it would be to code."

"You looked up the regulations through the county?"

She sits back and takes another sip. "I just—I was curious," she says with a shrug. And it should absolutely not be *arousing*. This is not seductive LaRynn, fucking-thong-bikini LaRynn, or even sexy-angry LaRynn. But the way she studies her mug, her hair mussed in a heart-shaped halo around her face, the way she tucks some of it behind her ear. Fuck, I'm going to have to fake another reason to use the camp shower like a goddamn creep.

I try to steer my thoughts back to the conversation, think about all the times I've wanted a quick lunch out and had to drive somewhere or sit down at one of the other restaurants nearby, or hit the taco shack for the millionth time. "LaRynn, that sounds really great. You should absolutely talk to her about this."

Her knee bounces erratically. "You think?" she asks.

"Yeah, I definitely think."

She starts picking at her nails. "I know I need to meet

with an advisor of some kind and I'd want to go over the numbers, and it's a long shot anyway—who knows if June would even be interested in doing *anything* with me—she probably wouldn't. But . . . I think I would love to do something like that with my money when we sell. Invest in something like that. Some kind of place that makes people happy that way."

God, I want that for her, too. Her discomfort at simply sharing ideas and admitting to *wanting* something makes me want it for her ferociously.

"Talk to June about it. I think you should do it."

She goes back to her nails, but smiles uncomfortably. "Thank you," she says without looking back at me. She checks the clock on the wall. "I better get in the shower. You need the bathroom at all?"

"Nah, you're good. Just remember to text Sal," I reply.

She waves her phone at me. "Always do. I'll see you in a little while?" she asks. The hope in her voice feels like a light in my chest.

"Yeah, I better get over there. I'll see you later."

"Let me know if you need anything on the way or anything."

"Thanks Lar–*LaRynn,* I mean."

She tosses me a look over her shoulder. "You can call me Larry, Deacon. It's managed to grow on me. Don't tell anyone else, though."

I laugh and blow out a long breath as she walks away.

"Turn on the music before you head out, please!" she calls.

"Got it!" I grab what I gather is her favorite Elvis compilation and put it on, grinning stupidly to myself. The journey from last night to this morning . . . from quietly attempting to communicate through our shit to her soft confessions and shy smiles . . . it feels like we've scaled a small mountain. Or maybe just found a new path around it. Talking about her ideas and her wanting things feels huge, either way.

I HOP DOWN THE STAIRS with a little pep in my step and catch Elyse by the laundry as I pass.

"We'll see you in a bit," she says brightly.

"Sounds good!" I head into the garage and get into the car.

And then it hits me.

Oh. Fuck.

I race back inside just as Elyse turns to walk away from the washing machine, and I hear it filling.

"*Fuck,* fuck fuckfuckfuck—"

"What?!" She spins around in a panic just as the scream echoes down from upstairs.

I groan. "Oh God. Oh God," I say shakily. I nearly rip the machine out of the wall trying to get the water turned off from the back.

"*What the hell?!*" Elyse yells. "What's wrong? I just started some laundry because I heard you guys talking and didn't want to interrupt you!" And then, she remembers. "*Ohmygod* I forgot! That's still not fixed?! Shit!"

I can't take the time to talk her down right now, though. "She's absolutely going to think it was me and that I did this on purpose, isn't she?!" I say to myself, just as another wail sounds from above us.

"What do I do?!" Elyse squeals.

"I have to get up there," I tell her. "I may need you to corroborate that this was you, though. You'll back me up?" *Shit,* there's more screaming and some incantation in French being cursed above the sounds of Elvis in the background.

She thrusts her palms out helplessly at her sides. *"Duh!"*

Alright then. I leap up the stairs and sprint to the bathroom, taking no time to brace myself before I yank open the door.

A very naked creature from a horror movie slowly uncoils to her feet, hair plastered to her face, covered in chunks of gray matter.

"Larry?!"

"You," she growls.

"LaRynn, it wasn't me."

"Why would I believe you?!" She stomps a foot in the muck.

I try to get the words out as calmly and rapidly as possible. "It wasn't me. I swear, LaRynn. It was Elyse. She came back and heard us talking and she figured she'd start some laundry. I promise."

I go to reach for one of the towels in the basket and see that she's used them all. I track her quaking in rage out of the corner of my eye and wince.

"Probably a bad time to bring up the spare towels again, huh?" I say.

She bursts into tears. Full-body sobbing, shoulders curling inward. *Dammit. Shit. This place broke her.*

"LaRynn—"

"Stop! Just get *out!"* she screams.

"LaRynn, I promise it wasn't me, this was *not* on purpose. It was just bad timing."

"It's always bad timing!" she says, voice tight. "It's always when I start to trust you, when I open up to you. I'm somehow *always* left looking and feeling fucking *stupid!"*

And there's the leak. "Let me get you something, *please.*" I scramble out and grab the quilt from my bed and thrust it towards her. She rips off the rubber gloves and throws them down before she steps out and snatches it from me, wraps herself in it and collapses onto the toilet, tears still streaming down her face. My back hits the wall and I let myself slide down it until my ass settles on the ground across from her. She cries quietly, music playing behind us.

Every bit and piece we've chipped away from each other through kindness, through sharpness, through blunt force . . . now feels like we've managed to expose all our nerve endings. Raw, frayed. I should have known this would happen eventually. *Every* problem reveals itself at some point.

"I'm sorry," I say. Because it's clearly about more than the shower right now.

"You *broke* my heart," she says. And it's worse that it comes out as a whisper. I'd rather she scream it at me.

"I know," I croak. "And I mean it. I'm sorry. I'm so, so sorry, but you . . ." She looks up at me through angry red eyes and I pause. "LaRynn, you bled mine out in pieces that summer, too. You didn't want anyone to know about me, about us. *You* were the one who kept insisting there were no feelings, that it was just about sex. That was never my idea. You made me think you were *ashamed* of me."

Her eyes round, a light-switch shining on her features, a click that unlatches the tension in her entire face.

"What?" she replies in shock, voice breaking.

"And," I say, desperate to get the rest out, "I know you shared more of everything with me than you did with most. I do. But it was still only pieces, and I was *eighteen,* LaRynn. I'd just lost my dad, someone whom I felt deceived by. Someone who was out there with his own shameful secrets. I was

angry and felt like I was that for you. My brother was off at college and . . . doing big things. While I was here, working at a campground and fucking—tinkering." I breathe. "I already felt like I wasn't worth much, so every time you said something like that . . . I believed it." I look at the ground for the next part. "And then you told me you *loved* me, and I thought I might've felt that way too and it scared the fucking shit out of me, to think that love and shame could coexist that way. And then . . ." I have to work to swallow, my mouth is so dry. "And then you were off at college, and sometimes—sometimes I thought I should reach out to you, or I thought I'd get a chance to see you when you'd visit Cece again. I figured I could *talk* to you about it all. But you stopped coming here, and it just became something I wanted to forget, too. Especially after you didn't even come down for Nana's memorial, LaRynn. I convinced myself that none of it was a big deal, that I'd been right—that you were ashamed of me, that you were some selfish, spoiled brat. And I know that you're not, okay? I know you never were, now."

Her lower lip trembles. "I wasn't *ashamed* of you," she says with a sniffle. "I didn't mean to make you feel that way. I just don't know how . . ." She shakes her head and searches the ceiling. "I thought I *had* to be something convenient, Deacon. Casual. I thought I was making it *easier*." Another tear escapes.

"And I thought I was going along with what you needed, too," I say.

We regard one another for a moment longer in this smelly bathroom, with Elvis and our honesty still singing in the air.

"Let me be your friend?" I ask, gently. "Let me get to know you again, and you me? I think we're both self-aware enough to know we're worthy of that for one another." At least, that's what I'm trying to tell myself. "Can you try to trust me? Enough to believe that I want to make this house project work for us both. Let me show you I want to be your friend."

Her teeth saw into her lip. "You still want that? With me?"

"I basically *made* you marry me, Larry. I'd really like for something good to come of this. I'd like to be your friend even . . . after. I think our grandmothers would've liked that, too."

She looks down at her lap, blowing out a long breath. "Okay," she says, quiet and firm. And more quickly than I would've thought. "I want to be your friend, too, Deacon. And before—before was never about *you*. That was about me, and I'm sorry. I'm trying to be better. I will be better." A deep breath. "I *like* you, which is as surprising to me as it is to you."

I blink and smile. "I like you, too."

TWENTY-FOUR

LARYNN

It's somehow both harder and easier to pretend at the barbecue tonight.

When he tosses anyone around the dance floor that comes within his reach, it's easy to laugh and smile from a distance. He's switched out his work boots for cowboy boots and it's too easy to laugh at those, in addition to the patriotic printed shirt he has on over another one of his tank tops.

But it's harder when he loops around and finds me as a slow song comes on, pulls me up from my haybale-perch between Sally and Macy, and drags me out onto the blacktop.

I turn to see Jensen pulling Elyse out to the floor, too, just as Deacon slips a palm around my lower back and cups my other hand in his. He's flushed from exertion, cheeks glistening. Eyes dark and full of glitter in the string lights. His stubble is already peeking through, his curls going crazier than normal.

"Having fun?" he asks with a bright, open smile.

I press my lips together to keep from beaming back nonsensically. The full force of his warmth makes me feel dozy.

"I am. I saw Mrs. Gold pelt her husband with a cornhole bean bag and he shoved a piece of pie into her face."

He makes a *tsk* noise and shakes his head. "I've told them time and time again to save the foreplay for their RV. There are *families*." He mimics her tone and expression with frightening accuracy, and I have to press my forehead into his rumbling chest to hide my laugh.

It's easy to be his friend on the beach, where we all light our sparklers before Jensen plays the national anthem on a portable speaker. It's more difficult when he holds my hand on the walk back because I'm certain he's only doing it for his mom, but it feels too good to me.

The more I let little memories of our past slip through—some of the things I'd said and done and how I perceived them versus how they must've made him feel—the more desperately I want to be his friend. He's charming and generous to a fault, to the point that he's bound himself to me, and I want him to feel that from me, too, somehow. I *want* to show him that I like him. That I see him.

"I'm sorry about Helena," I decide to blurt out now. He stops and lets the group continue past us, maintaining his grip on my hand. His brow furrows in confusion, so I press on. "I'm sorry I didn't show up. I was in the hospital with pneumonia at the time, and I lied. I just didn't want my grandma to worry; she had enough going on, you know?" I peel my hand away to tuck my jacket tighter around me.

"It's okay," he tells me. "I'm sorry you were sick and alone." He takes my hand back. And something crackles through me that he even recalls this from when Elyse mentioned it. That he was able to piece together that I'd been alone. "And I know she said she didn't want anything, but if you ever want to do something for Cece, I'd be happy to help you," he says.

There's more of that brittle feeling, tiny hot sparks popping in my chest like kindling. I try to see his face, but with the moon behind him he's mostly in shadow. "Thank you," I choke out. "I . . . I still have to go get her ashes. I haven't done it yet."

He drops my hand and tucks me into his side, rubs a palm up and down my arm. "I'll go with you when you're ready."

TWENTY-FIVE

LARYNN

Elyse stays with us for two more days before she heads back to school, and it's strange, but it's almost as if summer disappears with her. We have to get back to working on the house. We become immersed in it.

And with each item we accomplish, it seems something else goes wrong.

We manage to stay on budget for cabinets and get those ordered, but then our garage door breaks and we have to take that from our rapidly disappearing funds.

I find and order appliances within our means, but then a small mudslide takes out part of the road heading into the campground. And though no one was hurt and he puts on a brave face, I can tell it weighs on Deacon. He spends the better part of two weeks arguing with the county on whether or not that section of road belongs to the campground or if it's publicly maintained. He brings up plot maps and Macy tracks down every piece of literature regarding the easement. They eventually win the argument, but they get jerked around and redirected time and time again when they try to get information on when it will be fixed and what they're supposed to do in the interim. Deacon eventually charms someone enough to come out and deem the intact part of the road safe for temporary use, and someone follows behind to place concrete pillars around the chunk that's missing.

And with him otherwise occupied, I pick up most of the tasks at the house so we can continue momentum on that front.

I record everything the plumber tells me—things that I might not understand, but know Deacon will. Apparently our block is on septic that ran down to the street, and roots closed it off. The entire thing has to be replaced. Another devastating punch to our budget. And Deacon was right before; when Grandma and Hel did their renovation years ago, some things were done wonky and corners were cut, so we end up going over our overall plumbing allowance by more than double.

To ease that particular blow, Deacon decides he'll be the one to do the installation on all the floors, despite that being "fucking terrible, and the one thing I would always rather pay someone else to do," he says.

And I do my best to stay determined. The harder I watch him work, the more motivated I am to carry my weight, too. I stick to four shifts a week at the café and spend all my free time working on the house.

I also buy him a new toothbrush, which I can tell puzzles him to no end, but I throw out some made-up dental hygiene statistic to ease any suspicions. I will be taking that low moment to my grave.

Once we have two working toilets and I figure out an agreeable system for keeping things organized amid the chaos (thank you YouTube), I finish wrecking out the main bathroom and kitchen cabinets on my own. Deacon has to step in after I buy all of our sinks and faucets to help me determine correct measurements, but before the end of July we've got everything off to the fabricators for the countertops, too.

By August, we can no longer park in our garage, and we have to halt progress to install the new door so we can keep it closed off. It starts looking like something out of a serial killer show, with white tarps over the cabinets and the vanities that arrive, along with the bathtub I picked out for the master.

And though it's clear that it isn't always easy for us both, with each new obstacle that pops up (surprise, your windows are delayed by a month, and literally everything is more expensive than what you were originally told) we continue to work at being good friends to each other.

It feels like we start to create our own soundtrack along the way, too. I start to think that maybe it won't just be my low moments set to song, but those better, or happier parts of life, as well. Each time one of us gets home, there's something playing. We have a running joke on the nights we don't want to do a damn thing that "Jump in the Line" is the only song with enough pep to perk us up. It gets played regularly until we get sick of it, and we default back to Redbone, or Elvis, sometimes Fleetwood.

With the kitchen and our finances in shambles, we spend three weeks straight eating snacks and cold items for dinner. And I'm hurtling toward my breaking point, so I know he must be, too. Not to mention I'm becoming concerned for his well-being because his go-to rummage meal is a peanut butter and marshmallow fluff sandwich. *Yeah.*

It's in the second week of August, when I trudge upstairs and find him napping on the subfloor (since *of course* the hardwood we tried to restore ended up being beyond repair), snoring despite Harry Belafonte blasting through the room, that I finally reach that point.

"That's *it*! I'm calling it!" I yell above the song. His eyes fly open and he jerks up to his feet, the half-eaten sandwich that had been on his chest falling to the ground with a sad little splat.

"What?! What happened?" he says back groggily.

"I'm calling a team-building day. We need to get the *fuck* out of here. And we are eating out. If I have to make another microwave quesadilla, I'll put metal spoons in instead. I want a real meal, and I want *out* of this house."

He dusts the crumbs from his shirt as a hangdog smile parts his face. "Oh thank *God* you said it. I spent like forty-five minutes today looking up stuff online about how to just burn this fucker down to collect the insurance money and get away with it, but then I realized that I'd compromised myself by my search history." He lets out an exhausted laugh. "What do you want to do?"

I'm kicking myself that I hadn't remembered it was my turn to plan something sooner. Our last team day may have gone a bit haywire, but it ended up *leading* to something good, at least. "Wait, what day is it?" I ask out loud before I check my watch. Wednesday. "It's a resident's day at the Boardwalk. It won't be nearly as packed as normal."

"Sold."

We waste no time walking down to the amusement park after we change out of our work clothes. I go with my tiniest black romper with some white tennis shoes, and he goes with his favorite redwood-printed shirt and shorts.

While the best part of being in a more northern area of the west coast is how it rarely gets too hot for too long, today is one of those days that flares with the sticky heat of August.

"You mind holding my stuff?" I ask. "I hate carrying a purse."

"No pockets in that thing, huh?" He laughs, holding out his hand. I feel his eyes scan me from behind his sunglasses and a hazy warmth ebbs across my skin where they land. I'd really love to get to a point where those small comments and touches feel less loaded to my brain—to my libido. I can only hope it'll come in time, where my *like* for him isn't quite so easily drowned by my *want*. Any harmless remark that could loosely be interpreted as flirting might've been a game to me before, something I'd try to one-up or turn on him. But that was before I knew that I'd once made him feel as used as I had, and I just can't bring myself to play again. These last six weeks have been an exercise in restraint, in throwing myself into work in any way that I can, in trying to show him I value *him,* this place . . . this opportunity. Even if it hurts me sometimes. Like when he does a sad, tired little cha-cha dance to a silly song to try and cheer us up, or when he gives me a sideways hug after I hand him some coffee in the morning. It makes regret burn through me, that I ever fucked things up or mistook him so thoroughly.

"Thank you," I say as I pass my cards and a Chapstick his way.

"Rides, arcade, or food first?" he asks.

"Rides, absolutely." I want to be catapulted and flung to the point that I *can't* control or resist it. Tossed around and overwhelmed by so much feeling that my mind goes euphorically blank from thinking.

"Giant Dipper first or save it?"

"First so we can go on it more than once."

"Smart girl." He smiles. And my steps bounce so much that I doubt my heels touch the ground.

But when we get near it we see that the line is already wrapped and twisted in a mile-long chain.

He sighs. "Food for the line, then?"

"Let's do it." I fist pump the air, desperately clambering to keep our spirits up.

Our eyes oversell what our stomachs and hands can handle, so I get a plate of fried artichoke hearts with a vanilla custard cone while he gets a plate of caramel apple nachos and buffalo tater tots.

When we get in line we look at each other at the same time. "How are we even supposed to eat all this?" I laugh. "Like, not figuratively. I mean with what mechanisms will we?" I have something in each hand, and so does he, and neither of us thought this through.

"Mouths only?" He laughs, then illustrates by leaning over and running his tongue up my cone.

Lust zips through me and I choke on nothing, but I manage to quell it with a cough. "Help me finish this first since it'll melt anyway and then I'll have one free hand at least." I nod to the custard.

We do just that, moving along in the line. When I've got a free hand I use it to feed us both.

"Tot me," he says after I've just fed him one of my artichoke hearts. I use surgical precision to avoid my fingertips touching his lips.

"So," I start. "We're not stuck talking about cabinet colors or re-measuring the same thing seven times until we pass out from exhaustion right now. Want to tell me what else you've been up to these last eight years?" He uses the door frame leading into the indoor part of the line to nudge his glasses up onto his head, and I laugh. "I could've helped you with that," I say.

"Greasy fingers," he replies, scrunching his nose in mock disgust.

"You've always been so finicky about that hair. You better hope you don't lose it one day."

"Look at this hairline, woman. It hasn't receded a millimeter." He pouts. "And what do you mean by 'what else'?"

"I mean aside from work and the campground and stuff. Any girlfriends?" *God* I hope that sounded as casual as I tried to make it sound.

He hums lowly as we step farther down the line.

"Nothing serious. Longest girlfriend I had was a few months last year. How about you?"

I severely underestimated that petty, nasty part of me, because she rears up with lava-hot jealousy at that mere mention.

I manage to wrestle her down, and stick with honesty. "Nothing serious. Flings here and there. School took up even more of my time than it would for a normal law student."

He nods to a heart before he tilts his head. "Why's that?"

I feed him the artichoke before I pick at one of his caramel nachos. "I asked for special accommodations for most of my classes, and had tutors for just about everything, too," I say. "I'm dyslexic, so studying eons of written text . . . takes me longer."

His brows push together. "I never knew that."

I shrug. "It's not like it's something I'm ashamed of. I just was taught from very early on that advertising it made it seem like I was asking for sympathy or making excuses. When I got to college I learned pretty quickly that that's not the case, and that it's okay that I learn differently, and I started to advocate for myself . . . I had some great professors and tutors, but law was never something I was passionate about to begin with." A sigh whistles through me. "So, really, I was making myself miserable for years, for more hours of my day than I was ever free."

He rolls his lips together. "No wonder you were so cranky," he jokes.

I laugh through my nose and shove his pec lightly, the feel of his nipple through his shirt like a brand against my palm. *Great, now I'm hot for his nipples?*

He throws away the remaining tots and his empty plate of dessert nachos. "Still, time for a relationship or not, I'm sure you had plenty of guys fawning over you," he says.

"Want the last one?" I hold up the fried bit and he shakes his head. "And not really. I'm usually too mean or too tall for anyone to *fawn* over."

"Too *tall?*" he says. I'm tempted to huff about the lack of shock regarding the other point, but refrain. We get called forward for our turn. "What do you mean too tall?"

"I'm roughly six foot, Deacon. I've been told *many* times that I'm too tall." He snorts in disbelief as I shift uncomfortably in the seat, our knees knocking together—ironically.

His eyes cut over to mine as the lap bar locks into place. "Those are the same kinds of small-minded people that say there's such a thing as too much money, or too much time. They just don't know what to do with all of it."

My mind short-circuits even before the ride jerks forward, before it's filled with laugh-screaming in delight, or the rattling of the coaster flying over the tracks with every dip and turn.

TWENTY-SIX

DEACON

"Okay, but do you like Sand Dollar White more or do you like White Sand more? And are you absolutely certain you don't like Greek Villa?" LaRynn asks me.

I look back at the wall with numerous white stripes painted on it. If I'm honest, I don't think I can tell the fucking difference between a single one. I think the paint place might be screwing with her and giving her all the same sample. I scrub my palms up and down my face hard enough to see spots. *Don't tell her you don't give a shit. Don't tell her you don't give a shit.* "Rynn, honestly, I do not give a shit." *Recover.* "I mean, I trust your judgment."

She bevels her head my way with an unimpressed look.

"I'm sorry," I say, laughing. "I'm trying, I swear. I truly can't tell the difference. You want to go with a different shade of white for every room? We can always do that, too."

She cocks a hip and a brow. "Are you making fun of me?"

I hold up my palms and laugh some more. "Not at all. I just genuinely can't tell."

She sighs and her shoulders slump, ponytail slipping over her collarbone with the movement. "Good. I can't take another man thinking I'm crazy over this." She swipes an arm at the wall.

"Oh, don't get it twisted, I *definitely* think you're crazy, but I kinda like it."

"*Ha.*"

"Who *else* is making you feel crazy?" I ask.

"The paint guy at the shop *you* recommended. Howie of the Howie's Paints establishment. Grumbles about every sample I ask for and rolls his eyes in a way that lets me know he thinks I'm a monumental pain in the ass."

I make a noncommittal noise and file that in my brain to address later.

"Alright, I'm off to work," she announces.

"Are you gonna do it today?" I ask, and she groans. "Quit being chicken and just start the conversation with her, LaRynn." She has yet to talk to June about any potential plans.

"I don't want to bug her *at* work about it."

"You're not *bugging* her, you're talking about investing in her business."

"I just want to approach it outside of work. And we haven't been doing much outside of here lately." She spins in a circle for emphasis before she starts walking away.

She grabs her apron off the room divider across the landing before she continues. "I was actually thinking we should plan something for your birthday, though. So maybe I'll bring it up then?"

I feel my face pinch into a frown. "You remembered my birthday?" I ask in surprise.

She slips on one of those athletic wear jackets, the zipper pressing her cleavage in together before it's concealed. Folds her arms across her middle. "I do. I had to get it on all the bank paperwork, remember?"

Oh. So she doesn't just remember it because it was the same day she told me she loved me. "That's right."

"So . . . so I know we're just about broke, here, and I'm sure we need to have a conversation about delaying everything else so we can get caught up. But we could still do *something* to celebrate, don't you think? Something that doesn't cost much?" She grabs her purse and steps toward the door.

It warms something in me that it doesn't seem to upset her that we'll have to slow down. Because she's right—we *are* nearly broke and we both will have to work to come up with the money to pay for the rest of the renovations. But she doesn't seem upset by the idea of living here together longer, and that makes me feel like we're succeeding in some way, even if we're failing in terms of the budget.

"Sure," I say. "Nothing big. Maybe have some dinner and some beers."

"We could go to the campground since we can't exactly host anyone here?"

That warmth simmers at how much she uses *we*.

"I'd like that," I tell her.

Her mouth bends into a smirk. "Sounds good. I'll see you later."

I PUTTER AROUND THE HOUSE aimlessly for a bit, but can't seem to focus on a single task, so I eventually decide to go for a drive. Maybe I'll go on a nice walk through Henry Cowell Park or something.

But right as I get to the edge of town, I see the paint store.

I screech into a parking spot and head in, only to find an exasperated looking man frowning at me. "I take it you're Howie?" I ask.

He grunts. "Yup. Can I help you?"

"I referred a woman here. Tall, long dark hair."

He shrugs through a bored look.

"Uh—" I guess I'll continue. "—bright green eyes. I'm talking eyes you'd remember." *Small constellation of freckles, a smile that's rare and sweet.*

"No idea."

Jesus. I refuse to describe her other parts to this asshat. "Hang on." I scoop my phone of my pocket. Find a picture of her dead asleep on the ground, white paint swatch tiles scattered on her chest. One second she'd been holding them aloft, kicking a socked foot and humming along to Leon Bridges. Her hair was spread around her, tank top creeping up her waist. And the next minute she was out like a light, softly snoring with her mouth open.

On second thought, it's probably not the most flattering picture of her and it might only be cute to me. "She comes in asking for white paint," I ram out. "Like, *all* white. Different shades of it."

Howie's lips pale and thin and his glare narrows. "That broad is a pain in my ass."

I slip my phone back into my pocket and slowly place my hands on the counter.

"I referred her to you because you're a local shop, and I figured you'd be grateful for the support." I cock my head and return his glare. "And she pays for those small samples, does she not?"

"Sure, but she takes over an hour every time she waltzes in here asking for this one or that one. It's goddamn white, tell the chick to pick one already."

I look around the empty store. "Seems she's doing you a favor." He gives me an incredulous look, and I blow out a breath. "Here's the thing, Howard. She's bringing you business. I also do *all* my business locally as a contractor. Either you can be nice to the lady and appreciate her money and the other money you'll surely go on to make when I send more people this way, when I buy *my* paint from you in the future, too. *Or* I can make it my personal goal to tell everyone I do business with what a miserable bastard you are. You following me, Howie?"

He blinks and nods.

"Now I don't care if she comes in here and asks you to mix Sand Dollar with Moonbeam and two parts Yelp-Lady-White, even if she turns around and asks you to reduce it to 75 percent or add yellow to it or some shit, I expect you to do it with a *smile* in the future. *Capiche?*"

A muscle contracts in his jaw and his face reddens, but his shoulders drop, resigned. "Understood."

"Thanks, Howie, appreciate you." I tap the counter before I smile and leave.

And instead of going for a hike, I turn the Bronco around and jam back into town because I have the sudden urge to visit my *friend* at work.

Maybe I should tell her so she can have a laugh, but it feels too close to bragging, or like I didn't think she could handle it herself—dealing with someone unpleasant. The truth is, I know she can hold her own better than most, but I also know, on some level, that she'd do the same for me—for *anyone* else—before she'd ever stand up for herself.

WHEN I WALK INTO THE side entrance of the café, I spot her from a distance, and am immediately transfixed on the sight of her. She's bopping around behind the counter, her hair swinging, smiling softly to herself as she straightens mugs so that their handles are all at the same angle. Some deconstructed version of "Friday I'm in Love" plays through the speakers as she sings along.

Jesus, she looks . . . she looks so at *home* here. It's the first time that I let myself acknowledge the full scope of sadness that I know I'll feel when she's gone, when a roof and a contract aren't binding us closer.

I believe we'll stay friends—I think we're doing that well enough now, but I also know she'll be more distant based on logistics alone. And I already miss her, even though she's standing yards away.

She still doesn't notice me as a customer walks in, the bell tinkling over the door. Instead she turns and fucking beams at them. A smile I've only been able to see a handful of times since she came back. Her full lips stretched, the apples of her cheeks filling. Fuck. *For a stranger?!*

I plop down next to someone at the end of the bar, my eyes still stuck on LaRynn.

"Hey, Deac," comes a voice from my right. I turn and recognize Rafe.

"How's it going?" I ask offhandedly before I turn back to LaRynn.

"I see you've spotted our newest addition here," he drawls. I slowly swivel my head his way. I barely know the guy—a local surfer, played a few pickup games on the beach with him in the past. A greasy feeling pours through my skull at the familiarity in *his* tone, though.

"Let me warn you now, my dude," he continues, looking pointedly in LaRynn's direction again. "That right there is an exotic, but highly venomous creature. Not sure the bite is worth it if you catch my drift."

My teeth clamp together. "Is that so?"

He looks back her way and jumps in his seat. I follow his eyes and find her now staring back, scowling from the other end of the room.

"Yeah, that's so," Rafe replies.

I keep my eyes locked on LaRynn as I talk to him. "She doesn't like most pet names. Don't call her sweetheart or babe or any of that shit. And don't *gesture* for her. It's not a full service restaurant. It's not a cocktail bar. If you need something, you'll have to get up and go to the register like anyone else. She can't stand feeling like she's being summoned because she's not your butler or your maid."

I see him whip toward me in my peripheral. "How the hell would you know?" he asks.

LaRynn starts marching our way, scowl only growing more fierce, more breathtaking the closer she gets. I can't help but grin, stupid heart floating around like a helium balloon in my chest.

"Because that's my wife."

I get up from the bar and intercept her halfway so she doesn't have to come all the way down.

"Hey, love," I say, before I lean over the counter and kiss her cheek. Soft, smells like coffee and burnt sugar. Maybe something coconut today, too. "Just go with it. It'll make him stop bugging you," I whisper, full of hope. I clock the goosebumps on her arms and slide my hand along her wrist, noting the way her frown whisks into a stiff smile.

She chuckles breathily, the tiny sound like lightning in my veins. "He looks like he's seen a ghost," she says.

"I love it when you scare people."

Oh *fuck me,* it was the wrong—or *right*—thing to say. She bites into her lip happily and I zero in on it. On the places where her teeth leave little indentations. I want to make my own. Everywhere. To watch the skin pale before blood rushes back to it. She traces her palm up my bicep and I resist the urge to flex under it, track her black-polished nails as her fingers spread.

And then she leans over and kisses my shoulder through my shirt in such a soft and familiar way that something splinters inside of me.

I have the asinine thought that I want to curl up, have her cradle me against her chest or hold my head in her lap. A thought that's immediately followed by a booming inner voice that screams *She's not yours, though. You are not really hers, either. You didn't want this. She didn't want this. Someday she'll intertwine her hands, her life, her soul with somebody else, and you'll have to stand by and be happy for her.*

And while we joke about our dysfunction, and high-five on our better communication these days, I feel like I have to continue to show her I value her in my life, even in a painful capacity. That even if I'm starting to want all of it—all of *her*—I need her to understand that I would be okay if all I ever got was this piece.

When we were young we shared our bodies, only baring other parts with a constant sense of self-preservation that kept it all in check. We shared an angsty-sarcastic view of the world, a false roof over us for shelter. Now that we're being real, that self-preservation's all stripping away, and I'm fucking terrified that I'll mess this up somehow and lose her altogether. The idea of being without her when I've only just got her is enough to make me wrangle the hope back down.

A kiss on the shoulder and a smile undoes me this way, I guess.

But then her eyes land on my throat, my jaw, then meet mine. "I'll see you at home," she says.

Home. Home. Home. Three months together in a ripped-up building and nothing's ever felt more like it.

"I'll see you at home."

TWENTY-SEVEN

LARYNN

It's amazing how quickly time passes under the monotony of being busy, yet the moment you're free and a little listless, it slows to a glacial pace. Since we're at an almost-standstill on house progress, I've taken up trying to teach myself to cook, have finalized our shower tile choice (something that was quite literally keeping me awake at night), and I even found Helena's old kiln buried in the garage. I've dedicated a good amount of thought toward potentially trying that out soon, too.

A few days after I mentioned it the first time, Deacon and I have the conversation about where we're at on money and what we need to do about it.

He scratches the back of his neck in discomfort when I bring it up. "I can't pull anything out of my retirement without a pretty hefty penalty," he says.

"No, no. I don't want you to do that anyway," I urge. "We just have the new walls to drywall, then have to match texture and paint. What else?"

"Floors," he grouses and I lift a brow.

"We *have* floors." I nod to the boxes containing the planks. "We just have to install them."

His face falls into a pout. "We also need to install hardware for everything. Hot mops and tile. Hook up the bathtub. And the new doors. And—"

"Okay, okay. So, a *lot*." Neither of us mentions that we could technically sell it as is right now. With the new layout, the plumbing and electrical up to code, plus the updated cabinets and appliances, we'd be fine. Someone else could come in and finish it. I've looked into what multi-unit homes are going for in the area, and even with Sal's place remaining mostly outdated, we could very easily *each* clear half a million dollars. "So, we just take our time. No biggie." I shrug.

"I guess we need to tell Sal where we're at, too. I don't need to move her over to Santa Sea if we're still here for . . . a bit longer."

"For sure," I agree, my voice a caricature of a cheer captain. "That'd keep it easy on us since we give her rides everywhere and all that."

"Exactly. Look at us, continuing to be agreeable." He flips me a thumbs up like a cornball and I shake my head.

Agreeable and fucking awkward, apparently.

"Why are we so weird whenever we have one of these chats?" he asks, and I have to toss my head back and bark out a laugh.

"I listened to a podcast interview with a comedian once," I say. "And she said that sometimes making adult choices and even advocating for her own career felt like doing an impression of someone else until she got used to it. Maybe we're just not very good at *our* impressions yet."

He chuckles back, the sound warm and rough. A memory echoes distantly in my brain, that rumble vibrating against the inside of my thighs. I look away and wipe my palms down my skirt.

"I'm still glad we're trying," he quietly replies.

I try to pivot the subject. "Have you thought about what you want for your birthday at all? Make it cheap. Ideally free."

A look slips across his features and I can almost hear the old, flirty reply he'd have given me once. Instead he goes with, "Pretzel pie."

"Pardon?"

"Pretzel. Pie. That's what I want. The peach kind."

"What in god's name is peach pretzel pie?" I ask dubiously.

"My grandma never made it for you? She called it pretzel Jell-O, but—"

"Hold on. There's *Jell-O* involved?!"

"I can't believe you never tried it! Cece loved it, too. Nana made it for everything."

"You're telling me that my grandmother, with her very French roots, loved an American dessert called pretzel Jell-O pie?"

"If you can't make it it's fine, Lar," he teases.

I laugh through my nose at his proud little pout. "That's really what you want for your birthday? For *me* to make you something?"

The pout morphs into a veritable frown. "You've been cooking a lot. I think you're great."

I roll my eyes. "For like a week. And I undercooked *pasta*." I paw my hands through the air to brush it off before he can say something placating about the crunchy spaghetti I made us two nights ago. "It doesn't matter. I don't mind making you your . . . very delicious sounding dessert."

His mouth curves in a goofy smile and he rubs his palms

together gleefully. "You're gonna love it. Make enough for leftovers!"

THERE ARE TWO MORE DAYS until his birthday, August 22, but I decide I'll look up recipes today, and I promptly take the bike to go get everything from the store while Deacon's off picking up the shower tile we ordered.

I take the long loop home so I can watch the sunset. Surfers dot the water like peppercorns in foam, ice plants spread over the sandy cliffs, their flowers already gone for the summer. And when I pass the lighthouse on West Cliff, an idea hits me—a cost-*free* idea—for our next team-building day.

DEACON'S BACK AND UNLOADING BOXES by the time I pull up beside the garage.

"You free tomorrow?" I ask him after I take off my helmet and grab a load to help.

"I can be," he says with a grin.

"I figured since we got behind, and since you planned two team days in a row, I could plan our next one, too. Two for Two."

The retreating day casts him in an orange glow and makes his eyes look like honey. The breeze picks up a lock of his floppy hair as he smiles. "Time and place, Lavigne. Just name it."

THE FOLLOWING MORNING FEELS LIKE the curtain has been peeled back on autumn for a few hours. Fine hairs rise on my arms when I step onto the chilly balcony off of the living room, tendrils of steam curling up from my coffee. I reach back inside and snag the flannel Deacon's left draped over the chaise, pull it tight around myself before I rest my elbows on the dewy railing and clasp the mug in my hands.

Only, when I lean forward and take a deep inhale of the dawn, I catch Deacon on the other side of the wall, on his respective balcony, doing the same thing. We laugh in synchrony, three feet and a wall between us.

"Morning," he says, his voice gritty with sleep. The happy expression fumbles when his eyes land somewhere near my collar.

"Oh, sorry," I say when I look back down at the jacket. "It was cooler than I realized and I just saw it—"

"It's fine," he rasps. "It's—good. Totally okay." Nods and clears his throat. "What time do you want to head out?"

"Is a half hour okay?"

He nods his agreement. "Meet you at the landing."

I HAND HIM A TRAVEL mug of coffee at the landing twenty-nine minutes later, and we head out on our walk, side by side.

The silence is comfortable, in spite of the conflicting emotions that have been gurgling their way through me lately. It's a great thing just to be his friend.

"Before I forget," he starts after we've cleared our first block. "Mom keeps hinting at coming by and seeing what we've done with the place." He sighs wearily. "I gather that she's already under the impression that you inherited the money to fund it since she hasn't asked, but I, uh . . . I didn't want you to think you had to keep lying to her. If it comes up for any reason, I want to tell her the truth."

I scuff my shoe against the pavement. "That's fine. It *was* inherited. We don't have to share any of the terms or anything . . . That's our business anyway, right?"

Something about that seems to delight him. He turns to search my face and smiles with a nod.

We continue on, passing the lighthouse on West Cliff before we round the corner where it continues.

"Alright," I say with a happy sigh. "Pick one." I jut out my arms toward the row of homes. Multi-millions of dollars, each one an eclectic style all its own. Some have a partial view of the park off to the side in the distance, but all of them have a view of miles and miles of ocean out the front.

"What do you mean?" He laughs, his head canting to the side.

"I used to play this game when I was little, where I'd pick the house that looked like it was meant for me. Like, maybe it was green and green was my favorite color at that time, or maybe because it was a tall, lanky-looking house it felt like I should live in it because *I* was lanky and tall. Maybe it was fancy and had a big wrought iron gate out front and I thought I was fancy. I want to know which one you see yourself as."

He doesn't hesitate. "I want you to pick it for me."

I dip my chin and glance up at him through my lashes. "That's cheating."

"You pick for me," he says firmly.

"Fine," I reply with a long sigh. I chew my lip and study as we continue walking along, before I stop and act like I'm deeply considering the singular less-than-gorgeous house on a corner. It's painted a Pepto-pink and has eight wind chimes hanging on the front porch.

"*Really?*" He groans, and I laugh before I keep going.

"Hey," I chide, "every house deserves *someone* to love it."

* * *

AT SOME POINT WE COME to my favorite house—the most beautiful home I've ever seen. It's one I remember from my childhood here. The cedar shingles that cover it have weathered a bit, but to me it only makes it look more homey. It's set back farther from the road than most of the others, so it has an expansive green lawn out front. There are thick, white casings on all the windows, and flower boxes brimming with spilling vines. A lofty brick chimney hugs its side, with billowing hydrangea bushes along the porch that have begun to patina for fall. A black bench-swing lined with fat, cushy pillows rocks gently on the porch. Five bicycles lay on the right half of the lawn, scattered: two adult-sized and three smaller ones. A playhouse and a slide on the other.

It's warm, inviting, cozy. It's the kind of house that no one ever wants to leave or move away from, the kind that everyone gravitates back to, a North Star for home. I'd bet anything that there's a concrete square somewhere with an entire family's handprints molded into it.

The one to the left of it is what I pick for Deacon, and it's just as lovely in its own way. It's a craftsman style, with oversized paneled windows, rounded dormers, and stacked fieldstone around the base. Ferns and boxwoods and everything in shades of green. Something sturdy and substantial, well-crafted and charming.

He looks back at me, surprised when I point it out. Grins smugly and taps a finger against his stubble as he considers it. "That's a damn good-looking house," he says.

I laugh through my nose and roll my eyes. "Yeah, yeah, it is."

"Which one is yours?" he asks.

Two more homes down stands a newer build. It's a stunning dark gray, with black framed windows and modern, sleek finishes. All sharp angles and lines. Out front is a rock garden—minimalist, with only a few tall cactuses jutting up. It's polished, with a black painted gate closing off the driveway. It's likely the most expensive one on the entire strip.

"That one's probably mine," I say, pointing to it.

He frowns. "*That's* your favorite? Really?"

I pause and squirm, suddenly a little uncomfortable with this game I chose. "It's more about which one *looks* like it would be mine. Not just my favorite one."

"So, not the one you were mooning over a few houses back, then? You think *this* one feels more like you?"

I flap my hand at the modern mansion. "I mean, that's an extremely luxurious house, Deacon," I say, forcefully cavalier. "Anyone would think this dark one was more my style. *No one* would guess that the storybook home was mine. No one else would think that one looks like me."

He shakes his head and drags his eyes my way, something hardening in his expression. "It looks like you to me."

God, I know it's a stupid game. Poor little rich girl daydreaming of a new home and a new life. I know that in terms of relativity, I have way too much in this life to be grateful for, and I used to hate myself for feeling like I wanted something else, for not just being happy with what I did have. And even though I've started being a little easier on myself, and I *know* it's silly . . . I still can't get a full breath at the idea that Deacon could see me as that lovely home.

"You could see me with the flowers and the porch swing?" I ask. "Not just some cactuses and rocks?" I feel like I'm always so jagged and sharp.

"Hey, don't knock cactuses. They're incredibly resilient. Hard to kill," he says. He turns away from me and closes his eyes, his face tilted up to the sun. "But I could see you with a whole garden of them, and flowers everywhere, too. With the lawn and the swing and all of it, Lar."

The warmth of the morning starts to burn through the fog, bathing my cheeks. I close my eyes and let myself imagine that for a minute, too.

TWENTY-EIGHT

LARYNN

I wake up on Deacon's birthday to an email from my mom.

> From: Allison Lavigne Edwards
> To: LaRynn Lavigne
>
> LaRynn,
>
> I am coming to California for three days over the
> third weekend in September and would very much
> like to see you. I will be staying at The Dream Inn so
> that it's easy for us to get together.
>
> Love,
> Mom

I read it over and over again. Trying to pick up some kind of inflection somewhere. Trying to decide if she meant this as a soft request, or if it's an irritated demand. I toggle the screen like more information might load before I read it again.

"Hey, you okay?"

I jump at the sound of Deacon's voice at my side, spilling my coffee and dropping my phone in the movement. "Shit, sorry."

"It's alright. Here, let me help you—"

"I got it, I got it." I clamber for some paper towels and jerk down, my head smacking into his face with a thud.

He falls back on his ass and holds his hand against his eye. "Ow."

I try to blink away the bright spots popping in my vision. "You okay? Sorry." I rub at my forehead.

"I'm good. Are *you*? Looked like you went somewhere for a minute." He squints my way and helps me wipe up the spilled coffee.

Shit. His birthday. "Yeah, totally. Just needed the caffeine to hit, you know?" I try to brush it off. "Um. Happy birthday."

He grins and stands, holding out a palm to help me up. "Thank you. Can't wait for dessert."

I wince after he pulls me to my feet. "It's certainly . . . ready." I made it last night and then fretted when I went to bed, trying to think of how I could make it less of an *ugly* dish. I think I'll toss some fresh peach slices on top, or maybe some raspberries in powdered sugar to break up the gelatin layer.

Fuck. I can't believe my mom is coming into town.

"You sure you're good?" Deacon asks.

I remember how his ability to read me so clearly would've aggravated me before. Now I'm just annoyed that anything else is taking away from a day to celebrate him.

"My mom emailed me today. She's coming into town to stay next month," I confess.

"Here?!"

"That was my reaction, too, but no. She says she's staying at The Dream Inn." I sigh.

"What's with your parents and my birthday, huh?" he asks. The tone is light and fun, but my shoulders immediately tense.

The last time we spent this day together, a tsunami warning had all the residents in or around the Boardwalk evacuated. We'd all ended up at Santa Sea, since it was high and far enough away from where the wave was predicted to hit. But Deacon and I thought we could get away with sneaking off while Macy, our grandmothers, and the twins were busy reading or playing cards. We did not, however, account for my mother announcing that she would not be returning home with my father, or for him to show up back in town, more than a week early.

Neither of us had our phones, since we were both more concerned with finding somewhere we could get naked. Meanwhile, my dad came stomping into the campground, igniting everyone to form a search party to come and find us.

"Sorry. Shouldn't have brought that up," Deacon says.

"No, stop. Stop. It's—" I give his thick wrist a quick squeeze, before I drop it like a hot iron. "It's okay. *We're* okay. We can laugh about it now, right?" Please laugh with me about it now.

He inspects my face for a moment. "Yeah, we can laugh about it now."

I can't help but notice that neither of us does, though.

AND SINCE THE ANXIETY OVER the email won't settle in me unless I address it, I sigh and hit Reply.

Okay, Mom. I'd like to see you, too.

Love,
LaRynn

The dessert is fucking delicious.

I eat my words, along with a third helping, sitting at a picnic table with the twins, Sally, Deacon, and Macy (who insists that we sing happy birthday despite the fact that he's twenty-seven).

"Make a wish," she teases when she sets the only remaining sliver of pie in front of him with a lone candle.

He looks at me as he blows it out.

HE CATCHES ME A WHILE later in the hallway, looking at the pictures of him growing up.

"Now *this*," I say, "this one is my favorite." I point out the frame that holds a tiny version of him, I'd guess maybe age four or five. He's sporting a cast up to his elbow on each arm, glowering at the camera and holding a single green balloon in a bandaged hand. "How on earth did you manage to break *both* arms?" I chuckle.

He laughs through his nose. "They weren't broken, actually. We lived on some property back then and had burn days once in a while. There'd been one the day before, and I was out playing with my brother. I, uh . . . I thought it was a pile of sand and reached my hands into it. Turns out it was ash, and was still *very* hot in the center."

My stomach loops. "Oh my god, Deacon. That had to be *awful*."

"It's okay. I don't remember the pain at all anymore, and the scars are very rarely noticeable. Sometimes in summer when I'm tanner you can see the ones between my fingers, where the skin's thinner." He smiles softly. "This girl I once knew still told me my hands were the sexiest thing about me."

This girl. I believe I'd followed the observation with *aside from your dick*. It was a sweet and sexy moment that we'd seemed happy in back then, and I'm glad he's laughing about it now. But it just . . . doesn't sound as nice, anymore. He does have the best hands, and yeah—*that,* as well . . . but he's also got the best mind and spirit. He works harder than anyone I've ever met. He can look at *anything* and find a way to figure it out or tackle it with enough time. He can dance and isn't one of those men who will stand off on the sidelines. He's playful. He makes mundane things fun and indulges me in my silly games. He'll . . .

He'll make a great husband for someone else, someday. When someone *else* gets to do life with him.

I feel like I've swallowed acid at the thought, the dessert going sour in my gut, and have to blink rapidly. "That why you got the tattoo there?" I ask. My voice sounds throttled.

"Honestly? Yeah, kinda." He shrugs and laughs. "I almost got a different one in Vegas, first. Went there to celebrate when Jensen got accepted to med school. We were drunk and I was flipping through a book, about to pick something random when a guy wandered in and *shamed* me."

"Shamed you?"

"Yeah," he scoffs. "Jensen swears he was someone famous but there's no way. This guy was just as hammered, and he asked me 'Are you just *picking* something like an idiot?' And when I shrugged he told me I'd regret it. That I better get something that would *mean* something to me. Made me give him my slot because he needed to have something *worthwhile* inked onto him. When I asked him what his was about, you know what he told me?"

"What?"

"He said it was for a *girl*." He shakes his head and rolls his lips.

"What a chump," I snicker. "Did you see what he got?"

"Fuck, I don't know. I think it was an umbrella or something. Like I said—he was hammered." He chuckles. "Anyway. When I got home I started thinking about it more." He gives it a wistful look. "The octopus is adaptable. Can look at circumstances and flex, stretch, find a creative or strategic way to make them better. Damned things can lose an arm and find a way to grow it back.

"Plus, I still am and will forever be fucking terrified of actually going in the ocean, so this is probably as close as I'll ever get to one." He turns his hand over and continues to give it an appraising look, bandages on multiple fingers. He's merciless on those hands. Sacrifices them for every single one of our tasks. Keeps on going no matter how many times he gets a metal splinter in one or hits another with a hammer.

"*And,* it just looks cool," I say.

He smiles. "And it just looks cool."

We fall into a cloud of silence and I search for a path out. "So . . . you having a good birthday?"

He blinks and his jaw works. "I'm having a *great* birthday, but . . . I did think of something else I want."

Static fizzing fills my ears when my thoughts trip into something hopeful. "Yeah?"

"I want you to talk to June."

I exhale. "Deacon—"

"*Talk* to her. You're a dreamer *and* a fighter, LaRynn Cecelia. I know you can do it. Let yourself dream a bit and at least ask."

A dreamer *and* a fighter.

It's enough to bolster me.

TWENTY-NINE

DEACON

I manage to herd Sally, Jensen, and my mother inside so that June and LaRynn can be left alone for a bit, but I find myself checking out the window periodically, trying to read their lips.

And then I decide that I'm okay with being a nosy asshole when I see both of their expressions fall, and I slide open the window.

"When?" LaRynn asks her.

"I'd have to renew my lease before the end of November. I could ask them to hold on to next door, too, but I don't know if they will or not. If you think you'd be able to close before November thirtieth, I'll ask," June replies.

LaRynn's eyes find mine. We'd need a thirty-day closing on the property, at minimum. So, realistically, that'd mean that we would need to get the place on the market by late September. Earlier would be a safer bet. It'd be a rush, and we'd be selling it unfinished.

This whole thing would be over in a matter of weeks. Not the six months or so I was hoping for.

"You're losing your lease?" I ask. Because screw subtlety.

"Not yet," June replies. "But with Otto leaving next door, the building management for the strip is raising prices. I'm doing fine, but honestly . . . I won't be able to afford to stay there if I don't change something, and that'll take an injection of money I don't have. If LaRynn wants to do this with me. . . ." Her eyes fill and she chokes on tears. "I don't want *any* of you to think you *have* to, though. I would not have even said a damn thing. I *haven't* said anything, because I just figured I'd have to move farther into town and find a smaller setup, you know. I would not be saying any of this if you hadn't started this conversation." She looks back at LaRynn. "But you're right about everything, and I'm desperate to stay there. It's the best location and I'm not afraid to beg them to hold off on signing over Otto's to anyone else for a bit, too. If you want to do this—I'm sorry, I know it'd be rushed—but if you want to do this I would *love* to be in business with you."

"What if I can't get the money in time?" LaRynn asks. "Would you still be interested if we had to move locations?"

June sniffs. "Absolutely. But know that that would entail a bigger start-over process. Being by the Boardwalk and the pier and on the main strip would be ideal. I know it would be a mad dash, but I'd be lying if I said I didn't want to stay in that spot."

IT FEELS LIKE PICKING UP a bag of groceries and watching them collapse through the bottom. A little dumb and helpless. I try to scoop up all the goddamn pieces rolling away, and attempt to enjoy the remainder of the night. But every time I look at LaRynn her eyes are already there to meet me, their corners sad. I can tell that she's stressed about it, too, but wants to keep the night upbeat. And I'd love to be solid for her, to alle-viate any of her worries and be supportive. I don't want to be selfish, but . . . fuck.

Yes I do. I really *do* want to be selfish. I want to say fuck the location and *wait*. Beg her to wait and to stay with me. Plead with her to stay in our house together a while longer until I convince her to be mine. *Dream and fight with me, let me dream and fight with you, too.*

She finds me after we say our goodbyes to June, rubbing an arm self-consciously. "Hey, I feel terrible, but I, um . . . I think I drank too much. I know it's your birthday, I'm so sorry, but any chance you're okay to drive?" she asks.

I'm . . . not. I also drank too much in too short a time frame in my efforts to stay collected.

"I—shouldn't." I wince.

"Well," she declares. "We're a mess, aren't we?" She tries to laugh but it dies on a sigh.

"I've only got the two-seater," Jensen offers, pointing at his Jeep. "I can give Sal a ride, though."

"Works for me," Sal agrees.

"The Mystery Spot's open tonight. You two can stay in there," my mom decrees, and I feel the blood leave my brain.

"What's the Mystery Spot?" LaRynn asks.

"The Airstream sites are all named after different land-marks or attractions around Santa Cruz," Mom explains cheerfully. "It's rented tomorrow, so you'll have to replace the sheets, but it's open."

I catch LaRynn's expression, her eyes closing in pain.

Yep, we're a mess.

* * *

WE'RE HOVERING ON OPPOSITE SIDES of the double bed in the trailer. Standing over it and studying it like we hope it'll sprout wheels and carry us home.

"Do you mind if I take my jeans off?" she asks.

"N-no. Not at all. Please do. You're good." *So smooth, jackass.*

"You can too," she adds. "I mean, like—don't feel like you have to sleep in *your* jeans or anything. Be comfortable." She undoes a button. "Or don't. Don't let me make you feel like you have to strip or something." She pulls down her zipper and I'm aware that I should be responding but my mind is a blinking cursor. "You know what, I think I'm going to take the dining bench." She turns to leave. "On second thought. Or third. Whatever the fuck. We can absolutely be adults about this, can't we? I'm spiraling and I don't spiral like this so anytime you wanna chime in here and stop me would be truly wonderful—"

"We can definitely be adults about this," I say. And then I laugh a high-pitched sound when I take off my pants.

She removes hers and laugh-snorts before she slaps a palm to her lips. "Okay, okay. We *are* mature enough for this," she declares.

"If you say so," I reply. But when I take off my shirt I lose her eyes, her laugh fading away with them. I want her to look at me, the way I'm always dying to look at her. But instead, she quickly turns around without a courtesy warning and I just about need to gag myself and grit my teeth in my shirt.

String thong.

White.

A black bow at the top.

The birthmark in perfect palm placement.

She settles backwards into the bed.

I spin around and follow behind.

When I try to adjust, our asses kiss. "Sorry," we say in unison.

Eventually, one entire side of my body goes numb, pins and needles from shoulder to hip. I roll over, and I can tell she's already asleep, her breathing even and steady. She's always been one of those people who can fall asleep anywhere, under any circumstance. Probably the result of being conditioned and desensitized to stress.

I, however, feel fucking desolate and out of control. Still trying to catch all those rolling pieces and find a way to carry them with me.

I DON'T SLEEP A SINGLE solitary minute—something that I know will bite me in the ass later. Especially when she wakes up with a smile that only makes me feel more helpless. Because I don't know if she's happy that we're going to be speeding through the remaining things at the house, onward through the finish line of this arrangement, or if she's just trying to be positive for my sake.

I worry that asking has the potential to make her feel guilty about the quick sale, too. Like maybe she knows how much I want more time to prepare, to grieve a bit longer, but she also wants to jump on this opportunity.

I wish I didn't feel the *need* to try to take everything apart and figure out a situation so much. It feels like that's all I've been doing since Dad died. Figuring out how to *fix* things. Figuring out how to keep them together. Trying to make myself useful, or valuable, or important.

But it's like LaRynn said: people aren't houses or projects.

You can't disassemble them and find out how they operate, identify their broken bits and replace them. You can do your best to understand them as they are, but . . . *people* change. They grow. They learn. They just . . . *are*.

I feel that husk-like sensation again. Something dried up, easily crumpled to dust.

"You ready?" she asks me after she's put her jeans back on. I've been dressed and waiting at the dining table since sometime in the night, when she let out a breathy sound in her sleep that sent me flying out of that tiny fucking bed. So yeah, I'm fucking ready.

But I just say, "Yeah."

We replace the sheets together, and for some reason even that action makes the cracks in me pull wider.

When we quietly finish closing up the trailer, we walk back to the car.

"Jensen asked if we wanted to pick up a few matches today," she says to me after we pull away from the campground. "He said he texted you, but you didn't reply. Coffee shop is closed for Sunday, so June's probably free, too?"

"Sure." I try to smile. "Sounds good."

Then, because I'm only growing more tired by the second and know if I don't say something now, I won't muster it up later, I say, "Don't worry about the house, okay? I've got some money in savings I can access, and you can always just pay it back to me when we close. We'll get the new doors put up and the shower tile done, and we can get the kitchen tile figured out this week, too. I'll cancel the windows . . . We'll get the important stuff done and get it sold in time."

She nods and smiles shakily. "Thanks. You're right. I know we can do it." When I look back her eyes are glassy. Out of relief or gratitude, I suppose. I swallow convulsively for the opposite reason.

THE AFTERNOONS HAVE ALREADY STARTED to cool off earlier, today especially. We stretch and warm up at the beach for a bit with layers over our suits, until our blood pumps enough to cut the chill from the breeze.

"Same teams as before, yeah?" Jensen says. "Since it brings our height average equal."

He's still six foot two, but whatever, I guess. It irritates me more than it should that LaRynn casually agrees to be on his team. Like it's another kind of smug foreshadowing for how it's *all* going to be easy to part from. Like she's not desperate to stay near me for what little time we have left, unlike myself.

And *fuck*, I'm sluggish. And so fucking sullen. I serve a ball low into the net and kick the sand like a toddler.

And I *keep* fucking up. Spike the ball a mile out of bounds, trip into the net on an easy pass. All while Jensen and LaRynn perform a choreographed sequence of high-fiving and hip-bumping in celebration.

God I'm tired, and I feel like such a fucking baby, but she's slipping through my fingers and even though she's *right there,* she still feels so out of reach. And fucking *Jensen.* With his happy-go-lucky, nothing-gets-me-down, everything's-great, *I'm-a-goddamn-doctor,* I'd-*never-let-my-own-insecurities-or-fears-get-in-the-way-of-something-I-want* persona. How *nice,* to be so well-adjusted and levelheaded.

She's going to find someone like him someday. Someone who didn't hurt her, who didn't fuck up. Someone who'll always be able to say the right thing, to do the right thing.

It's easy for her to laugh with *him*. I don't see her dropping *his* hands like they're on fire when they brush. I don't see her stiffening up when *he* does a celebratory shimmy.

They fucking chest bump when they win the second match in a row by eight points and *shit*, I feel like I'm an idiot teen again, but I have to get the fuck out of here. I mutter something unintelligible and grab my shirt, flinging sand up into my own face in the movement.

I can't fucking imagine making it another second on this court and I have got to get some air because how the *fuck* am I going to last even another week with her in that house? Having to mourn her while she's only feet away from me.

I think my promise from earlier was a lie.

I don't think I can do this.

THIRTY

LARYNN

His stomping picks up ahead of me, almost too fast for me to keep up, shoulders strung tight, the veins in his arms standing at attention. Despite the wind picking up and the sweat cooling on his skin, he doesn't replace his shirt, and neither do I, afraid to miss him running away from me.

When we make it home in record time he tramples the steps like he's trying to wreck them, my heart gathering speed alongside. And when we finally make it home, he slams his palms into his hair, gripping it at the roots before he rakes his fingers through it until it's standing on end in every direction—as wild as the look in his bloodshot eyes.

"*What* Deacon?! What is it? What's wrong with you?!" I'm nearly shouting, but I can't seem to get myself under control. My chest heaves, his agitation siphoning the air from this room.

"I just—*fuck!*" He bolts up from the couch and paces a few steps before he collapses back down and looks up at me, hands clasped together in front of him. "Fuck it. I—I can't do it anymore, LaRynn. I'm begging you, alright? Please, *please* stop," he groans.

"Stop what?!"

"Stop *flirting* with him, please. Stop it." It's a quiet, pained request—his face buried in his banged-up hands.

I attempt to slow my heart, inhale deeply. Rub at something sore in my chest. This sweet, oblivious man thought that was flirting? "Tell me why," I say, desperate to cut right to the bottom of this.

He looks back up at me and shakes his head angrily. "Because it fucking *hurts*. It makes me feel like I'm in pain, like I'm being choked by my own goddamn fury. *Please*, LaRynn. Fuck my pride, I want you to stop because I want you for *me*, and even if I can't have that I just—need to be able to make it through the rest of this without wanting to put my head through the floor, alright?! I'm flat out begging you, please don't—not in front of me anymore." He blows out a trembling breath. "I'm sorry, I didn't sleep and I just can't pretend. I'll calm down. I'm sorry."

He's vibrating with it, with the need to rage against something, some*one*. And my palms are stinging with the need to grab for him. But I'm still utterly confused. What was it about the harmless afternoon that got to him? Why was *this* the time? What about a silly game on the beach?

"What was it? What changed?" I have to ask.

Our gazes clash, his dark eyes so clear in this moment that their brown is liquid bronze.

"It's the way you fucking *smiled* at him. You didn't try to hide it. You didn't turn around so he couldn't see it, like you usually do to me. You let it stick to your face and didn't try to stuff it away. You didn't have to second guess every touch. It was that he made you *happy* and you didn't have to think about it. It's that it was *easy* and this thing between us hasn't been. It's that I've had to work so goddamn hard for those smiles, and now I'm fucking greedy for them. And *nothing* has changed, not really. I just want you worse. And it *hurts*. God, this feeling, LaRynn." He fists his hair again, rocking in his seat. "*Jesus,* I'm so sorry, I can't believe I'm acting like this. I know I should just be happy to be your friend, and I am, okay? I get that we weren't good to each other before and *I* took this off the table, but I can't do it anymore, I'm sorry I don't think I can stand it, I—"

"Show me," I say shakily, heart swelling. "Show me where it hurts."

His head snaps up to mine and I step to him, between his parted knees.

He studies me for one more echoing beat before he exhales, lets his forehead fall against my lower stomach with a groan. His shoulders drop with something like relief. "Show me," I repeat, my fingers knitting in his curls.

He tips his head back as he snakes up a hand to grasp at my hip, places the other against his chest. "Here," he croaks.

I look at his splayed fingers against his heart, those two that are bandaged, and something twinges through me. At the reality of this man who works so hard and feels so much harder. "Here?" I ask, laying my hand over his. He nods.

I gently push him back into the couch before I climb onto his lap, straddling his hips with my thighs. I slide our hands aside and dip my chin, kissing the spot on his warm chest. A breath huffs out of him, warm against the shell of my ear. "Better?" I ask. His throat bounces, one side of his mouth ticking up, but he shakes his head in denial.

So, I confess. "I sometimes hid my smiles because I was afraid of everything else you'd see. I thought *I* took this off the table and that I had to be happy to be your friend, too." His grip on me tightens. "I thought I had to be okay with *just* being your friend. But I want you too, Deacon. I want everything."

And I smile now as I trace my hand along his jaw. Allow a small laugh to escape at his concentrated, enamored expression. His beautiful face. He barely grins back, not full-out, but his eyes widen just slightly, like he's amazed or afraid to miss whatever this is. He places a hand on either side of my neck, thumbs meeting in the middle to trace a line up to my lips. The bosom-heaving begins anew, and my nipples press through my swimsuit into his bare chest, cool air swirling in the space between us on each exhale and making me desperate to press in.

"I want it all, LaRynn. You're a fine friend, but I can't take having less than all of it with you," he says, thickly.

I nod solemnly. "Nothing less."

His thumbs drop to the base of my throat, fingers knitting themselves around the back. And every other thought is silenced when he tugs me by that grip to close the distance between us, his lips meeting mine.

Deacon's always kissed like it's the finale. Like the kiss is what we've been climbing and torquing ourselves toward all this time. Like he'd be content to only do this tonight, tomorrow, forever.

It's like slipping into a bath; warm and wet and makes every muscle in my body feel languid and pliant. Even when we come apart for air we don't allow more than centimeters between us. When I pull back he lightly bites. He holds me by my neck like he's freeing my head for the moment, like he's got me, and *God*, I want all of this; this and more. Everything.

I start to chase friction with my hips and he's up in an instant, carrying us to the bedroom.

"Deacon." I want him to have my words. "Deacon, I'm in this. Us."

"I'm trying to be in something, LaRynn, believe me."

"Don't," I say with a small laugh, our noses brushing. I know he's excited because I feel the same, like I want to be everywhere all at once, but he knows what I mean. *Don't try to lighten this for my benefit. I don't need it.* "I mean it. I'm in this and I want to know that we both are. That you feel like I do."

He sobers and nods once, mapping my face. "I think I've been in this since I saw you kicking one of the planter boxes out front," he says with a quick pant, hot against my mouth. "Since you showed up in town again. In one way or another I have."

And then he brings my mouth back down, and my legs wrap and squeeze around his hips. A grunt of approval rasps out of him, and frantic need rips through me. Our hands fist in each other's hair, just shy of pain.

When we make it into the room, he lays me down with heartbreaking gentleness—onto the bed he built, among the pillows I picked for their colors because I think they reminded me of us. Tans, blues, blacks. Sand, ocean, leather. Night skies and back seats. Maybe I picked the green tile for the redwoods and the buildings around Santa Sea. Maybe he and this place are part of me again.

He slides onto his knees between my legs, big and beautiful with his unruly hair and wicked grin and thrumming pulse—a force of nature himself.

"Untie me," I say, and his lips press together like he's trying to contain his excitement. I follow his palm from my ankle, up my shin, up my thigh. Our gazes clash when he teases a thumb inside my swimsuit bottom and I hiss through my teeth, heat licking through me like a whip.

"Untie me," I say again, and this time he doesn't stop the smile.

His hand smooths the rest of its path up my stomach to the bow between my breasts. He gives it a precise tug and it slides apart, grazing my nipples with frustrating lightness. We both let out a groan.

"Put your mouth on me," I say, my voice so husky it should make me self-conscious. I could not care less.

"I've got plans to. Have plans for your mouth, too."

"Yes."

He licks a line from my belly button to my nipple, circling me with his tongue and plucking me with his teeth before he switches to the other side. I need *more.* There's a buzz under my skin that pulses every time he does that but settles every time he breaks free. And then he plants sucking kisses that bring it roaring back.

"Are we doing this? Is this happening?" he suddenly asks.

When I look down at his face against my chest he's wearing that crooked grin, mouth open with his teeth still resting against my nipple. And there's something so lewd about him smiling at me that way with *me* still in his mouth, that the moment begs for some levity.

"We could look at more tile samples for the kitchen, if you want? Go over the budget?" I say.

"Fuck the budget," he growls.

A shocked and lusty gasp breaks free from me, and he cuts it off with a kiss.

"God, I'm so in this with you, LaRynn," he says against my jaw, fingertips tracing their way down my face.

I slip my hands inside the top of his shorts and push meaningfully.

He laughs, shoving them down and kicking them off, a

pillow flying off the bed with them. He rolls back to kneel beside my hip, pulls one of my knees into his lap to part me wider. "Can I?" he asks.

"Please," I whisper.

His eyes close only briefly before they're back on me everywhere: On his hand as he pulls the delicate string on my bikini bottoms and slides them away. On my face when his fingertips find me, watching me while he moves them against me, groaning against my neck when we hear the wet sound of it.

"Keep going," I say, even though it's what he's already doing; I'm lost to chasing down that sensation, a wave I'm desperate to ride until it crests over me. Up, down, circle. And then he's pinning my knee to the bed and folding himself across it, replacing his fingers with his mouth, their motions with his tongue. The wave takes me over and back around and I cry out, my fingers knitting themselves in his hair.

"Please," I pant as I float down, even as my blood rushes in my ears. "I want you."

He reaches up past me to the nightstand, tears the wrapper in his teeth on his way back. I watch him roll it onto himself before he drags his body back over me, bracing on one trembling arm.

"Jesus you're beautiful, LaRynn," he says, his thumb sliding along my collarbone.

"So are you," I tell him before I tug him back to my lips by his hair.

And at the first nudge into me I start to babble and shake. "I *missed* you," I admit with a moan. Emotion twists in my throat. I hope he knows what I mean. That even though I've lived with him for months, I've missed him even when he's been close. That I missed him so fucking much after I left the first time. He pushes in farther and I lose my breath.

"I missed you, too," he replies hoarsely, pausing to kiss the corners of my face.

"I thought I was crazy to miss you. Told myself I was ridiculous. Tried to pretend it was less than it was." A breathy whine when he retreats.

"I did too, love," he says. "*God,* I thought about you." He slides in again. "Thought about how I missed that mouth and your glare. Thought about your laugh . . . Thought about this." He slides home and I whimper at the complete and total fullness, the rightness.

I capture his bottom lip in my teeth and drag out a bite. "You ruined me for anyone else, you know," I tell him, voice tight because not only has it been a long time for me, but also because it's *him.* "The ones after you made me feel bad for directing them, but I never knew anything different."

He goes utterly still above me, lashes pressed against his cheeks, nostrils flaring. And I realize that I've just alluded to being with other people with him buried deep inside me. "Shit, I'm—"

"Shhh, shh, shh," he shushes me. "Just—just give me a second here."

"I'm sorry," I say, voice hitching, eyes filling.

His lids crack open and he tips down to kiss me, like he can't help himself. Thumbs my cheekbone in reverence. "Telling me I ruined you for anyone else is causing me to have—a *moment*—and I just need you to be still for a second, please." He smiles self-deprecatingly and my teeth sink into my lip to stifle a laugh. I clench around him and his eyes roll back on a groan.

"Evil witch." He recovers with a smile and a sharp thrust of his hips that scoots me up the bed.

And with each push he builds more of that exquisite ache.

He's as steady as a metronome against me, agonizingly tender. His mouth on mine, my teeth grazing his warm shoulders, his lips down to my chest.

The steadiness of it makes me desperate. My hands rake and squeeze against everything they touch. His backside, the sheets, my own breasts.

He levers up and drags me by my thighs until I hang just off the bed, nibbling the inside of my ankle before he bends my knees up and pushes himself back in. The change in position pulls a cry of bliss from me, his name pealing from my lips when heat tightens behind my ribs again. And then he swipes his thumb against me and takes me apart once more, piece by piece, so deep that I could never forget he was here, as if I ever did.

He clasps his hands around my waist and drags them down, thumbs hooking into my hips while he pumps and grinds my body against his, working me over, eyes locked on mine, my name whispered roughly against the inside of my knee when he finally lets go, before he collapses onto shaking arms above me.

"Rynn," he breathes again into my damp skin, his jaw grating against mine, my heels crossed around his lower back. I feel utterly wrung out and feverish, the sights and sounds of him still replaying through my brain. I want to hold him here, to keep him this way.

We stay as long as we can before we're forced to deal with the human aspect of things. He scoops me up as soon as I reemerge from the bathroom and lays me back down, studies me like I'm something both old and cherished, new and exciting. Sun shines through the windows and doors, illuminating a half-framed wall covered in swatches of white paint behind him. His eyes glaze and warm and I feel lush and indulgent under them. I don't want to hide under a sheet or turn away. I only want him to see how he makes me feel, only want to make him feel even half of what I do.

I think I might be in too deep all over again, but . . . it really feels too good to make myself care or be scared anymore. At least for now.

He settles beside me, tracks a finger down my cheek.

"Tell me what you're thinking," he says.

I answer without preamble, "That I'm happy." A tear springs loose and slides away. "That I'm happy here with you, in our half torn apart house. That I think—I think I'd be content to serve coffee every day and watch the waves and never do anything extraordinary and still feel like I have the best life."

He inhales sharply before a smile blooms. "I'd give you that house if I could, you know. That one on West Cliff." More tears bubble up from my eyes, because his words make my chest throb. He's so *good*. Good at so much, so much more intelligent than anyone ever gives him credit for. Than I ever gave him credit for. It makes me burn, thinking about it—I should *know* how that feels, to be put in a box and for assumptions to be built around me. But instead of closing himself off and turning into an angry, imposing fortress, he just gives more of himself to people. It makes me want to tuck him away and snarl at anything that tries to come for him.

He weaves a lock of my hair through the fingers on his tattooed hand. When his eyes meet mine again, they're damp, but he's smiling. "Instead I've got a double wide on a campground and a half-done half of a duplex to offer. But the view is pretty great."

"Don't forget about the planter boxes," I say with a wet chuckle.

"Oh, right, how could I? The planter boxes are fucking pristine."

We dissolve into laugh-crying until enough of our bare skin collides to turn it all to hunger again.

THIRTY-ONE

DEACON

"Would you stop petting it, Deacon?"

"What?" I say innocently, swinging the tie to her silk robe like a lasso. "It's so smooth and slippery. I want one."

"It does look good on you, I suppose," she says, taking an overly large bite of her cereal.

I look at her sitting on a dining chair, feet propped up in my lap. She's wearing one of my Santa Sea shirts—this one dotted in sand dollars—left completely unbuttoned, the mass of her hair swaying behind her. We woke up sometime in the night, starving, and shuffled our way out here, each grabbing something to throw on as we went.

"Not as good as that looks on you," I tell her before I take my own bite. I stare down at my Cheerios and try to calm, immediately dying to dip my hand under that shirt and slip it off her. *Cheerios. Milk. Cereal. Spoon. She's gonna get tired of you if you keep at it like this.*

"Silk feeling a little *too* good, *mon coeur*?" she asks, bending over to set her bowl on the table beside me. I try to adjust the robe but just end up sliding it along my now-stiffening cock—*she knows I can't think straight when she slips into French—and shit, I think I might be blushing*—

"Fuck—" I hiss when she glides her foot along me, spoon clattering to the ground. But then she parts the robe and slides onto her knees and *Jesus Christ* I knock over my bowl and the rest of the milk off the table when she takes me in her mouth.

Milk and cereal splatter across the subfloor, and we don't bother to clean it up until morning.

THIRTY-TWO

DEACON

We should be frantically working to get everything done at the house. Instead, the last week of August slips away in a different kind of frenzy.

We make a valiant attempt at the floor installation. But I ask her to step on a plank to hold it in place for me while I lock it in with a mallet, and in doing so she rubs her silky calf against my jaw. "Oops," she says huskily.

I exercise saint-like restraint for two more planks.

On the third, she drops a pen that I'm fairly certain she just grabbed off the counter, looks down at me, and innocently says, "Oops," again.

And then she delicately steps over my shoulder with her long legs, drops to all fours in front of me and slowly reaches for it, stretching and presenting her baby blue thong under a black miniskirt, six inches from my face like an offering. I knee the mallet aside and grab her hips, drag her to me as she squeals.

I press my face to her and kiss her slowly through the material at first, pinning and sucking until she starts circling and arching back against my face. Until she's pleading with me—filthy, unintelligible things in two languages. I nearly weep at the sight of her hand creeping back, her fingers sneaking inside. I pull the fabric to the side crudely to watch her touch herself. Lick her lazily when she stills.

"Do you remember when you called me out for my premature hallway incident, love?" I say against her birthmark, giving her an appreciative squeeze. "I think I should make you come with your clothes still on to even the score."

"*I* think you should rip these off with your teeth and bend me over the table," she replies.

Next time. Next time I'll make her come with her clothes on. *This* time I toss her over my shoulder and haul her to the part of the living room where all the furniture is pushed together, kicking off my boots as I go. And as I settle her down to her feet again, I slide and grind every curve of her against me before I drop back to my knees at her front.

She looks down and bites her lip, her chest rising in a rush, curling a fist against my scalp as I ruck her skirt up to her waist.

"Too pretty to rip," I grit out, kissing the jut of her hip before I bite the band of her panties and drag them down, down, down her thighs.

I take my time kissing, licking, and massaging my way back up her legs, until I start to feel little tremors quivering across her skin. Until I think she's as worked up as I am, when she's squeezing her legs together and whimpering, dying to relieve an ache.

I fish out a condom from my wallet when I eventually make my way back to her neck, and she grabs at my belt and shoves at my jeans. And then I spin her around and step between her spread feet.

The sight of her in the mirror that's also been shoved over

here nearly undoes me, and I have to gulp down air. Flushed cheeks, nipples pressing through her white shirt, palms splayed across the table. The ends of her hair graze my hand against her lower back when she lifts her chin with a heavy-lidded gaze, finding mine in the reflection.

She holds my eyes, her breath hitching when I slide myself into her, when I cup my hand around her long throat.

"Tell me how good I have it, LaRynn. Tell me how lucky I am." I groan, every strand of my control strung to capacity.

She scores her nails up my wrist, the pads of her fingers smoothing along the lines of the tattoo, until her palm comes to rest over the top of mine. Colors flash in my vision when she squeezes both our hands around her neck, and her expression melts into a slow smile.

"You've got it so fucking good. You'll *always* have it so good, Deacon. Always the best."

I thrust into her messily, our hips bumping and rattling against the table, every sound that escapes her fraying at my restraint. My spine aches with the effort it takes to hold back, while one hand stays at her pulse and I work the other between her legs, endlessly dragging and squeezing, playing and pushing, until her eyes finally stutter closed, thighs going limp when she chokes out my name. She pulls me over the edge with her, nerves detonating through my limbs until I'm thoroughly, completely spent, and I cave in, my hands collapsing against the table beside hers to catch my weight.

I wrap her in a hug from behind and take her with me to the floor, my pants still at my ankles, her skirt still around her waist, sweaty and breathless and laughing deliriously, stacked on top of one another like the records she has piled in the corner.

"I love you," I say. Because it's what I feel and *fuck it*. I've tried to think of a hundred ways to tell her more romantically, but there's nothing else to it.

She rolls off of me with a tiny thud and searches my face.

I scramble to say more. "I love you and I know I don't always . . ." I falter through an inhale, frustrated with how difficult it is to find the right words, my mind blanking with emotion. "I've been trying to show you. I thought it was more important to show you, first, and I promise I'm going to keep doing that. But I also wanted to *say* it first." I feel raw when the words hang between us. Raw, and a little sick. A lot sick when I think of how she must've felt eight years ago.

"I know you do," she says simply, smiling shyly. "You've been showing me. With your patience and your trying. Your partnership." She catches her breath and inches up to my face, kissing me sweetly. "And I love you. I plan to keep showing you, too."

THIRTY-THREE

LARYNN

Everything feels like fall. The weather turns cool early in September. Morning walks require one of Deacon's hoodies or flannels—largely because the way he looks at me in them warms me up enough to stave off the cold.

The beach isn't exactly known for its fall foliage or anything, but it *feels* like the colors are changing, turning over and brightening.

If summer had been a song on our soundtrack, it was something with a chaotic rhythm—some galloping chorus, full of longing. "A Little Less Conversation" and a lot of "Suspicious Minds." But autumn . . . autumn starts to feel like whatever Etta meant by "A Sunday Kind of Love." An "Unchained Melody" full of fucking and fun, with long, languishing rests in between short bursts of productivity.

June and I agree for me to go down to two shifts a week for the time being, and Macy and Deacon agree to call a local handyman for anything that comes up over at the campground. Which *should* substantially free us up to finish things at the house.

It still takes us about two weeks to settle into a system that actually works, though.

I am promptly kicked off of the floor installation crew, but he and Jensen end up knocking it out together in under a week.

I stick to painting during that period, which isn't so bad. I must've intimidated Howie from the paint store enough because he ends up giving me a nicely discounted rate on all ten gallons of Seashell.

And we do really well, most of the time. The first night Jensen was there helping us we were a bit intense. But *he* took a little while to get the hint—was trying to hang out and chat while we shifted restlessly on our feet, our palms opening and closing at our sides, until Deacon eventually lost patience and blurted out, "Jay, I'm sorry man, but I'm gonna need you to leave now. I'm trying to get inside my wife's overalls, if you catch my drift."

"*Jesus,* Deacon, there was no *drift* in that. That was fairly unsubtle!" I shouted, but Jensen laughed and immediately left, backing out of the doorway with his hands in the air. "I'm sorry!" I called out behind him before Deacon lunged for me in three great strides. I flung the paintbrush and splattered him by accident, then screamed in delight when he chased me down and proceeded to smear me back.

That was also the same night Deacon and I received a group text from Sally that stated:

I love you both dearly, and I'm happy to hear that things are going well. But I'd like to HEAR slightly less. Please put a new door higher up on your priority list.

* * *

THEREAFTER, WE START TO SET small daily goals *before* we indulge ourselves in rewards.

He frames in the new doorway at the top of the landing and installs the door, so we treat ourselves to pizza before I ride him into oblivion on top of the chaise.

We finish installing cabinets, so he makes good on his promise and makes me come on his lap with all of my clothes still on.

The bathrooms are a bit like musical chairs. We need at least one functional shower, so we have to time our hot-mopping and tiling perfectly so there's not a huge overlap in days. When we succeed, we wash each other's hair before he takes me against the shower wall, our skin slick and soapy.

We finish the install on the kitchen backsplash before we spend that afternoon making deliciously slow, lazy love in bed. Tucked together on our sides like spoons, legs and arms tangled in four-way braids. We fall asleep in the same position immediately after, and don't wake up until the following morning.

Most days we're sore and exhausted down to our bones, but we find ways to lean on one another and keep going.

Sometimes he stops by the shop while I'm working just to quickly tug me into a kiss before he returns to his own tasks. Other times I massage his palms until he falls asleep.

THE ONLY PROBLEM WITH ALL this happiness is the worry that lurks in the background over losing it. Like how fall feels bright and colorful, but you know that winter is going to eventually show up.

As such, my anxiety builds the closer we get to my mother coming into town.

The night before I'm scheduled to meet her for lunch, Sally invites us over for dinner and cards, and I'm grateful for the distraction.

We eat outside until the cold seeps in, but Sally and I lose Deacon to her patio in the transition. The door is mildly squeaky, and the drip system on her plants isn't working, so of course he's incapable of leaving it alone. Inevitably it'll lead to him fixing three more problems that no one else realizes even exist. We watch him through the glass as he starts wiggling a fence board.

Sally laughs through a sigh. "Should we remind him that this will all be someone else's issue soon?"

The words zap through my chest, and I feel my expression pinch. "No," I say hoarsely. "No, I don't think we should remind him."

I feel her turn to me before I look back at her. "Did I say something, sweetheart?" she asks.

"No, no. Nothing that isn't true," I mutter, patting her arm. "It's just a house. It's just a—*thing*. A possession. I just . . . I've had to let go of things before, and in those other cases I didn't get to take something with me, like I'm getting to with him." I smile when I see him pop back through her gate with his tools and a new lightbulb. "But this one feels a bit like letting go of a whole little *world*, I guess. Does that make sense?"

Her wrinkled brows gather tighter. "I would've thought you'd be thrilled to be rid of it after all this. You'll have all that money to start something new, add to the shop with June."

"I am. Really, I am, Sal. I promise. I don't mean to sound ungrateful or dramatic," I assure her. "It'll be nice to be somewhere quieter for a while, too." I shrug. "For us, and especially for you. You won't have to listen to us stomping around or the constant shot of the nail gun going off above your head. The never-ending sound of that damned table saw." I laugh.

"Mm-hmm," she hums in agreement, just as Deacon peeks back in from the patio.

"I'll be right back. I have to hit the hardware store for some new tubing for this," he tells us.

"Deacon, it *really* doesn't need to get done tonight," Sally urges.

"I've got the time. I'll be right back." He shuts the door and disappears, Sal and I shaking our heads good-humoredly.

And then her front door flings open behind us and we jump in our seats as Deacon crosses the room, tips me back in my chair, and plants a chaste kiss on my lips.

"Sorry, almost forgot that," he says with a grin. Then he disappears once more, leaving Sally and I laughing in his wake.

THIRTY-FOUR

DEACON

In the dark hours of the morning I lurch awake, disoriented like I'd been falling through a dream. I feel further off-course when I find LaRynn's side of the bed empty. There's a knot in my neck that rivals the one in my stomach as I pad out to the kitchen, where I find her sitting with a mug of coffee, staring at the empty table.

"Hey," I say groggily. "You okay?"

She looks up at me with a haunted expression. "I'm okay. Couldn't sleep."

"Here." I motion for her to make room so I can slide under and set her on my lap. When we twist into something comfortable, she rests an arm over my shoulders and skates her fingertips through my hair in circles. I wait quietly with her for a few moments until she's ready to talk.

"I'm anxious about seeing my mom," she says after a while.

I kiss her collarbone through her shirt, my chest stinging for her. No one should be this apprehensive about *seeing* a parent. "Do you want me to come with you?" I ask. Because I can't tell her what to do in this situation. I couldn't demand explanations or apologies from my own dad even when I knew I was running out of time, so I understand her struggle with this relationship with her mom.

She fidgets on my legs, like the idea that someone would want to hold her hand in an uncomfortable setting makes her twitchy. "No, that's okay," she says. "But please don't think it's because I'm ashamed—or anything less than proud to be with you. I'm so, so proud of you."

I kiss the worried crease between her brows. "Thank you for telling me that, but you don't need to worry about me, love. You do what you gotta do, tell her whatever you need to. And I'll be here for you when you get home."

At that, she starts crying in earnest.

THIRTY-FIVE

LARYNN

She's already waiting for me when I get to the restaurant, staring out the window with a far-off expression on her face, her hands worrying at a napkin. It's a look she wore so often before, and I always got the sense that she was dreaming up another escape.

But in this moment, when she looks soft and unsure, I also remember the mom from my early childhood, the one who painted on the driveway with me and put flowers in my hair.

When she spots me she stands and smiles politely, but her posture hardens, her chin lifting like she's fortifying herself with every step I take.

She pulls me into a stiff hug. "You look great," she says when we pull apart, eyeing me from head to toe.

Not *hello*. Not *I've missed you*. A remark on my appearance.

"Thanks," I reply darkly.

She huffs out a prim sigh. "What, LaRynn? Did I already say something wrong?"

I sit back in my chair and blink. Outside of my outburst a few months ago, I'd normally have cowed at the reaction.

Followed it up with something placating, gaslighting my own emotions in the process. Immediately tried to make myself easier for her. Something like, "I'm sorry, I've just had a bad day," or "I'm sorry, I'm not feeling well."

I've never felt like I *could* be messy, could be less than perfect, or could show my anger to either of my parents and still be loved. I've contorted and diminished myself to try to keep them happy. Or just to keep her *there*. And then every time I inevitably failed and exploded, I was the one with the mess to clean up. The one who was spoiled rotten, dramatic, the one who needed too much attention.

But someone loves me at home. Someone who loves my sharp edges as much as all my softer ones, too, and even the ones I haven't quite got figured out yet. And I'm no longer afraid. I'm tired of acting fine just to spare her feelings.

"I haven't seen you in over ten months, and we've barely spoken in that time. So yes, Mom. I *don't* like that the first thing you do when I see you is make a comment about my appearance." I blow out a breath. "When you say that to me, what comes to my mind is that of course you think I look great now. Because the last time I saw you, I'd just gotten out of the hospital the month before. I was weak and too thin and living on my friend's couch. I had to sell my car to pay for that hospital bill because I didn't have medical insurance. All because I quit *school*. That's what comes into my mind."

She rears back, shaking her head in disbelief. "How was I supposed to *know* you were in the hospital? You didn't call me. You didn't tell me."

"And that is something I am working on. I own that. But why would I think you'd come?"

"Because I *did* come back. I did. I signed every document your father bullied me into, ensuring I'd never have access to you, never have a *thing* if I ever left again. I did all of that so that I could be stuck there in that life for *you*."

"And you never let me forget it," I say helplessly.

She sits back and blinks rapidly. Our waiter comes by and fills our waters, tells us about the specials. We make quiet selections while we stare awkwardly at our menus.

When we're alone again I look back up at her.

She blows out a wobbly breath. "I'm . . . trying. I want to try to be in your life, and it feels like you won't let me," she says.

"Then I think . . . I think we have to stop trying to skip over the past. You can't expect someone to forgive you without ever apologizing." A few tears fall to my napkin. "You act like we have something we never really had, because I think you'd rather just pretend and start over. It feels like now that *you're* happy, you want me in your life. But I don't think this should get to be circumstantial that way, Mom."

Her brow crumples as she hiccups through a cry, too. "I know." She gives a broken shrug. "I just don't know where we start."

"I think *here*," I say, voice fragmented. "Maybe *here* is where we get to start."

Just like the house that once felt like it would never be done, like there was more to fix or address around every corner . . . even in the mess, I think *this* is still livable, too. There's something to love here, in this place where our relationship exists. And maybe if we keep working at it, eventually it will be somewhere comfortable—maybe even lovely—too.

THIRTY-SIX

DEACON

I hear the front door open and sit back on my heels excitedly. She's been gone for over four hours, so in my anxiety I turned on Solomon Burke and distracted myself by touching up some baseboards. Turned the volume on full blast, ready for her to come home to.

When I sit up to greet her, my smile falters because she walks in, tear-stained and skittish-looking . . . but the surprising part is that she's not alone.

A woman who is unmistakably her mother trails in at her side. Sharp eyes start cataloging the space, lips rolled together in a line. I immediately feel self-conscious.

I've got one of LaRynn's athletic wear headbands on my head to keep my hair out of my eyes, for fuck's sake. Which probably means that it's time for a trim, but I've been a little preoccupied with other matters lately. I try to brush at a peanut butter stain on my shirt when I clamber to my feet.

LaRynn's gaze meets mine and my hands twitch at my sides helplessly.

I would've changed if I'd known, I try to convey through my eyes.

Her head tilts in a sweet smirk, pride rising in her expression.

I dust off my hands and cross the room to turn down the music before I meet them.

"Hi," I say, reaching out a hand. I look down and see the paint stains and calluses and almost take it back. *Fuck it.* I refused to let my insecurities get in the way when LaRynn didn't want me to come with her before, but the fact that she was proud enough to bring her mother here. . . .

It might not be *for* me—she might not have even told her we're married or any of it—but even if it's just to show her this chunk of life we've carved out . . . it feels like something wooly expands in my chest. "I'm Deacon."

Her mother smiles back, even though it looks like it takes some effort. "I'm Allison. It's nice to meet you."

LaRynn tucks herself against my side, wraps both of her arms around one of mine. It's oddly protective. "This is my husband," she says to her mom.

There's no hint of surprise on her face, but Allison's shoulders lift with the returning smile, like she's gathering her whole strength for it.

"The place looks lovely, LaRynn." She nods to me. "And Deacon. Everything looks wonderful."

I can feel LaRynn's heart pounding against my bicep and her smile against my shoulder.

DURING THE VISIT THE WOMEN start out orbiting each other a bit awkwardly, but after a time, Allison's personality starts to come through. LaRynn asks her about her husband, about New York. Allison shows her photos of their dog and her husband's kids. LaRynn's responses are reserved and polite, but it's clear that both women are trying. They hug tightly when she leaves.

When we shuffle together after, I turn the music back on before I pull her head to my chest and fold her fingers with mine. I smile into her hair while we dance in the kitchen.

"You called me your husband," I say.

She laughs quietly. "Like that, did you?"

"I fucking loved it."

THIRTY-SEVEN

DEACON

The house should feel like a monumental success. We're most likely a month away from doing just about everything we set out to do. I've made sure the rental over at Santa Sea will be tenant-free around the same time, so there's no additional stress over finding a place. Cheryl Gold offered to be our realtor.

But as everything comes together, I find myself growing even more attached. The more it looks like a completed house, the more I realize how much we've been making it our *home* this entire time. With our messes and our music. All the memories from our past with our grandmothers, and the ones we've made together.

ALMOST FIVE MONTHS FROM THE day she showed up in town, LaRynn and I get a phone call with an offer on our grandmothers' house. It's over the listing price, and all cash. Thirty-day closing.

It *should* be the dream, really. Maybe if I believed in fate or destiny or signs it would feel like an affirmation that we're doing the right thing.

Cheryl tells us to take our allotted time to consider, which we intended to do anyway.

When we get off the call, we fasten ourselves into a hug. Rock gently back and forth, stockinged feet on warm wood floors. Not quite a dance. Holding on to what we've gained.

THIRTY-EIGHT

LARYNN

After we reach our seventy-two-hour deadline and send our acceptance, Deacon and I drag a woven blanket and a bottle of our favorite cheap wine to the beach to watch the sunset.

He tucks my back against his chest, wraps me in the cradle of his hips. We sit quietly that way for a while, my head resting in that spot where his collarbone meets his throat. And then he reaches up and tugs my beanie down over my eyes playfully.

"What's on your mind, love?" His voice rumbles against my cheek before he presses his lips to it.

I readjust my hat. "I was just wondering what made you go with 'love'? Is it just short for Lavigne?" I ask with a smirk.

He scratches his jaw against mine and I hum happily. "I just want to say it as much as possible. Want to say it enough times to make you forget the one time I didn't."

I squeeze his arms tighter around my body, try to contain this frothy feeling before I reach back to run my palm along his face. He turns and places a kiss against its center.

"What's on *your* mind, love?" I ask him back. I feel him smile briefly into my skin.

"Something a little sad," he admits.

I know it is. But maybe if he says it out loud, I can, too. I squeeze his hand while we stare out at a fiery sky together. "Tell me."

He sighs. "I'm thinking about Nan and Cece. How I'm glad the house waited until they were gone to really fall apart. That I wish they could see it now."

Something heavy catches beneath my sternum and my heart thunders in my chest.

"Do you ever worry it'll be *us* that falls apart when we're gone?" I whisper. He tilts my chin up to him and a tear slips down my temple with the motion. "Because I worry, Deacon," I blubber. "I worry because I don't understand how someone could ever feel the way I feel about you, could feel anything close to it, and end up so far from it like our parents did. I worry that we're selling this house because of me, because of something I want, and one day this is going to wear off and you're going to hate me for it." More tears slide away.

"Sure, I worry," he says quietly, thumb drawing shapes against my cheek. "But then I remember that *we're not them.* I know we're not perfect. . . ." He laughs and his eyes shine. "We might have bad tempers and some baggage, we're probably way too self-indulgent, and even though for some reason I actually *like* it right now, no doubt that hair in the shower thing will make me fucking crazy someday." He kisses a tear away. "But *look* at us, LaRynn. We've had to do so much shit backwards. We had to fall back in love while tackling a renovation *and* some demons. If we can do that, we can do anything." He kisses the corners of my eyes again. "What if I told you I was scared I'd get lost in myself again? That I'm scared of changing, too. What would you say?"

My brows pinch together. "I'd *find* you," I tell him, firmly. "And I don't think there's a version of you I couldn't love."

He lets out a watery laugh, shakes his head with a smile. "*See?*"

I kiss the thumb he slides against my lips. "And the house? You don't think you'll regret it?"

At that he looks back out over the water, like he's searching for the right words. "I think I've become more . . . connected to the place, but I think that's because it's been *ours*. And, yeah . . . I wish we could hold on to it and still have everything. But it's not just you who needs—or *wants*—the money. And I think as far as the grans go . . . I think they'd be happy for us."

And I don't know why I can't seem to stop blubbering, or why I'm grasping on to him so tight and needing his reassurance, but I ask, "And you won't hate me again someday?"

He frowns as he looks at my lips, my nose, my eyes. "Hate you? LaRynn, I never hated you. I don't think I could have. You want to know what I hate?" He wipes at more of my tears. "I hate that I married you on some nothing Wednesday, in a short-sleeved shirt and jeans. You deserve a *Saturday*, Rynn. You deserve the Friday night that leads into the entire Saturday, and the whole Sunday in bed after." He sighs. "I hate that I've never danced with you on a *proper* dance floor." At that, I smile. "I wish I could say I hated that you wore black to our wedding, but the truth is, you ripped the air out of my lungs in that dress, too." I breathe a laugh and his face sobers. "I hate that I did that to you when we were younger. I hate that we wasted any time not loving one another. Hate that you thought I was anything less than gone for you. Because I'm so fucking gone for you, LaRynn. I'm so stupidly in love with you."

I turn in his arms until I can face him fully, settle my knees outside his hips. "I hate that I did that to *you* when we were younger," I say. "I hate when I have to spend my days waiting for my nights with you. Or my nights waiting for my days with you. And I'm so stupidly in love with you, too." I cradle his face in my hands and kiss him. "I'm so gone for you that sometimes I want to tear this place apart just so we can do this all over again." We laugh inside another kiss, our teeth bumping. "And even though I know you'd be devastating in a suit, I don't care about a wedding. I'd rather have a kitchen floor."

"I can do that," he promises.

THIRTY-NINE

LARYNN

Five days after we accept the offer, I decide that there's one more thing I need to do for closure.

I get carsick on Highway 17 like I always do, but Deacon holds my hair and rubs my back, waiting patiently until I'm ready to keep going.

And when we arrive at the funeral home, we clutch hands as we walk through the parking lot. All the way inside, up until the very last moment when I have to take my hand back to accept my grandmother's ashes from the woman behind the desk.

I don't cry when we settle in the car, or on the entire ride home. Deacon drives at a snail's pace the whole way back, slow enough that I don't get sick for once. We do weather our fair share of honking and middle fingers from people as they speed around us, though.

It's when we get to the front patio gate, woody branches and orange-green leaves lining the fence instead of the bright flowers of summer, that I let the grief crash over me.

I let myself feel as if she has died all over again, as if it's only just happened.

I let myself hear the sound of her voice in my mind, think of her standing at the gate to greet me every year. Let myself remember her teaching me to make beignets, and how she'd let me go on the Fireball ride at the Boardwalk even though we both knew I would puke after. I cry for how she let me spend hundreds of dollars at the arcade one summer in order to win enough tickets for a skateboard from the prize center, even though it was a complete piece of shit and would have been cheaper to purchase outright.

I cry for Helena and how I never had *her* peach-pretzel-Jell-O-pie, and then cry some more when I wonder if she would've liked that I made it for Deacon. I cry for how I wasn't there for my grandma when Helena passed.

I cry for how *lucky* I feel that, even though my childhood may not have been particularly happy, I had her and this place and those summers.

I even cry for my dad when I think about how miserable and lonely he must be, how he must have let his anger fester so deeply that he has no idea how to reach out. How much he missed out on with his mother, me, and his life. I allow myself to feel it and let go, to be okay with the knowledge that I'll never welcome that relationship back into my life, even while I feel sad for him because of it.

I cry on the sidewalk until I notice the goosebumps on Deacon's forearms and feel the cold bleeding through our clothes.

When I look up at his face, I see that he's been crying, too. I lean up and kiss him before we head inside, my little box tucked under my arm.

We step into the main hall and find Sally waiting for us, sitting on the foot of the stairs, oxygen tank at her feet.

"You know, what's the point of these damn cell phones if

you two never answer them?!" she asks. Deacon and I look at each other, dumbfounded.

"Everything okay, Sal?"

"Do you have a few minutes?" she huffs, pushing herself up to her feet.

We exchange another confused look. "Yeah, we're just tired. I finally picked up Grandma." I nod dumbly to the box at my side.

"Oh good!" she says, over-bright. "She can join us, then."

AFTER WE SETTLE IN OUR seats around her table, she proceeds to catch her breath while she pours herself a drink.

"I have an offer for you on the house," she says.

Deacon widens his eyes at me. I can almost hear his thoughts. Something like *Uh, help. Is Sal losing it? She knows we already accepted an offer.*

"Sal," I start, uneasy. "We already got a full-priced offer. We accepted it almost a week ago now."

"Well, this offer is *half* of the asking price."

Now Deacon rubs at his forehead and I wince at her. We're both exhausted and already emotional and if Sal really is cracking right now, I suppose we'll just have to handle it, but—

"The offer is from me. I'm able to give you the full market value for my unit, but I am offering to buy my unit, only. So you would get to keep yours."

Blood rushes through my ears.

Sal explains further, "I only didn't speak up earlier because I didn't realize how much you might *want* to hold onto it. I also didn't know if I *could* do it, but I was able to move some things around, and—"

"*No,*" Deacon says firmly. "No, Sal. You can't do that."

"Deacon, my rent has been nearly the same since the nineties. I was surprised at just how much I *can* do it." She sighs happily. "Would I if you were anyone else? No, but I kinda look at it as buying into a co-op of sorts—with how much you help me anyway. Now I'll *really* get to lord this over you. Maybe we put bingo back in the rotation."

He gives her a helpless look. "Sal, that's a *lot* of money." Neither of us would have ever thought she could afford it.

"Would it be enough for what you need? For the shop and for everything else you want to do?"

"Yes, but . . . *Sal*."

She pats his face sweetly and looks at me. "It would have been yours someday anyway. May as well give it to you both now and have the chance to see what you do with it."

He looks my way. "I don't know if we even *can* back out now, though. Can we?"

My shoulders lift in a weak shrug. "I really don't know, Deacon. I think Cheryl would have to get us out of it somehow."

A smile plays at his lips. "Do you want to?"

"I don't want to get our hopes up, Deacon."

But he's already grinning.

FORTY

OCTOBER 31ST

LARYNN

Turns out, Cheryl Gold got to be a hero in our story.

And now Deacon is beholden to her for every summer for the foreseeable future.

Still worth it.

She coached us through writing a letter that she took to the other agent for us. In that letter, we wrote about our grandmothers' history here, and even shared what happened with us, explaining why we were changing our minds and hoping to pull out.

They agreed to dissolve the contract without penalty.

We were able to turn around and enter into an agreement with Sal, which we will close on in mid-November, just in time to renew the lease at the café, and pay the deposit to hold the shop next door.

Today, though. Today there's a candied apple candle blazing on the tray that sits on our freestanding tub, a decorative skeleton hand holding up a peace sign next to the sink. "Witchcraft" by Frank Sinatra floats through the room.

"How long has it been since we've waltzed?" I hear Deacon say to me from outside the bathroom door.

I fling it open to find him in a perfectly cut suit, the shirt left partially unbuttoned, a rose dangling from his teeth. Pieces of his hair are already escaping its slicked-back style.

I laugh before I smooth it over and intone the next line back to him with the appropriate amount of drama. "Oh, Gomez . . . *hours*."

He's taking this whole Halloween thing much more seriously than I anticipated. Borderline out of hand, really. Once we landed on Gomez and Morticia, the man immediately committed to growing out a mustache and started slipping into character around the house at random times.

He wags his brows. *"Cara mia."*

"Mon sauvage," I reply.

He lifts my hand and begins kissing a path up my arm. "You almost ready birthday girl?"

"Yes, yes. Don't rush me." Especially since it was *his* idea to "take the mustache for a test drive" for an hour, thus causing my (very happy, five-stars, totally worth it) delay. He delicately brushes my hair from my shoulder before he nips at a spot on my neck that makes my breath hitch. *"Deacon,"* I breathe.

"I'm in *character*. Can't be helped," he murmurs beneath my ear. One palm comes to slowly wrap around my throat while the other slips inside the top of my dress. He tips my head back against his shoulder and kisses me deeply.

A frustrated sound growls out of him before he pops away, hands in the air like I've burned him. "I *told* you, love, we *can't*. We gotta go."

"Oh, you told me, huh?" I laugh at his retreating form.

I touch up the red lipstick he's just smeared and check my reflection.

Sometimes I have these moments where I boomerang out of my own body and back. The kind of moments that make my reflection feel a bit like déjà vu, both unrecognizable and yet familiar, like this is what I was meant to have, meant to feel. And yet I wonder if this is sustainable. If one body can really contain so much love. Happiness. Hope.

Having Deacon on my side has made me feel invincible, which has made me feel brave enough to be vulnerable, too. To other relationships in my life, and to betting on myself.

I don't know if we'll always get what we wish for. I know that life is going to come with its battles. I know that love will, too. But I'm starting to think that's the whole point— finding the person, or people, who'll fight and dream *with* you.

I pass the flowers and the birthday card from my mom on the way to the living room, where I'm warmly surprised to see that he's divested the kitchen of the beignet mess from this morning. He woke me up with breakfast in bed before he brought me onto the balcony to show me my gift. I'd laughed until tears leaked from the corners of my eyes.

A cactus garden. New planter boxes, full of all kinds. Some are shaped like flowers, others are spiked and untouchable. A mosaic of sharp and soft.

I see him waiting for me at the landing now. My beautiful, brave, generous husband. Past him, alone in my old room-that-was-not-a-room, sits Helena's kiln. Since we've already made ourselves cozy in the spaces we've been using, we plan to make that a project area. When we close on Sal's unit I'm hoping to talk him into building me some big shelves in there. Things I can stuff full of albums and art and pictures.

Eventually I'll get good enough at throwing clay to make some vases and knickknacks.

"Ah!" I squeal when Deacon takes my hand and spins me into a low dip.

"I love you," he tells me, suspending me in air.

"I love you, too."

WE MAKE OUR WAY DOWN the stairs, out onto the patio. Past the pumpkins we carved three nights ago because I told him I never had before. Instead of regular carving knives he insisted we use electric drills and tools, so we were still finding pumpkin guts in our hair two days later.

"Oh, shit. I need my tie," he says suddenly. "I don't know where I left it."

I spare him a vaguely annoyed look. "Do you need help finding it?"

"Probably will make it faster," he says, wincing, and I have to laugh. The man will walk past his own keys (in the spot I told him they were in) five times before he registers them.

I head back up after him and start looking around the living area while he checks the bedroom. "Look under the bed!" I call. "Did you hang it up somewhere after the other night?!" *When I wore nothing but it.*

"Check the house nipples!"

I scoff. "*Stop* calling them that or I'll take them down!" I yell back. The first thing I successfully made on the kiln. My attempt at new key hooks. To be fair, they do look a little bit like nipples, but they work.

Sure enough, I see his tie. "Found it!" I call.

When I slip it off, something clatters to the ground with it.

I pick it up and nearly drop it again. A ring. Three stones, an oval in the middle with little trapezoids on the sides. I whirl around and find Deacon down on one knee, tears in his eyes. More of his hair has escaped the confines of its gel.

"I know I'm in a costume right now, and that I have a very distracting mustache—which I think is growing on us both—but I'm still open to discussion as far as that's concerned . . . and I know you said you don't care about a wedding or any of that. I know it's your birthday *and* Halloween and I know you always said you never got to feel special because everyone was always celebrating something else." He takes a shaky breath. "I also know that you're already my wife, but . . . I wanted to maybe give you something extra today, too. I wanted to propose to you properly, at least." He takes the ring and my hand and tries to clear his throat. "Be my wife. *Stay* my wife. Forever, LaRynn. I don't care where we end up or what we do as long as I have you."

He's a blur in front of me, until my smile spills the tears from my eyes. "Yes," I tell him. "Yes. I'm yours, forever."

WE DO END UP MAKING it to the Halloween-slash-birthday party over at Santa Sea, eventually. Sal was waiting for us downstairs, dressed as a nun of all things, with tears already trailing down her face.

We hang out by a fire and watch kids buzz around the decorated sites in their costumes, knocking on trailer doors for tricks and treats.

Macy gifts me Helena's old recipe book and I cry.

* * *

THAT NIGHT, WHEN DEACON STRIPS off my dress and proceeds to kiss every inch of me, I tell him, "I thought of one more thing I want for my birthday."

He laughs into a particularly sensitive spot. "Yes, love?"

"Your name."

EPILOGUE

DEACON

"Ow."

I'm awoken by a heavy thud against my temple, just before the unmistakable ringing of a toy screeches inches from my face.

I crack open an eyelid to see a head of black curls and bright green eyes staring at me from the side of the bed.

"Daddy, I'm calling you," Dot says, tapping the phone that's still laid against my cheek. She holds her toy up to her ear.

I grab my phone and adjust it accordingly. "Hello?" I whisper.

"Can you talk?"

"*If* you can whisper, I can. Let's let Mommy sleep."

She pulls her pink cell away from her ear and frowns at it. "I can't hear you good." She gives an Oscar-worthy show of slamming on buttons—truly impressive for a five-year-old. "Sorry, Daddy, I think I'm losing you. Phone must be broken."

"Hey, Dottie?"

"Yeah?" She brings the phone back to her chubby cheek. "Can you hear me now, Daddy?"

"Yes, baby. I can also *smell* your morning breath. Go brush your teeth."

She pouts fiercely but keeps the phone pressed up to her ear. "You can't smell through a phone."

I sigh. "Are your brothers awake?"

"*Yes.*" And *now* she chooses to whisper, the muted volume making it sound sinister. "I made them breakfast."

"You *what?!*" I say, louder than I intended. LaRynn groans and rolls into my back, presses a kiss between my shoulder blades.

"What'd you make for them?" LaRynn asks, muffled in my skin.

"I'll have to call you back, Dad."

"No problem, kid." I sigh-laugh and toss my phone on the nightstand before Dot crawls onto our bed, shoving a sharp knee into my ribs as she wedges her way to Rynn's arms.

And just like clockwork, I hear more feet drum up the stairs in a stampede. It's been this way since each of them was born—like LaRynn is the sun our family orbits around. The moment her eyes open, they're drawn in, and she welcomes them with open arms.

Sully's the first to slide through the doorway on his socks before Leo knocks in behind him.

"Don't worry! We already took care of it, and it wasn't as bad as it sounds," Sully swears.

Ah, fuck. That can't be good.

"*Nope!*" Rynn shouts. "If it's already been dealt with, I don't even wanna know the details. Not today." Probably a good call.

We found out about Leo only six months after the

expanded café opened, which was unexpected, and . . . *not* easy. Sullivan came only fifteen months after him, and that didn't exactly *un*complicate matters. But, even when it felt like we were ships passing in the night, grazing palms and tiredly passing bundles . . . my wife and I have always found a way to dance.

Sometimes in a very literal sense since Sully especially would not be settled to sleep without music.

We've opened our businesses alongside each other and experienced great successes, while we've simultaneously found ways to cope with huge loss, too.

Sally only lived to meet Leo before she passed, and to see LaRynn and I fulfill a few dreams. And even though she'd backhand us for it, sometimes we still let ourselves feel deeply sad that our kids won't grow up knowing or remembering her.

Dot decided to be our biggest surprise yet, and she also decided to show up while we were in the middle of our second renovation on the house. When we converted the entire thing to a single-family home—our biggest project to date. . . . *So*, batting a thousand as far as taking on too much at one time is concerned.

When she was born and we settled on her name, LaRynn vehemently stated that she be called *"Just Dot, because she is IT. Period. No more."* I was the very proud recipient of a vasectomy when she turned two.

"You have all your gear packed for Gran's?" I ask Leo.

"Yup."

"Both jerseys? Cleats, pants, belts?" LaRynn asks.

It's the first weekend we're leaving extended family in charge of the sports shuffle, and it's a bit daunting to say the least. But we've been extremely lucky with our village. My mom can't be pried away, and even LaRynn's mother has made herself a regular fixture. She spent summers here when the kids were babies, until she and her husband Liam relocated to California when he retired three years ago.

"Yup, got everything packed," he confirms.

"Sullivan?" I ask.

"Yep! We got Dot packed up, too," Sully replies.

At that, Dot folds her arms and gives them an exacting stare. "Did you pack my sasquatch pajamas?"

Both boys roll their eyes and say *"Yes, Dot,"* at the same time.

If LaRynn is our sun, Dottie's our moon.

The new(ish) doorbell chimes from downstairs, and the boys scramble out of our room right before two dachshunds come flying in and my mom's voice follows from below.

"I'm here for the goods!" she yells.

"Grammie!" Dottie shrieks, using my face to leverage herself off of the bed.

"Jesus, you'd think my mother would value the concept of a door," I mutter. LaRynn laughs as Hilde and Greta weasel under the comforter.

"Are you decent?!" Mom calls from the top of the stairs. I snort and shake my head. She has *never* dropped that joke.

"All clear!" LaRynn shouts back.

She appears in the doorway to our room with Dot buckled to her leg and her typical perma-grin.

Macy Leeds has somehow stopped aging since grandchildren came into her life; a concept I am baffled by, since I seem to wake up grayer by the day.

"The boys are already in the car. You didn't make them any promises on my behalf that I don't know about, did you?" she asks, looking bewildered.

"I think they're just excited to actually *camp* at the camp-ground," LaRynn explains. "And to hang out with their cousins."

Mom looks back down at her leg-barnacle cheerfully. "You ready for some girl time Dottie Reine?"

"Ready!"

"Alright, we'll see you two on Sunday, then! Come on, girls!" The dogs dart back out from the covers, skittering behind.

LaRynn and I sit up, her chin balanced on my shoulder as we watch out the window until they pull away.

And just like that, we're alone.

"More sleep? Or do we get up and get going now?" she asks with a yawn.

I press her down with a kiss until her head hits the pillow once more. "You get some more sleep. I'll make us some breakfast."

She hums a noise that makes it difficult to leave, but I manage like the seasoned hero I am.

I head downstairs into the new kitchen. Start prepping beignets and get the coffee going, turn on some quiet music while I work.

After only a few minutes I feel her eyes on my back: another one of those wonders of marriage—the way you start to become so accustomed to the other's presence that you recognize the way spaces change when they walk into a room. A personal source of gravity.

The song changes and grows louder behind me and I start to laugh, right as I dust a final pastry with some powdered sugar.

The tune calls up one of our early memories from the first phase of renovation. Back when we only *thought* we knew what exhaustion was. When we were throwing ourselves into the house, but we didn't yet realize just how much we were throwing ourselves into each other, too.

She'd fallen to the ground dramatically, tossing aside a hammer and pushing the safety glasses back up on her head. "Go on without me," she'd wailed. I was completely caught off guard because it was normally *me* calling for a break.

"Let's at least get this last half done, Lar," I replied. I had, like, seven things to fix over at Santa Sea that weekend and didn't want to lose steam. But when I looked down at her, she was well and truly smoked. I'd accidentally busted my lip with a hammer the day before, along with my hands—*who knows* how many times. We were a sight to behold.

"We need music," I declared.

"We need drugs," she deadpanned, before she snorted a short laugh at the ceiling. "Music will do just fine, though. You pick."

I dragged my feet across the floor and looked through the records, quickly registering that everything there consisted of oldies. I picked the one that I thought had the most life. Anything to invigorate us. Turned it up as loud as possible.

"Jump in the Line," with blaring trumpets and echoing drums and a happy, clapping rhythm, began playing. I'd hauled her to her feet and made her march a lap around the entire space with me.

Dancing—albeit not very enthusiastically.

We let the song bounce off of the busted walls and lift our broken spirits.

It became a small routine we established. One of so many little things that we've collected over the years—things that seemed molecular at the time but have spun up and gathered like cotton candy until it's become this great, fluffy, us-shaped life.

I turn around with a smile to find her beaming back just as brightly. And *God*, I'm struck all over again. By her same incredible witch hair and her sea glass eyes. The same constellation of freckles. The addition of a few laugh lines. She's only grown more stunning, and it's even more overwhelming because I get to know her soul.

She shimmies to the song as she makes her way over to me, and even though it's meant to be silly, she pulls off deeply sexy. She always does. Even when she's swimming in one of my shirts and sporting some of her tiny sleep shorts.

We make out like teens until I have to set down the plate of beignets. She scoops one up and pops a corner into her mouth, leaning a hip on the counter next to me.

We eat standing up, like we so often did for those months that summer.

"You sure you don't want to go anywhere, love?" I ask her, dusting some powdered sugar off her lip with my thumb.

"Never been more sure of anything. Happy anniversary."

AND THIS IS HOW WE spend it. We blast our music—all the songs we've added to our life's soundtrack so far—and we dance in our home. In our kitchen and in our beautiful kids' rooms, on our patio and our balcony. In our bedroom, down the halls that are lined with photographs and memories, and in all the places where we'll keep making more.

ACKNOWLEDGMENTS

First and foremost: Thank *you* for spending your time in this story.

Thank you to everyone who encouraged me to pick this one up again and finish it despite setting it aside two times before. I was just scared, but it was worth it.

Britt: You have been nothing but joy and sunshine to work with on this. Thank you for forgiving me my many, many errors and fixing this up to be the best it can be. Your encouragement along the way has been priceless. If there are any mistakes in the final version of this, please know that they were my own and that Britt caught them, but I failed at applying them to the right Google Doc.

Danielle: Forever the first person who took a chance on my DM—thank you, thank you, thank you.

Krys: Thank you for your friendship and for letting me whine and verbalize all of my imposter syndrome on a near-daily basis. And for fist-pumping the air with me on the good days. Endlessly grateful to have found you on this corner of the internet.

Kelsey: From blue alien genitalia to here, huh? Sorry if you didn't think I would put this in writing, but I'm nothing if not a professional. Thank you for wanting to give me and my books (and my unhinged DMs) a piece of your time, for beta reading and helping me find those weak spots, and for sharing your platform. You're a *gift* to so many—including me.

Kenz: Thank you for being a sounding board, for beta reading and giving me essential feedback—even when it was just the applause I desperately needed. You're a rare and special gem and I'm so grateful for you. You'll never be rid of me.

Hannah and Tabitha: The most amazing part of this entire author experience is how letters on paper manage to string together real-life connections. I'm pumped and so lucky to know you. You are both hired for beta reading for life and for friendship even longer.

My gosh, there are too many people I would love to thank for simply sharing their energy and spaces with my characters. For someone who finds the social media aspect of this job a bit difficult, I am forever in awe and indebted to those who take the time to make videos and beautiful photos that showcase my words. At the risk of sounding earnest or like a try-hard-wannabe-cool-mom, *you* guys have given my stories your time and shared your passion for them in one way or another—be it your posts, videos, or beta reading—and it has all helped me make a dream look like a reality. Specifically, I want to thank Logan, Alex, Marisol, Ashley, Ariana, Stephanie, Sil, Julia, Alahni, Jill, Pauline, Brooke, Kristen, Hannah, Molly, Jamie, Rose, Crystal, Katie, Teresa, and Storygram Tours. I wish I could thank *everyone* else individually, too, but I think that might entail a whole other book. Even if none of you ever read this one, or if you hate everything else I write in the future, you helped bring new people to my little worlds, and for that I'm sincerely grateful.

Thank you to everyone else who shouted from the rooftops about *Funny Feelings*, too. Those messages and voice notes carried me on through the end of this one.

To my friends and my family: Oops, I did it again. My bad. I *promise* one day I will take smaller bites and bigger timelines so that I'm not quite such a special wreck. During this book especially we had to navigate a whole lot of "life," and I'm thankful that we (like Deacon and LaRynn) found a way to dance through it.

Thank you **all** for supporting my dreams. I hope to forever create stories that make people feel seen and characters that bring them some amount of joy.

Don't miss out on the rest of Tarah DeWitt's
steamy romances . . .

Available now from

PIATKUS

Do you love contemporary romance?

Want the chance to hear news about your favourite
authors (and the chance to win free books)?

Kristen Ashley
Ashley Herring Blake
Meg Cabot
Olivia Dade
Rosie Danan
J. Daniels
Farah Heron
Talia Hibbert
Sarah Hogle
Helena Hunting
Abby Jimenez
Elle Kennedy
Christina Lauren
Alisha Rai
Sally Thorne
Lacie Waldon
Denise Williams
Meryl Wilsner
Samantha Young

Then visit the Piatkus website
www.yourswithlove.co.uk

And follow us on Facebook and Instagram
www.facebook.com/yourswithlovex | @yourswithlovex

PIATKUS